D0858687

Rattlesnake Brother
A Gabriel Hawke Novel
Book 3

Paty Jager

Windtree Press
Hillsboro, OR

This is a work of fiction, names, characters, places, and incidents either are the product of the author's imagination or are used fictitiously, and any resemblance to actual persons living or dead, business establishments, events, or locales, is entirely coincidental.

RATTLESNAKE BROTHER

Copyright © 2019 Patricia Jager

All rights reserved. No part of this book may be used or reproduced in any manner whatsoever without written permission of the author or Windtree Press except in the case of brief quotations in critical articles or reviews.

Contact Information: info@windtreepress.com

Windtree Press
Hillsboro, Oregon
http://windtreepress.com

Cover Art by Christina Keerins
CoveredbyCLKeerins

Published in the United States of America

ISBN 978-1-950387-06-9

Special Acknowledgements

I'd like to thank the Oregon State Police Fish and Wildlife division for allowing me to ride along with an officer to learn all the ins and outs of the job. Special thanks also go out to Judy Melinek, M.D. for answering my pathology questions, Dr, Lowell Euhus for explaining about the Wallowa County Medical Examiner's job, my son-in-law for answering my strange questions about law and weapons, and my niece, who helped with the legal information.

Author Comments

While this book and other books in the series are set in Wallowa County, Oregon, I have changed the town names to old forgotten towns that were in the county at one time. I also took the liberty of changing the towns up and populating the county with my own characters, none of which are in anyway a representation of anyone who is or has ever lived in Wallowa County. Other than the towns, I have tried to use the real names of all the geographical locations.

Chapter One

Two large objects wrapped in brown sacking hung in a pine tree twenty feet off the dirt road. Two bull elk heads leaned against the base of the tree. A lone camp trailer, closed up as if no one were there, sat thirty feet from the pine with a fire pit between the camp trailer and hanging carcasses. There wasn't a vehicle in sight.

Fish and Wildlife State Trooper Gabriel Hawke stopped his vehicle. He started to type the trailer's license plate number into his computer. No signal. His right hand settled on his radio mic at his left shoulder. "Dispatch. This is Hawke. I'm about five miles from Coyote Springs on Forest Service Road forty-eight-sixty."

"Copy."

"I have a lone camp trailer and two elk hanging in a tree. Trailer license is Oregon- ..." He called in the number and scanned the area waiting for the dispatcher's reply.

"The trailer belongs to Duane Sigler of Eagle, Oregon."

Sigler. The man had a penchant for poaching. "Copy."

Hawke turned off his vehicle and stepped out, putting his cap on his head. He tucked his head down in the fur-lined collar of his coat. The first of November in Wallowa County always had a bite in the air. At this elevation, three inches of snow covered the ground.

No one appeared to be in the camp trailer. There wasn't the hiss of a propane furnace. No sound, no movement. He knocked on the door just in case someone was sleeping.

No answer.

He scanned the area. Two folding chairs leaned up against the trailer. Two elk, two people, that was okay. But then why were they out driving around if they'd already filled their tags?

The antlers were a three-point and a four-point. Either one would make a nice trophy of the hunt on a wall.

Hawke walked over. There were tags tied to the base of the antlers. Just as required. That was a good sign, considering one of the hunters liked to not play by the hunting rules.

He untied the string around one tag and opened it. The month and date hadn't been notched out. Not a good sign. He glanced at the name on the tag. Duane Sigler. That matched the trailer license. He tied that tag back on and untied the other one.

Again, the tag wasn't notched out. Benjamin Lange. Hawke stared at the name. The county district attorney wouldn't be hunting with a known poacher, would he? It could be someone with the same name.

A glance at the address and he was pretty sure it was the district attorney. The D.A. lived on the west side of Wallowa Lake and that was the address listed.

Hawke replaced the tag and decided he'd wait for the hunters to return.

《》《》《》

Thirty minutes later as Hawke finished off a cup of coffee, Sigler's pickup slowly drove up the road. There had been two pickups with hunters and a jeep come by while he waited. He'd talked to the people in each vehicle and wrote them down in his logbook.

The late nineties, faded red, Ford pickup crept up to the trailer. Two men stepped out.

Neither one was D.A. Lange.

Hawke slipped out of his vehicle after turning on his recording device.

"Morning. Looks like you've had a good season," he said, motioning toward the elk hanging in the tree.

Sigler walked over to him cautiously. "Yeah. Bagged them yesterday. Season started two days ago. We're legal."

That the man was already on the defensive didn't surprise Hawke. "I didn't say you weren't. Could I see your hunting licenses and tags?"

The other person with Sigler pulled his wallet out of his pocket. Sigler remained still. They'd had their share of run-ins over the years. The man never helped himself by cooperating.

Hawke took the other man's hunting license, opened his logbook, and wrote down his name and address. Barney Price. His address was Gresham,

Oregon.

"Can I see your hunting tag?" Hawke asked, handing the license back. The man headed to the elk with the D.A.'s tag.

Sigler's lips pressed together and his face grew redder with each step the other man took back to them.

"Thank you." Hawke unfolded the tag already knowing what he'd find. "Mr. Price, why didn't you notch out the date you killed this animal?"

The man glanced at Sigler. "I didn't know I was supposed to."

"And why is the name Benjamin Lange on a hunting tag you put on your elk? Your hunting license states you are Barney Price." Hawke held his gaze on the man, but kept Sigler in his peripheral vision.

Price faced Sigler. "You told me this wasn't a problem. That the person who owned the tag sold it to you."

Hawke put up a hand to stop the man's outrage. "Mr. Price, hunting tags can't be bought and sold among hunters. Only the person who puts in for the tag and purchases it can use it to shoot the animal defined on the tag." He tucked his logbook back in his pocket. "I'm afraid you have violated several hunting regulations. The worst being you used a tag that isn't yours and," he glanced at Sigler, "you provided him with the tag."

"Why you!" Price took a step toward Sigler. "I'm not paying any fines or going to jail. You are! And I'll make sure everyone knows what an unethical hunting guide you are."

Hawke stepped between the two men. "Take those elk down. You'll help me put them in the back of my truck," Hawke told both men.

Once the elk, heads and all, were stowed in the back of Hawke's pickup, he cuffed the two men and put them in the back seat of his vehicle.

While they sat in the back glaring at one another, Hawke confiscated their weapons from Sigler's pickup. He checked to see if they were unloaded. Price's still had a cartridge in the chamber. He ejected that, shaking his head.

Stowing the rifles in the tool box in the bed of his pickup, he heard the two men arguing inside the vehicle but couldn't make out exactly what was being said.

Hawke locked Sigler's pickup and camp trailer, hoping the man had the trailer key in his pocket or in the pickup.

When he slipped in behind the steering wheel, both men stopped talking.

Hawke peered into the review mirror at Sigler as he started the vehicle. "How did you get a hold of D.A. Lange's hunting tag?"

Sigler peered back at him. "Lange gave it to me. He said I could use his tag."

Hawke chuckled. "The District Attorney knows you can't gift tags."

Sigler glared at him. "He gave it to me."

"You might want to rethink that story on the way to jail." Hawke put the vehicle in gear and headed back to Alder. Looked like there wouldn't be any more time spent out here. By the time he booked these two and dropped the elk off at the local butcher, he'd have just enough time to catch D.A. Lange at work and ask him about "gifting" the tag to a known poacher.

《》《》《》

11

Hawke walked from the county jail next door to the courthouse in Alder, the county seat. He wanted to have a talk with D.A. Lange.

He walked up the concrete steps, admiring the original two-story courthouse built in 1909. The stone for the building had been cut at a quarry on the slope southwest of Alder. The lower level housed the court room and the county offices that took payments. Tax collector. Water Master.

Hawke walked up the narrow staircase to the offices on the second floor. He'd always thought it was interesting that the D.A.'s office looked out over the city park.

The receptionist, a young woman who had grown up in the area and stepped into her grandmother's footsteps, pulled her gaze from the computer monitor on her desk. "May I help you?"

"I wondered if the district attorney would have a moment to speak with me." He held his State Police ball cap in his hands.

"Just a moment, let me see if he has a moment, Trooper…"

"Hawke."

She nodded and picked up the phone, pressing a button.

He'd given testimony at several of the attorney's trials. He couldn't say he disliked the man, but Lange didn't have a personality that rallied people around him. He was a damn good D.A. He nearly always won his cases.

The receptionist replaced the phone. "If you can wait about fifteen minutes, he'll be through with the meeting in his office."

Hawke nodded and took a seat across from her desk. A magazine rack hung on the wall beside the chair. There was a hodge-podge of interests. Women's magazines, athletic, food and nutrition, cars, and hunting. It appeared they wanted to keep anyone who had to wait entertained. What he didn't see were the kind that gossiped about celebrities. After noting the types, he scanned the dates. Some were nearly three years old. It appeared they didn't have a subscription to any of the magazines.

He pulled out his phone and popped one earbud in his ear. He'd downloaded Sigler's recorded account of how he came to have the tag with D.A. Lange's name on it. Hawke had worked enough with the district attorney to know he'd only believe what he heard.

As he was setting the recording to the section where the man named Lange, the Assistant D.A., Rachel Wallen, stalked out of the district attorney's office.

"Terri, I'll be out of the office until tomorrow morning." Without even looking his direction the woman whipped into her small office, grabbed her coat and purse, and left.

Hawke stood. "She didn't look happy."

"She rarely is. The boss and her clash over everything. Not sure why he hired her." Terri, the receptionist, picked up the phone again. "Do you still have time for the State Trooper?"

Her brown hair, piled on her head, bounced as her head did one nod. She replaced the phone and pointed to the office behind her.

Hawke stood and strode into the room.

District Attorney Lange wasn't a big man. The top

of his head came to Hawke's shoulder and his frame appeared as if it would break in a strong wind. He did have a deep powerful voice that carried well in the courtroom.

Lange stood and reached across his desk with his right hand.

Hawke grasped the fine bones in his and released quickly.

"What brings you to my office, Trooper Hawke?" The man sat back down in his chair.

Hawke remained standing. "I ran across a poacher today. Duane Sigler."

The D.A. nodded. "I know of him."

"Just know of him?"

The man's eyes narrowed behind his heavy-rimmed glasses. "Is that an accusation?"

"He had a bull elk tag with your name and residence on it and said you gave it to him." Hawke didn't imagine the flare of anger in the man's eyes.

"I don't know what you're talking about." Lange shot to his feet.

Hawke held up his phone and hit the play button.

"Lange gave it to me. He said I could use his tag." Sigler's voice rang loud and clear.

"Even the District Attorney knows you can't gift tags." Hawke's voice.

"He gave it to me." Sigler's voice held conviction.

D.A. Lange's face was red. "I didn't give that man a tag. I didn't even put in for a tag this year. I didn't have time last year so saw no sense in taking a tag from someone who did have the time to hunt."

"I'm going to look into it." Hawke said, pivoting and striding out of the room, down the hall and stairs, and across to the front door. The man's desperation to make him believe he'd not even put in for a tag had Hawke wondering if the man protested too strongly.

Chapter Two

Hawke spent the rest of the afternoon on the computer at the state police office in Winslow, following the trail of the elk tag registered to Benjamin Lange. All of the paperwork, right down to his credit card paying for the tag, proved he did put in and later paid for the tag.

What did Sigler have on the D.A. that made the man give his tag to the known poacher? It was evident by the D.A.'s fabrication of how he didn't even put in for a tag that the poacher would be easier to extract the truth from. Maybe. He was in the Alder jail and going up for arraignment in the morning. Knowing Sigler, he was more apt to get information out of the poacher after he'd been arraigned and let go. That meant catching Sigler sometime tomorrow afternoon.

Hawke logged in his contacts and his citations. A glance at his sergeant's office revealed the man had gone home already. He'd catch up with him in the morning and tell him about the tag.

Hawke left the building, climbed into his work vehicle, and drove to the Trembleys. His landlords were sure to have a few insights into why the D.A. might be paying off a poacher with an elk tag. He parked beside his personal vehicle.

Dog, his large breed mutt, charged out of the barn.

"Hey, how was your day? Did you keep the horses company?" Hawke walked into the barn and over to the stall where his two horses and mule stood with their heads over the gate.

"You three look hungry. Didn't I give you enough early this morning?" He rubbed their foreheads. "I'll get out of my uniform and get you some grain."

He headed up the steps to his apartment over the indoor riding arena. Darlene Trembley gave riding lessons and boarded horses while her husband farmed their hundred acres.

Inside, he tossed his coat and hat on the one chair, and began stripping out of his shirt and Kevlar vest. He hated doing vehicle patrols because he had to wear the vest. When he patrolled on horseback in the mountains in civilian clothing, he didn't have to wear the restraining protective gear.

He pulled on a t-shirt and changed his slacks for jeans and shoved his feet into his old cowboy boots. All the hours he spent in his uniform, his body shouldn't want to shed it so quickly.

"Do I pop something in the microwave or hope Herb comes by with an invitation to dinner?" he asked Dog, who sat by the door, waiting for them to go back out.

He decided to wait to nuke something until he'd

finished taking care of the horses.

The animals in the stall crunched the grain and swished their tails. Hawke leaned over the top rail of the gate, his head between Jack and Horse. He enjoyed the company of his animals over people.

"You had dinner yet?"

Hawke jumped slightly. He hadn't heard Herb walk up behind him. Dog banged his wagging tail against Hawke's leg.

He turned from the stall and smiled. "No, I haven't had dinner."

"Darlene made a roast. If you don't come help eat it, I'll be having roast something all week."

Hawke knew the man didn't mind leftovers, but it was Herb's way of making Hawke not feel like he ate at their house too often. "Sounds good to me. I was going to heat up some soup."

"How's keeping an eye on the elk hunters going?" Herb asked as they walked toward the house.

"Not too many drunks. Mostly honest hunters out there." He'd wait to bring up Sigler and Lange when they'd finished dinner.

Herb stopped at the back door and looked at him. "Mostly honest. There was a time when there were a few families that took deer or elk out of season, but it was to feed their families. Now it's the damn hunters that think they are above the laws that ruin it for everyone else."

Hawke knew better than to get the man started on this subject. "Did your grandson's football team make it to state?"

The change of subject took them right through the beginning of the meal. The conversation in the middle was led by Darlene talking about the gossip at the quilting club.

"Selma said that new Assistant District Attorney was in her daughter, Cynthia's, clothing shop buying a suit that looked a lot like a man's." Darlene stood to clear the table.

"What do you mean, that looked like a man's?" The vision Hawke had was the curvy assistant in a man's suit that hung like a sack on her.

"You know. These days they make suits like a man's, but they are built for a woman's body shape." Darlene studied him. "Have you met the assistant district attorney?"

"Not met, but I saw her today." He remembered how angry she'd looked when she'd left Lange's office.

"And?" Darlene had her gaze on him as if she thought he should say more.

"And what? She stalked out of the D.A's office, went into her office, and left." He shrugged and put the last bite of potatoes and gravy in his mouth.

"Didn't you see how she's built? A man's dress suit on her would be like painting a bathing suit on Marilyn Monroe. All her bits and pieces are going to be more evident than when she wears a dress."

Hawke wasn't sure what the woman was getting at. He was more interested in why Ms. Wallen wanted a new suit. "How long has she been here?" he asked, thinking about a year, but he didn't keep track of the judicial employees. Only the ones he needed for warrants, the D.A. and Judge Vickers.

"She's been here nearly eighteen months," Darlene said, glancing at her husband as if she expected him to agree.

And he did. "Lange is on his second term. She came when his last assistant up and left without a word." Herb stood, grabbing the coffee pot.

"No more for me." Hawke put his hand over his cup. He wanted to sleep tonight. "No one knows where the other assistant went or why he left?"

"Nope." Herb sat back down.

Darlene placed a piece of apple pie in front of Hawke. "Peggy Greeley said she heard the D.A. and his old assistant having an argument the day before the assistant left."

"Who's Peggy Greeley?" Hawke scooped a bite of pie up with his fork.

"She worked in the recorder's office until eight months ago when she retired." Darlene sat down once they all had pie in front of them.

"This is really good. What did you do different?" Hawke asked, digging in for another bite.

"I changed up the spices. Added a little brown sugar instead of the granulated." She took a bite and smiled. "This is going to win first place at next year's fair."

Hawke glanced at Herb. They shared a grin. This past August had been the first time in ten years that Darlene hadn't won the prize for best pie with two crusts. She'd left the fair, steaming and vowing she'd come up with a better pie. They were the lucky recipients of her new recipes.

"Where could I find Peggy?" Hawke asked. He knew the argument nearly two years ago was unlikely to have anything to do with Lange and Sigler. However, the D.A. may have been doing other unscrupulous things that caused the man to leave. It would give

Hawke more groundwork for bringing up the fact the district attorney gave a hunting tag to a poacher.

"She lives in Alder. Now that she's retired, she and her husband, Bob, go off fishing a lot. And they go to Arizona for the winter." Darlene put her fork down. "Why are you interested in Peggy?"

Hawke shrugged and finished his pie. No sense in telling these two his suspicions about the D.A. Everyone in the county would know about it by morning if he did.

He helped clear the rest of the dishes from the table and excused himself.

Back in his apartment, Dog plopped across the end of his bed. Hawke wasn't ready to retire. He had too many thoughts tumbling around in his head. Opening his laptop, he googled Benjamin Lange.

The man had grown up in western Oregon, acquired his law degree at the University of Oregon and worked at several places on the west side of the state as an assistant district attorney before applying for the assistant district attorney opening in Wallowa County. The county commissioners and the previous D.A. hired him. He'd moved up to district attorney when the judge retired and D.A. Vickers became Judge Vickers. Lange was voted in by the county constituents for a second term.

Hawke pulled up newspaper accounts of several trials. Lange appeared to be hardnosed on those who broke the laws. It didn't make sense that he would break the law himself, but if Sigler were blackmailing him, that could have skewed the D.A.'s way of thinking.

He yawned, closed the computer, and chased Dog

into his bed on the floor. He'd have a talk with Sigler tomorrow afternoon and have breakfast at the Rusty Nail in the morning.

《》《》《》

After feeding his animals, Hawke climbed into his work vehicle. Dog's head drooped as he slowly walked back into the barn. He'd better take a trek on horseback into the mountains to check on hunters soon. Dog was getting depressed not getting to go with him.

He headed to Winslow, the small town six miles from the Trembley's and where the state police office resided. Hawke liked the Rusty Nail Café. Locals from Winslow and Eagle gathered there in the morning for coffee and gossip. He'd learned shortly after being assigned in the county that nine times out of ten there was some truth to the rumors floating around. Or at least you could use a rumor to discover the truth.

Merrilee, the seventy-something owner of the place, stood at her usual spot behind the counter. His friend Justine, who he'd been avoiding since she'd made it clear she was willing to open the shutters she had on getting involved with a man, looked up from where she stood taking an order. Her gaze latched onto him and then back to her order pad.

Hawke took his usual seat at the counter.

"Catching many illegal hunters?" Merrilee asked in her loud, gravelly voice.

He had a pretty good idea she'd just turned everyone's attention on them. While the old woman was rough around the edges and didn't give her employees enough time off, she was the one people went to when they wanted to get something off their minds or spill about someone else.

"Brought in a couple yesterday." He sipped the coffee she'd poured in a cup and placed in front of him.

"Anyone we know or some yayhoo from the city?" She picked up an order pad. "Same as usual?"

He nodded and ignored her first question.

She placed the order on the spinner at the kitchen window and turned back to him. "Cat got your tongue?"

"Something like that." He grinned at her over the cup. It was always the same. She tried to get information out of him. He clammed up. But he usually left having learned something helpful.

Justine placed an order on the spinner and faced him. "Haven't seen you in a while. The hunters must be keeping you busy." She plopped a blob of butter in a little dish and picked up a dispenser of syrup.

Before he could comment, she headed out to the tables.

Every muscle in his body wanted to turn and watch her. See if the coldness he'd felt in her tone showed in her body.

Damn! He hated the verbal and non-verbal dance women did when they were upset. He didn't have the time or the emotions for any of that. One of the reasons he'd never remarried. Once his wife left him for arresting her brother for selling drugs, he'd discovered that it was easier doing his job when he didn't have to worry about someone wondering where he was and if he was arresting a friend or family member.

He decided to let it go. They weren't a couple, but if he responded to her there would be a discussion and the whole county would think they were more than friends.

Merrilee placed his food in front of him. "You

know there was a fight in the jail last night?"

Hawke peered at the woman. "How do you know?"

"Darnell was in earlier. His wife said the jail sent for a doctor last night. When he came back, he said a couple of the people in jail got into it." Merrilee watched him close.

He shook his head. "Didn't hear about it." But he scooped his food in as fast as he could and as soon as he was in his vehicle, he called the county jail.

"This is Trooper Hawke. Can you tell me about the fight in the jail last night?"

"The two you brought in yesterday. We should have split them up when they started yelling at each other, but we didn't think they'd try to tear each other apart," the young jailer, Ralph, said.

"Are they well enough to go to arraignment and be released?" Hawke wondered if he should go speak with Sigler this morning before arraignment.

"Yeah. The doctor fixed 'em up, and we put them in separate cells."

"Okay. Thanks." Hawke disconnected and peered out the front window. He'd go have a talk with Sergeant Spruel.

Chapter Three

While Hawke sat in the office talking with his sergeant, they received word that the two he'd arrested the day before were out on bail and had been given plea dates.

"You'll need to tread lightly, if you think D.A. Lange did give that tag to Sigler," Sergeant Spruel warned him.

"I'll be careful. But if the D.A. did, he either sold it which means he needs money, something I can look into, or he gave it as a blackmail payment." Hawke tapped his pen against his logbook. "Either way, I'll find out."

"You're going to have to ask Judge Vickers, Lange's previous employer, for a warrant to get his bank records. How do you plan to keep him from telling the D.A.?"

"I'm not sure yet. But I'll work on it." Hawke left the sergeant's office and went over to his computer.

He opened the county site, only accessible by law enforcement, and looked for the video of Sigler's arraignment.

Sigler came into view. His left eye was black and blue. A cut on his cheek and his body sagged as if it hurt to stand straight. It appeared Price did a pretty good number on him.

District Attorney Lange read the list of violations and asked if Price had anything to say.

Hawke studied both men's body language and neither seemed to be avoiding one another or acting suspicious. He found it interesting that yesterday the man had been vehement that D.A. Lange gave him the tag. Today, when he could accuse the man to his face, he kept his mouth clamped shut.

He signed out of the court site and began carefully wording a warrant for Lange's financial records. He'd take the warrant to Judge Vickers and see if he couldn't get what he needed without the D.A. learning about it.

《》《》《》

"You want me to sign off on a warrant for you to look into my D.A.'s financial records?" Where Lange was a small, wiry man with a deep, loud voice, Vickers size and rotundness fit his bellowing presence.

Hawke was glad he'd cornered the judge in his office. "Sir, as I stated in the warrant, I want to make sure that the D.A. didn't receive any money for the exchange of his hunting license."

"I don't understand. Why would you even think such a thing?" Judge Vickers threw the warrant onto his desk top.

"I apprehended a man yesterday who had D.A. Lange's elk tag on an animal. He said the D.A. gave him the tag. Which we both know is illegal. I want to figure out how the man acquired the tag."

"Have you asked Lange? I don't like you cops going behind a man's back." The judge glared at him from behind rimless glasses.

"I did ask him. He swore he'd never even purchased a hunting tag this year. But I discovered he did and paid for it with a credit card." Hawke placed a copy of the tag registration and credit card purchase on the desk in front of the judge.

He picked them up, studied the pages, and shook his head. "I don't like this. But given the evidence, I'll sign off on this request. But keep it in house."

Hawke nodded. "I'll keep it quiet. Thank you, Judge."

He stood to leave.

"You do know if this backfires on you, you'll have a hard time working in this county?"

Hawke studied the Judge. "I know."

The man waved his hand in dismissal.

Hawke left his office and the courthouse. This could put him on early retirement if it came out the D.A. was crooked and then was vindicated.

《》《》《》

Hawke delivered the warrant to the bank manager and headed to the Shake Shack in Alder for lunch. The bank would email him the records he'd requested.

While he sat eating his burger in his vehicle, his phone buzzed. Justine.

The bite he'd just chewed stuck in his throat. He didn't want to talk to her on the phone. He let it ring and go to voicemail. What could she be calling him about?

He choked down the rest of his burger. When he'd slurped the last of his soft drink, he hit the voicemail button and listened.

"Hey, Hawke. I'm not sure what your cold shoulder was this morning at the café. Give me a call. I think we need to talk things out. As friends."

The phone clicked off.

As friends. That was what he'd thought they had, until recently. He'd deal with that later.

The radio crackled. "Twelve-sixteen ten miles out North Highway," dispatch said.

"Copy. One-zero-zero-two. I'm five minutes out." He turned on his lights and sirens and headed through town and out the North Highway.

It was easy to spot the bright blue jeep upside down about thirty feet off the highway. Two pickups and a car had stopped to assist.

"We think he's still alive," one man about forty-years-old said, walking up to Hawke as he stepped out of his truck.

"Anyone see what happened?" Hawke asked.

"We came around that corner in time to see the Jeep roll onto its back," a younger man said. The woman beside him nodded her head.

"Stay here and tell the next officer who arrives. Send the ambulance attendants down." Hawke grabbed his emergency kit and crossed the barbwire fence nearly flattened to the ground and walked through the dried grass and rocky pasture to the overturned vehicle.

There was a young man, barely driving age, suspended in air by his seatbelt. His head was bleeding and his eyes were closed.

"I'm Trooper Hawke. Can you hear me?" He

placed his fingers to the young man's neck, hoping to find a pulse.

A faint flutter under his fingertips told Hawke the driver was alive. The roll bar was all that kept him from being smashed under the vehicle.

Hawke tended to the cuts the best he could and waited. He didn't want to cut the driver loose until he had a professional medical team here to assist.

The wailing approach of sirens started the Samaritans by the road waving their arms.

That was one of the things he liked about this rural area. When someone was in need of help, you usually had more help than you wanted, but it was better than no help at all. Everyone looked out for each other in Wallowa County. The ruralness made it necessary.

The ambulance stopped alongside the road. Two attendants went to the back and were soon carrying a litter and emergency kit toward him. Two of the bystanders followed.

"Please, stay back," Hawke instructed the men as Roxie Paley and Bonnie Fletcher set the litter down.

"We came to help." The older man obviously didn't think the two emergency attendants could handle their job.

"Your help is better served up by the road." Hawke wasn't as nice this time. "Go back up there."

"What do we have?" Roxie asked. She was the plumper of the two.

"Male, Caucasian. Teens. Has been unconscious since I arrived about ten minutes ago. All I found were a few cuts and bruises. But as you can see, he's hanging."

While he was telling Roxie all of this, Bonnie had

been taking his vital signs. "We need to get him cut down and stabilized," she said.

"You do the cutting, we'll get him on the litter," Roxie said, placing a brace on the young man's neck.

The women set themselves ready to take the young man's weight.

Hawke pulled a knife out of a pocket of his vest and cut the seatbelt.

Just as the young man landed in the attendants' arms, the woman by the road called out. "Here! We need you here!"

Hawke made sure the EMTs were fine and headed back to the road.

The woman was on the other side of the highway, waving her arms.

Hawke crossed the highway and spotted what the woman was worried about. It appeared the Jeep had collided with a cow elk. "Go back to your vehicle," he told the woman.

"But she needs help." The woman continued to watch the animal.

"There is nothing anyone can do for her. Go." He grabbed the woman by the arm and pulled her to the highway.

A car rolled by slowly. Hawke waved it on by.

Roxie and Bonnie had the injured man in the ambulance.

"Think he'll be conscious for me to get his statement when I get through here?" he asked.

"He's starting to come around. There's a good chance," Bonnie said.

Hawke nodded. "Which is your vehicle?" he asked the woman.

She pointed to the car.

"Get in it and go on about your evening." He led her to the car and waited for her to get in and drive away.

The older man who first noticed the Jeep stood by his pickup. "You going to put the elk down?"

Hawke didn't like doing it anymore than these people. Elk were beautiful creatures who deserved to roam this country. But the cow's injuries were too severe for her to heal. "Unfortunately." He pulled his rifle from the overhead rack in his vehicle, loaded a round into the chamber, and walked across the highway.

The big animal was dying. As much as he hated to kill her, he knew she was suffering. He aimed, pulled the trigger, and only looked long enough to make sure she no longer suffered. The body was far enough off the road it shouldn't cause any problems. The trauma the animal had suffered wouldn't make it useful to anyone but predators. They would soon have the carcass cleaned up. This time of year, carcasses didn't last long.

He called it into dispatch and trudged back across the road to store his rifle back in his vehicle. It would be another hour before he could leave the scene. He had to take photos and assess the scene for the records and the driver's insurance company.

《》《》《》

Hawke walked into the state police office in Winslow two hours past the end of his shift. He still had to input the information from the traffic accident. He rotated his head, popping his neck, and sat down at his computer.

"I didn't think you were out in the field today,"

Ward Dillon, another Fish and Wildlife trooper said, walking in from the breakroom with a donut and cup of coffee.

"I didn't go out looking for game violations. I caught a traffic accident on the North Highway." He opened his document.

"I'd rather be after illegal hunters than deal with that." Dillon sat down at his computer and started tapping at the keys.

Hawke opened up his logbook and started entering all the information. The accident form was filled out and he was typing his follow up with the driver at the hospital when his phone buzzed.

Justine.

"Bad news?" Dillon asked.

Hawke stared at the man. Had he groaned out loud?

"No. Just someone I don't want to talk to." He ignored his phone and forced his mind back on the report.

He checked his emails and found one from Sergeant Spruel. His superior was a man of few words. *Sullen spotted Sigler picking up his vehicle and trailer this afternoon.*

Hawke clicked out of his email and turned off his computer. He'd go have a word with Sigler tomorrow morning.

Chapter Four

   The camp trailer, still hooked up to Sigler's pickup,
sat in front of his small house in Eagle. Hawke parked
his vehicle behind the trailer. He'd called in to dispatch
when he drove away from the Trembleys this morning
that he was headed to have a talk with Sigler.

   Hawke walked up to the door of the older, paint-
bare house and knocked. Peering up and down the
street, he made note of the old man peeking out of a
window two houses down and across the street. The
houses on this side of town weren't set up like regular
city blocks. Many were still on large lots with barns
that housed chickens, horses, and hogs.

   There wasn't a sound from the inside of the house.
He knocked harder and waited.

   Nothing.

   He tried the door knob.

   Locked.

   A stroll over to the camp trailer revealed it wasn't

Paty Jager

locked. He opened the door and looked in. Empty. Well, empty of Sigler, but full of camping gear and trash.

He closed the door and headed down the side of the pickup.

A cat hissed and jumped out of the bed of the vehicle. Hawke glanced in and found a spike elk head in the bed. There wasn't a tag on the antlers. Where had the man come across this? Or had he shot another elk while up getting his vehicle and camper?

Why had Sigler left the elk head in the back of his pickup? He would have known someone would come around to ask more questions since he'd implicated the district attorney.

Hawke strode to the barn in the back. The door was open slightly. He shoved it all the way open and stepped inside. An elk hung from the rafters. This man was going to have more violations for his next court appearance.

Sigler was a single man. There was no need for him to waste an animal by killing more than he needed.

Anger pushed Hawke to walk around inspecting everything in the building. There was a dark spot on the ground. It could be oil from a vehicle. He glanced up at the hanging carcass. Maybe when he backed in to hang the elk… But it was at an odd angle to the hanging carcass.

Hawke crouched, picked up a bit of the substance on his fingers, and sniffed. It wasn't oil. He rubbed his fingers together. It was red.

Like blood.

He glanced up. It wasn't under the elk. Hawke studied the rafter. And it didn't appear that there had

34

been a rope around the old dusty beam directly above the spot.

Finding so much fresh blood had him scanning the inside of the barn with a different intention. Instead of looking for a man, he was studying the area for what was out of place. A large amount of blood had pooled in this spot. Leaning closer, he spotted drops in the dirt and on the debris leading toward the door.

Hawke followed the blood trail to the front of the house. There was a patch about two inches wide as if the person had stood still. Closer inspection proved a vehicle had been parked in this area.

He slid into his vehicle and typed Sigler's name into the DMV records. Sigler also owned a 1985 Toyota Corolla hatchback. Pressing the mic on his shoulder, Hawke said, "Dispatch, this is Hawke. Put out an APB on Duane Sigler's 1985 Toyota Corolla hatchback."

The radio crackled and dispatch came back. "That car was found thirty minutes ago. Alder City Police are on the scene."

"Scene of what?" Hawke had a feeling he already knew the answer.

"Homicide."

"Location."

"Alder City Hospital parking lot."

"Copy." Hawke pulled out his phone and called Sergeant Spruel.

"I'm at Sigler's place and heard about his homicide." He explained how he had come to learn about the death. "Want me to contain the crime scene?"

"Yes. I'll send Detective Donner and a deputy to help collect evidence and question the neighbors."

Hawke ended the connection and stepped out of his

vehicle. He opened the back door of his four-door pickup and pulled out his evidence kit.

"What you doin' sneakin' around Duane's place?"

Hawke spun at the voice and discovered the old man who'd been watching him from down the road.

"State Trooper Hawke. Did you see anyone come by and visit Duane last night or this morning?" Hawke asked.

"There was a blue rig, looked like a suburban but smaller, pulled in here last night about an hour after Duane came back from hunting."

Hawke pulled out his logbook and started writing. It appeared his neighbor didn't know Sigler had been in jail overnight. "What time did he get back?"

"About six."

"After dark then?" Hawke glanced up at the man.

"Yeah."

"Could you see who was driving the car? Man or woman? Or get a look at them when they got out and walked up to his door?" The shrill wail of a siren grew in volume drawing closer.

"No. Didn't get a good look. Don't know if it was a man or a woman. But they didn't go to the house. Went straight back to the barn." The man narrowed his eyes. "Why are you asking all of these questions?"

"What's your name?"

"Jimmy Douglas, why?"

Hawke wrote the man's name down in his book as Deputy Larry Novak pulled up and parked beside his vehicle.

"Why is there another cop here? Duane do something wrong?" Mr. Douglas started backing away.

"Duane was found dead in his car at the hospital

parking lot." Hawke watched the man's reaction. He didn't seem distraught over the news. "Did you see when he left in his car?"

The man shoved his knitted cap back and scratched his bald head. "It had to have been last night. I don't recall seeing the car here this morning. Didn't think anything about it, until you said something."

"What do you want me to do?" Novak asked.

"Take statements from the rest of the neighbors. I'll take photos. I know where I've walked and interfered with the crime scene. I'll see if I can piece together any information for Donner." Hawke slipped his logbook back in his pocket and pulled out a camera.

As Novak moved Douglas back down the road, Hawke knelt and videoed where the car had parked, and the blood drops coming from the barn. He placed evidence markers by the car impressions and drops of blood and took photos. Digging in his bag, he pulled out a tube with a cotton swab in it and picked up one of the drops. He tagged the tube with the date, time, and location.

Shouldering his pack, he continued back to the barn, adding evidence markers and snapping photos as he went. Inside the barn, he videoed the interior and zoomed in on the puddle of blood. He clicked the camera from video to photo, added evidence markers, and snapped pictures of the whole building, hanging elk and all.

"Find anything interesting?" State Police Detective Donner asked, walking into the building.

"Blood. Pretty sure it doesn't belong to the critter hanging from the beam. That's a kill from several days ago and the blood is pretty fresh." Hawke walked over to the puddle, keeping away from the trail of drops. "I followed drops out to the front where it appeared he'd entered a vehicle."

Donner crouched. "Anything else?"

"I don't know if he was killed with a bullet or stabbed. Or something else. No one has reported what I'm looking for." Hawke scanned the area again, but nothing popped out as being out of place.

"You can look for a small caliber shell. He was shot, according to Dr. Vance. We'll know more when an autopsy is done." Donner stood. "Looks like you have things under control here. I'm headed to look at the body and the car."

Hawke waved his hand as his mind started working out where the shooter had stood. The neighbor had said the person who arrived came to the barn. Had they known to meet here or had the killer been in the barn waiting for Sigler to come out?

He noted a tall wooden structure hid one of the back corners a bit. A quick look and he could tell no one had stood in the corner. The layer of dust on the packed dirt floor hadn't been disturbed, nor the cobwebs about five feet off the ground.

Retracing his steps, he stood just inside the door. Scant pieces of straw, twigs, and leaves scattered across the entrance of the barn. Most likely debris from the back of Sigler's pickup when unloading the elk. The leaves didn't belong to any of the trees on the property. They were from an aspen. The twigs looked to also be aspen.

Hawke crouched, looking at the area from a different angle. That's when the sun glinted off of something just inside the opening. A click of the camera collected the location. He pulled out his pen and picked up the spent shell casing. A Smith & Wesson 380. The killer had used a handgun. One that was popular with conceal carry gun owners.

He put down an evidence marker, took a photo, and placed the shell in an evidence bag. Hawke marked the pertinent information on the bag and put it in his pack. Moving slowly along the walls, he looked for any sign someone might have been standing inside the door, waiting. Nothing.

He went back to where he'd found the casing. Using his pen, he moved the debris around, making a wider and wider circle until he spotted the indention of a shoe. From the definition of the heel and smooth sole, he thought the indention might have been caused by a dress shoe.

Hawke took a picture of the footprint, added a marker, and took several more photos. The print wasn't deep enough to try a plaster cast. When he couldn't find any more decent impressions of the shoe, he stood behind the print and took a photo of what the shooter would have seen.

The blood pool was directly in front of him. Had the person walked up to the door, said something to make Sigler turn toward them, and then shot? Or had Sigler been watching the door, waiting for the person, not expecting them to shoot?

Not one to leave a scene without thoroughly checking things, he made a wider circle from the area of the footprint and shell casing. Outside, just to the left of the door he spotted a chewed-up wad of gum. Sigler hadn't appeared to be the gum chewing type, and he doubted the poacher had many visitors who were either.

DNA testing being what it is today, he added the gum to the evidence. After bagging the chewed wad, he wandered back to his vehicle.

Deputy Novak walked toward him.

"Did you learn anything that will help?" Hawke asked.

"Not sure. Mrs. Ridley, down there." He pointed the opposite direction of Mr. Douglas's house. "She said she heard a shot about seven last night. She thinks. She said around here someone was always shooting at birds or skunks. She didn't think much about it. But knows it was shortly after she started watching television, which she does every night at seven."

"Anyone see Sigler drive away?" Hawke was curious that the man didn't call for help but instead drove himself to the hospital.

"No one noticed him driving away. One did notice a blue Tahoe here after Sigler came home. But they weren't sure of the time." Novak closed his notepad. "People in this area don't pay much attention to one another."

"Too bad. If they had been the nosey type, we'd have more information and a possible suspect." Hawke headed to his vehicle. He'd take the evidence to the State Police Office in Winslow and write up his report. Donner would need all his information to work on the murder investigation. He had a strong hunch the death was in connection to the fact the victim had pinched the D.A. with illegal actions.

《》《》《》

By the time he reached Winslow and the office, it was almost noon. His stomach growled, but he wanted to hand over the evidence. He didn't like carrying it around.

He stepped out of his vehicle as Donner drove into the parking lot.

The detective drove up to him and rolled down his window. "Find anything?"

Hawke handed him the evidence bags and the disk from his camera. "Shell casing, foot print, and a wad of gum. Not sure what all is relevant other than the shell, but that's all I found."

"It all helps. Dr. Vance was surprised the guy was able to drive from Eagle to Alder. She's going to start the autopsy this afternoon when she finishes with her patients." Donner motioned to the building. "I heard you saw the victim day before yesterday."

Hawke stepped away from the vehicle and Donner parked.

They walked into the back of the building together. The Wallowa County division of the Oregon Department of Fish and Wildlife shared the front half of the building, while the five-man Fish and Wildlife division of the Oregon State Police had rooms in the back.

Hawke slipped out of his coat and headed to the conference/break room. He poured two cups of coffee and noticed someone had brought cookies in. He snagged the cookie container and put it on the table.

Donner sat down, taking a cup of coffee.

Hawke took a seat across from him and grabbed a cookie to stop his stomach from growling. "Yeah. I caught him using someone else's tag on a bull elk, I confiscated and took the carcass to Jed Eagan."

"Whose tag did Sigler have?"

"Benjamin Lange." Hawke waited as the name

sunk in.

"District Attorney Lange?" Donner set his cup down.

"Sigler said Lange gave it to him. I went to Lange's office and asked him about the tag. The D.A. said he never even purchased a tag. When I checked, he'd purchased it with his credit card." Hawke waved his cookie. "It would be interesting to see who called who when Sigler came back from retrieving his pickup and camper last night."

Donner pulled out his notepad. "I'll get the deceased's phone records."

"I had Judge Vickers sign a warrant for Lange's financial records. I should have them today. I'll take a look and forward them on to you." Hawke sipped his coffee.

"You told Vickers what you suspect?" Donner whistled low.

"He said we needed to know one way or the other."

"I'll send you everything I dig up. You do the same." Donner finished off his coffee and grabbed a cookie. "I'm headed to tell the next of kin."

"He had family here?" Hawke had never heard anyone connect Sigler with a family.

"He has a sister in La Grande." Donner stood. "Keep in touch."

"I will." Hawke picked up his coffee and headed to his computer to input what he'd noted at the crime scene. He should have kept the disk to the camera. He could have uploaded the photos just as easy and faster than Donner. The detective wouldn't get them in the system till late today or tomorrow.

Sergeant Spruel walked out of his office and over

to Hawke. "You going back out on patrol today?"

Hawke could tell by the sergeant's tone he wasn't really asking. He was telling.

"Yes. I'm putting in my report on the crime scene. Then I'll grab lunch and head out to Sled Springs." Hawke turned on his screen and saw the email from the bank.

"It would be good if you took a trip up the Minam unit. We haven't had enough of a presence up there this season."

"Your order will make Dog and Jack happy. They're getting tired of staying at home."

Hawke waited until the sergeant walked away before he opened up Benjamin Lange's financial records. It appeared the man, while bringing in a good salary, was nearly broke. He made monthly payments to a retirement home in Oregon City. And it appeared to an ex-wife.

He hadn't had a chance to ask Sigler when he'd received the tag from Lange. Checking through the records, Hawke found a thousand dollars added to the account and a two thousand dollar deposit. Either one, but most likely the one thousand, could have been from Sigler for the tag. Some hunters wanted a trophy elk bad enough to pay big money. Not that Price had bagged a trophy bull.

Price.

This being one of the busiest times of the year for his office, he knew wandering around asking questions that should have been left up to Donner was a waste of his time. However, just like when he tracked a trail, looking for a wounded animal or lost person, he couldn't let the information he'd gleaned go. He had to follow the specks of knowledge and see what more he could learn.

One thing that nagged at him was the mention of a blue Tahoe having been seen at Sigler's.

He tapped the information he'd written down in his logbook about Price into his computer. Up popped the man's DMV record. He jotted down the vehicle license and wandered into Sergeant Spruel's office.

"Shouldn't you be out patrolling?" his superior asked, looking up from the paperwork on his desk.

"I'd like permission to follow up on the Sigler homicide. I don't know if my contacting D.A. Lange caused the man's death or if it was the hunter Sigler had duped."

Spruel gave Hawke his full attention. "You better not drag the D.A. into this investigation unless you are one hundred percent sure he is the murderer."

"I won't. I need to talk to some people. Ones that know more about the D.A. than we do. Also thought it might be a good idea for Donner to follow up on the hunter Sigler sold the D.A.'s hunting tag to. According to DMV records he owns a Tahoe. Sigler's neighbors saw a blue Tahoe on the street the night of the homicide." Hawke knew he was pushing his boss' limits by not going out and checking hunters. But a man he'd arrested was dead. And not by natural causes. He wanted to find out why.

"If you don't find anything more in the investigation by tomorrow, you get back out in the woods." Spruel studied him a minute before directing his gaze to the papers on his desk.

Hawke nodded and backed out of the office. There were only a few more hours left in his work day. But a lot more in the day all together.

He headed to his desk and found the address for Peggy Greeley. He'd see what the woman had to say about the D.A. and the cause of the last Assistant D.A.'s departure.

Contacting Price was also on his list. It would be good to know when he'd purchased his hunting expedition with Sigler. Also, Sigler's financial reports might show him withdrawing the same amount as the D.A. added.

Hawke looked up the information on Price and picked up his phone. He dialed the number the man gave him. The phone rang and voicemail picked up.

"Price, this is Trooper Hawke. I'd like to know when you purchased the hunting package from Sigler. You can call me at this number." He read off his number and ended the connection.

He called the Rusty Nail. His stomach wasn't going to wait much longer.

"Rusty Nail, what do you want?" Merrilee answered. It was a good thing the seventy-something woman went into the restaurant business because of her cooking. It wasn't her charm that brought people back.

"It's Hawke. Any chance I can get you to put together a turkey sandwich with chips and a coffee to go?"

"When will you be here?" Merrilee asked.

"Five minutes."

"I'm not a damn magician." She hung up on him.

Hawke laughed and knew she'd gone to make his sandwich.

He rolled up to the curb in front of the café. A glance through the big windows and he sighed. He'd just as well get this over with.

Justine strode out the café door and opened his passenger door, holding the bag with his food out to him.

"Thank you," he said, handing her a ten dollar bill.

"I see you've been too busy to return my calls." She stood on the sidewalk, holding his door open.

Everyone in the café would see if he pulled away, leaving her standing there. He couldn't do that to her. She was too good of a friend.

"Yeah. Caught a murder, and you know, it's elk season. I'll be heading back up the mountain."

"It's kind of late in the day isn't it?" The anger on her face softened to worry lines.

"I'm not going today, but will tomorrow. Check out camps along the way, hang around a bit, and come back." He pulled the cup of coffee out of the bag and placed it in the beverage holder.

"What did I do that has you avoiding me?"

"This is too long of a conversation for right now. I'm sure everyone in there is wondering why we're talking this long." He glanced at the windows, and sure enough, all faces were pointed toward them.

"I thought we were friends?" she said, ignoring his comment about people wondering.

"That's what I thought. Then you looked at me…like…well… like you wanted more." He didn't like talking about this stuff. "I gotta go." He motioned for her to close the door.

"This have anything to do with that new owner of Charlie's Lodge?" Her eyebrows nearly touched and deeper wrinkles covered her brow.

"Why do you say that?" He rolled the top of the

bag down, trying to make her realize he'd purchased a to go meal, to go.

"There's been things I've heard."

He wanted to know those things, but he really had to get going. "You'll have to tell me later, I really have to be somewhere. I'll call you on Monday."

"Promise?" Her dark eyes bored into him as if she could read his mind.

"Yes. I promise. Now close the door and let me get going."

She closed the door a little harder than was necessary.

He pulled away from the curb.

He didn't have time for this. And how did she learn about Dani? He'd have to talk to Darlene and see if the county gossips had he and Dani together. If he were to take the marriage plunge again, and he wasn't, it would be with the ex-Air Force officer. But he didn't have the time or the mental capacity to keep up with a woman.

Chapter Five

Once he was out of Winslow, he pulled out the sandwich and had it eaten by the time he'd slowed to enter Alder. He headed up Hurricane Creek Road and found the Greeley place easily.

The large old farm house had been well tended. The white sides didn't show any weathering, the green metal roof looked fairly new. The yard, for November, was short cropped and the flower beds all clipped back and mulched. The Greeley's took pride in their home.

Hawke walked up the paving stones to the front door and knocked. He liked that most of the rural houses didn't have doorbells. It seemed to be something that town dwellers used.

A dog barked. Not a big dog. A small yappy type. Hawke didn't care. He could get along with most animals.

The door opened. A woman in her sixties, wearing an apron like his mom wore a good deal of the time when she was cooking, peered at him from behind cat-eye spectacles. "May I help you?"

A white curly-haired dog stood behind her feet, yapping.

"Mrs. Greeley?" he asked, loud enough to be heard over the dog.

"Yes?" She reached down and picked up the dog. "Cotton, shush." The fluffy dog stopped barking and stretched its neck, sniffing.

"I'm State Trooper Hawke. I have some questions about D.A. Lange and the assistant that left right before you retired."

"Oh my!" She opened the screen door. "Come in. Has something happened to Travis?" She put the dog down and pivoted.

Hawke thought that was an interesting question. "Why would you think that?"

Mrs. Greeley glanced over her shoulder as she led him into the kitchen, the small dog following right behind. "Because usually when a policeman shows up, something has happened to someone. And you mentioned the assistant that left before I retired. I put two and two together."

A buzzer went off. "Just a minute. I have a cake in the oven."

He stood by the kitchen door as the woman pulled two round cake pans out of the oven. After placing them on the racks on the counter, she pushed buttons on the oven.

"Please, have a seat. I'll get you coffee, unless you prefer milk with your cookies?" she asked.

He grinned. He could see why Darlene and this woman were friends. "Coffee is fine." The kitchen was clean, neat, and cheery. He liked the whimsical birds on the curtains.

She placed the coffee and a plate of sugar cookies in front of him and untied her apron, placing it over a chair back before she sat down across from him with her own cup of coffee. "What do you want to know about Travis?"

"Nothing actually. I'm more interested in Benjamin Lange, but I heard there was an argument before Travis left the D.A.'s Office." He sipped his coffee and saw the wheels spinning behind the woman's eyes.

"I'm not sure what Travis' argument with Mr. Lange would have to do with whatever you want to know about the district attorney." She picked up a cookie and slid the plate closer to Hawke.

He took the hint and snagged a cookie. "I'm trying to find out why Travis left. Did it have anything to do with Mr. Lange's ethics?"

"Oh, I see. Not really. It was his telling Travis to do one thing, then turning around and telling Travis he should have done something different. It's as if the man couldn't make up his mind." She shook her head. "I know at the time Mr. Lange was dealing with his mother going into a home and his wife leaving him, but he really shouldn't have taken it all out on his assistant."

"His wife leaving? Did she have a large divorce settlement?" Besides paying for his mother's stay in a home, if he were doling out money to his ex, it would make sense about his need for money and selling the tag, even if it went against his morals.

"Not really. I know she did get something though. Afterall, she worked while Mr. Lange was going to college. She mainly just wanted out. I don't know how many times I heard her refer to him as a cold fish." Mrs. Greeley's eyebrows raised. "A marriage that is cold isn't worth keeping. And I told her that one day when she was pacing back and forth in the hallway trying to get up the nerve to tell him she wanted a divorce."

The woman's cheeks reddened. "That's also the day Travis came along and quieted her."

Hawke had a feeling he knew why Lange sent the assistant packing. "Were Travis and Mrs. Lange having an affair?"

Mrs. Greeley gave one brief nod. "They were good for one another."

"Are they still together?"

"I get a Christmas card from them every year. They are both quite happy. Travis is the District Attorney in Marion County." Mrs. Greeley narrowed her eyes. "What do you think Mr. Lange did?"

"I can't say. Did you ever see him do anything unethical?"

She shook her head. "No. That man was by-the-book."

"You don't think losing his wife to his assistant or anything else would have pushed him to do something unethical?"

"No. He might have been a bit scattered for a while, but he never did anything that would hurt his job or reputation."

That bothered Hawke. If he was so ethical, why did he give his hunting tag to Sigler, a known poacher?

"Thank you, I appreciate you visiting with me. And the cookies were delicious." He smiled as he picked up another one.

"You're welcome. I hope I was helpful." She walked him to the door.

"If you wouldn't mind. Could I get a phone number for Travis and the former Mrs. Lange?"

"Just a minute. They are Mr. and Mrs. Needham now." She reached into a rolltop desk in the living room and pulled out an address book.

Hawke opened his notepad and waited.

She rattled off their address and phone number. "Lorraine is pregnant. Something she wanted with Mr. Lange, but he wasn't ready. Or that's what he told her."

Hawke nodded. He understood the D.A. There was a time when he wasn't ready for kids either. After the way things turned out, he was glad he and his wife hadn't conceived. It had made her leaving him and disappearing completely from his life not as hard as it would have been had she taken the kids and never let him see them.

"Thank you for all your help." He left the house and climbed into his vehicle. He had one day to find something to link anyone with Sigler's death. Then he was back to patrol.

There had to be something.

His phone buzzed. The number was familiar.

"Hawke," he answered.

"This is Barney Price, you left a message to call you."

"Yes. Are you back home?" The background noise sounded like the man was in a moving vehicle.

"Headed there today. I stopped off at a friend's place... in Pendleton." The man's tone conveyed it wasn't any of Hawke's business.

"When did you purchase the hunting package from

Duane Sigler?"

"This have something to do with my court hearing?"

"No. It has to do with the death of Duane Sigler." It was blunt, but the man wasn't being all that cooperative.

"He's dead! Shit! I'll never get my money back." The man groaned. "My wife is going to kill me."

So much for any sympathy for the dead man.

"When did you send him money? I'm assuming it was before the hunt so he could stock up on food and essentials."

"He fed me canned stew and chili. Said it was the real hunting experience." Price scoffed. "I should have known when his price was half what most guides charged that it would be a hokey hunt. By the time I pay all the fines, it will have cost me more than a legit guide, and I'll have nothing."

"Does that make you mad?"

There was silence for several seconds. "Do you mean mad enough to kill Sigler? No. I'm mad I won't be able to take him to court and get my money back."

"When did you send him the money?"

"Why do you need to know?"

"It's part of his murder investigation." Hawke wasn't going into detail with the man. If he had an inkling Hawke suspected the D.A., the man could use that as recourse to get his fines thrown out. He was just as guilty of using another person's tag as Sigler was for telling him it was okay. Price should have read up on the rules and known.

"It was in September. I contacted several guides in the area. Sigler was the cheapest. My wife wasn't crazy about me spending money on a guide, but I hadn't gone hunting enough to feel confident on my own. I'd bragged to some buddies that I could bag an elk. After I said it, I had to do it." The man's bravado was weakening.

"Thank you. That will be helpful. Don't forget your court date. You don't want a warrant out after you." Hawke disconnected and put the date in his logbook.

He headed back to Alder. A look at the financial records might help him connect the dots. But what of Sigler's claim the D.A. gave him the tag? How had it been delivered? Face-to-face? He doubted that. Lange wouldn't be that careless when doing something illegal. The mess he'd witnessed in the camp trailer when he'd discovered the body, there was a good chance the evidence of the transaction was in Sigler's house.

Hawke contacted Donner.

"Donner."

"This is Hawke. I'd like to go through Sigler's house."

There were a couple seconds of silence. "You're not a detective, Hawke."

"I know. But if Sigler is telling the truth, Lange sent him or gave him the tag. There might be evidence in the house. I can see a man like Sigler hanging onto something that might get his butt out of trouble with the law."

"Have a look. But you bring me anything you find. I'm on another homicide in Union right now." Donner closed the connection.

It appeared the State Detective for this region was tied up. Good thing Hawke's need to know answers had been roused.

He continued through Alder and Winslow and arrived at Sigler's house in Eagle thirty minutes later. Standing in front of the house, he realized he didn't have a way to get in. He'd have to hope at least one window wasn't painted shut.

Even though the door had been locked when he'd visited two days before and the man who lived there was dead, he tried the front door. Locked. He started clockwise around the house checking windows and came to the back door. He stepped onto the three-by-four wooden platform that made up the backdoor stoop and grasped the door knob.

It turned.

Thankful he didn't have to climb through a window, Hawke pushed the door open. Musk and the sour odor of unwashed body sailed out the door on a rush of hot air.

He went in search of the heat source. It was an oil stove, nearly invisible for the clothing hanging over the chairs in front of it. It appeared Sigler had washed his clothes by hand either in the sink or the bathtub and hung them up to dry in front of the stove. He'd had the time to do his laundry before he'd met his killer.

Hawke switched the heater off and began searching the house for paperwork. Bills. Letters.

There were old bills in a drawer in a small desk that had seen better days. He didn't find any correspondence with Price. There should have been their contract and anyone else that Sigler may have duped into a hunting expedition.

He moved into the bedroom. The sheets on the bed had at one time been light blue. At least by the look of the sheet drawn over the corner of the bed. Hawke felt a pang of sympathy for the man. He lived alone and it appeared wasn't much good at doing household chores. It surprised him that the type of man Sigler was, he hadn't taken a wife just to do his laundry and keep the bed clean.

Maybe this day and age there weren't that many desperate women.

He picked at the piles of clothing. The third pile of towels, he kicked and heard what sounded like cardboard.

Hawke pulled on rubber gloves and picked the stained towels off a box of letters and papers. He packed the box into the kitchen, placing it on the table. The light over the table illuminated letters with postmarks from the past year.

He found the contract between Sigler and Price. The wording on the contract sounded legal and like the hunting trip would have been more extravagant than what Price received. Maybe Sigler's clients forgot the lousy food once they bagged a nice bull elk.

In what his mother called chicken scratches, the penmanship was so bad, Sigler had printed *paid 9/2*. That meant the money would have gone into his account that day or later. He'd check August and September for a payment into Lange's account.

But what he really wanted was something that proved the district attorney had given the tag to Sigler.

Hawke dug down in the box and found an envelope from the county court and District Attorney Benjamin Lange. After checking the envelope and finding it empty, Hawke pulled an evidence bag from his coat pocket. He slid the envelope inside the evidence bag and labeled it.

Could there have been a letter with the envelope? Possibly something unrelated to a hunting tag. Digging through all the papers in the box, he didn't find anything that appeared to have come from the district attorney.

It wasn't conclusive. They would only have Lange's word on why Sigler had an envelope from the D.A., but Hawke hoped it was enough to get more people, besides himself, involved in learning more about Lange.

Chapter Six

Hawke drove to Winslow and dropped the evidence he'd found off at the state police office after leaving a message for Donner.

Driving home, he thought about his conversation with Justine. He had to find a way to get them back to being friends. It was exhausting avoiding her. And, he needed to find out what kind of rumors his landlady was spreading.

But uppermost on his mind was returning to the D.A.'s office tomorrow and finding out from the receptionist what had been sent to Sigler. He'd written down the date of the postmark on the letter. 9/15.

Dog ran out to greet him as Hawke pulled up and parked alongside his pickup.

He gathered his work computer and coat and slid out of the vehicle. Dog jumped up, putting his muddy paws on his vest. "Thanks. Now I'll have to wash your mud off." He used his empty hand to ruffle the dog's ears.

Horse, his mule, brayed. Boy and Jack followed with nickers.

"I'm here. You can have your nightly treat," Hawke said, placing his things on the third step up to his apartment and heading to the tack room where the grain was stored.

The sun had set while he'd been at the office. The moonless night beyond the lights in the barn had an appeal to Hawke tonight. He fed the animals and walked back outside. The stars were bright lights in the nearly black sky. The moon; a golden C drawn on a black canvas.

Nights like this, reminded him of his childhood. First, when his father would argue with his mother, and he'd run outside to get away from the loud voices and accusing tones. His father had a roving eye. Something his mother found out about after their marriage and caused their divorce.

When they'd moved to the Umatilla Reservation, Hawke had believed he'd never have to listen to arguing again. But it happened, again, after his mother remarried and his sister was born. This time, his stepfather's other love was booze. He'd come home mean and nasty. Hawke would take his sister and leave the house. He'd tell her about the stars in the sky and how grandfather had told him the story of how the stars came to be.

When he was a teenager, he'd realized his stepfather did more than hurl words at his mother. He threw punches. Hawke stepped in. Then one night the reservation police came and said his stepfather had died in a car crash. Instead of tears of grief, his mother had shed tears of happiness. They did fine on their own. There were some lean times, but they didn't have to live in fear in their own house.

"You counting the stars?" Herb asked from behind him.

"No. Just enjoying the night."

"It's supposed to get down in the teens tonight. You might want to snuggle with Dog." The older man chuckled.

"Funny. Has your wife been telling people I'm dating Dani Singer from Charlie's Hunting Lodge?" It bothered him that Justine thought that was why he was avoiding her. Because he considered her a friend, he would have told her about Dani, if there were anything to tell.

"I don't know. You know women. When they get together, they think they can bring everyone together with love." Herb said the 'with love' in a flowery way.

Hawke laughed. "You can tell your wife, I'm not dating Dani or anyone. She's making my friendship with Justine weird."

"Are you sure it's something Darlene said and not something you did or didn't say?"

Hawke peered through the darkness at Herb. "What do you mean?"

"Word around the Rusty Nail is you've been avoiding Justine. Everyone wonders if maybe she's the one that caught your eye after all this time."

Hawke shook his head. "Everyone at the Rusty Nail thinks that? Then so does half of the county. Shit!" It looked like a visit with Justine was needed to get this all cleared up.

"Have you been avoiding her?" Herb tapped his

arm and started walking toward the house. "Come in for coffee."

"I haven't had dinner yet. I don't feel like talking." Hawke headed to the barn. This is why he avoided women. He should be thinking about who would want Sigler dead and how to approach Lange and his office for information about the letter.

In his apartment, Hawke microwaved a can of chili, buttered a slice of bread, and popped open a can of beer. While he ate, he listed the evidence they had so far and the allegations.

Smith & Wesson 380 bullet. A ding went off in his brain.

Hawke pulled his laptop over and checked out what guns were registered to Benjamin Lange. A Smith & Wesson 380. He left a message with Donner that Lange owned a gun like the bullet casing found at the scene of the crime.

《》《》《》

The next day Hawke called in to dispatch that he was headed to Alder and would be unavailable for an hour. He then dialed Justine's number, knowing she was working, and left a message that he would bring dinner over to her house at seven that night. Meeting at her house would make it easier for them to talk without others listening in. They had never gone out. They had both wanted to keep any rumors at bay about them being a couple. Yet, here, when they'd tried to avoid being in the gossip wire, they were.

He pulled up to the courthouse and parked. The receptionist at the D.A.'s office was on the phone. She glanced up, recognized him, and waved him to a chair.

After she hung up the phone she asked, "Do you

need to see Mr. Lange?"

"I'm hoping you can help me. Is there any way to know what correspondence was sent to a person from this office?" He walked over to the desk.

"If you have a name, I can pull up the files and see." She glanced at the closed door to the D.A.'s office. "But I can't tell you what exactly was in the correspondence."

"That's fine. It was postmarked September fifteenth and sent to Duane Sigler."

The young woman, Terri, frowned. "The name sounds familiar, but I don't think it's because of anything we sent." She typed on her computer. "No, nothing comes up on that name in September." She typed some more. "Not August either. Sorry."

"Who has access to the envelopes with the district attorney's name on them?" He knew the D.A. for sure, but if Lange was as by-the-book as Mrs. Greeley said, could there be someone trying to frame him?

"Anyone in this office." She rolled her chair to a cabinet behind the desk and slid the door open. "We keep all the stationery in here."

Rachel Wallen walked out of her office. Her eyes widened, then quickly lit up as she smiled at him. She walked up and held out her hand. "Rachel Wallen, Assistant District Attorney. What brings you here trooper?"

Her grip was firm.

"State Trooper Hawke with Fish and Wildlife. Just had a question."

Her gaze flashed over his face. "Hawke? Are you the trooper who is investigating the death of Duane Sigler?"

This was interesting. How did she know that? "I found the crime scene and am helping in the investigation. How did you hear about it?"

She narrowed her eyes. "I work in the District Attorney's Office. We hear about all the crimes committed in the county. Have you found any solid leads?"

"We're working on a couple."

"Is that why you're here? To fill us in?" She started toward Lange's office.

"No. Just gathering evidence."

"Here?"

He studied the woman. Was she playing dumb or was she egging him to say more? Bring up that he believed the D.A. might be involved.

"I've discovered enough. Thank you for your help, Terri." He nodded to the receptionist and walked out of the offices.

It wasn't until he sat in his vehicle, letting dispatch know he was available, that he noticed the D.A.'s investigator stood on the courthouse steps, watching him. Did Lange have the man keeping an eye on him or was it the Assistant D.A.? If something happened to Lange, she'd more than likely move up to fill his position until the next election.

A glance at his phone showed three messages. Two were from Donner. The third was from Justine. He listened to Donner's.

"Sent the envelope to forensics. We'll see if they can lift any prints, but more than likely they will be from people in the D.A.'s office. Without knowing what was inside, it's a dead end." Hawke listened to the second message. "Do you know how many people own

Smith and Wesson three-eighties? I really doubt I can get Judge Vickers to give me a warrant to confiscate Lange's pistol."

Hawke hit the off button and dialed Donner.

"Donner."

"This is Hawke. I was just at the D.A.'s office. They have no record of sending Sigler any kind of correspondence. So how did he get the envelope? And what's wrong with just walking in and asking Lange for his weapon? If he has nothing to hide, he'll hand it over."

Donner blew out a long breath. "The envelope is a real long shot. I can't see us tracing it to any kind of misconduct from the D.A.'s office. And for the gun. If you want to give it a try, you go for it. Me. I like my job."

Hawke liked his job, too. If the man handed the gun over, he'd stop pressing to find out if the D.A. was corrupt. "I'm in front of the courthouse now. I'll go ask."

"Let me know the outcome." Donner ended the connection.

Hawke drew in a breath and stepped out of the vehicle. Walking up the steps this time, they felt like they were three times as high. His job could be on the line.

"You're back. Did you forget to ask something?" Terri asked, glancing up from her computer screen.

"Is Lange busy?" He glanced at the closed door.

"I'll see." She picked up the phone. "Trooper Hawke would like to speak to you." She listened and put the phone down. "Go right in."

After his last encounter, he was surprised the man

was willing to see him. Hawke strode to the door and opened it, walking in.

Judge Vickers sat in the chair in front of the D.A.'s desk. He stood and held out his hand. "Hawke."

He shook hands with the judge. "Judge."

"What did you need to see me about today?" Lange's clipped tone said he didn't appreciate the visit and had more than likely asked the judge to stay to witness the encounter.

"I wondered if you would be willing to hand over your Smith and Wesson three-eighty for a ballistic test?"

The judge sputtered. "What is this request for?"

Hawke studied Lange. "The D.A. knows."

"My gun is down in the glove box of my car. I have a few minutes, you can walk down with me. Judge, you're welcome to come if you want." Lange moved from behind the desk and headed to the door.

"I'll leave you two to this." Judge Vickers walked out the open door and out into the hall.

"Terri, I'll be back in ten minutes," Lange said to his receptionist as they walked through the area.

Ms. Wallen stuck her head out the door as Hawke walked by.

He hoped she didn't decide to tag along. His intuition about her said she would do whatever it took to move up the ladder.

Hawke followed Lange down the stairs and out the back of the building to the county employees parking lot. A gray-blue Tahoe's lights blinked, and Lange walked up to it.

Tahoe. Just like the neighbors saw at Sigler's house. Hawke caught up to the man as he opened the passenger door and dropped the door to the glove box down. All the compartment contained were maps, a registration slip, and proof of insurance.

Lange tapped his hand around inside the compartment as if he thought the gun would miraculously appear. "I don't understand. It was here last week when I took it out and cleaned it."

Chapter Seven

This was the first time Hawke had witnessed a seed of fear on the man's face. "Why did you take it out and clean it?"

Lange stared at him. "I clean it once a month after practicing at the shooting range. It doesn't do any good to have a gun permit and carry if you aren't prepared to use it."

"Where were you Monday night between six and eight?" Hawke had a feeling the man wouldn't have an alibi.

"Monday night? I finished up in the office around six-thirty and drove home." The man peered straight in his eyes. "And I don't have anyone who can vouch for me. I live alone." Lange closed the glove box and stood. "I'm not stupid. You accused me of selling my hunting tag to Sigler and then he ends up dead. You're trying to pin his death on me." He slammed the vehicle door shut. "I didn't give or sell the tag to that man, and I didn't kill him."

Hawke almost believed him.

"Well?" Lange crossed his arms.

"Well, what?"

"Aren't you going to take down my statement about the stolen gun?" Now the man was tapping his right foot.

With a flourish, Hawke pulled out his logbook. "When was the last time you saw the Smith and Wesson three-eighty?"

"A week ago Sunday. I'd been to the shooting range and had cleaned the pistol. I put it back in the glove box around nine p.m."

"Who knows you keep a gun in your glove box?" Hawke asked.

The district attorney started to shake his head. "Dave Willard, the man who keeps tabs on the range. I believe he saw me putting it away one time. My previous assistant, Travis Needham." He said the name as if it left a bad taste in his mouth. "And my ex-wife, Lorraine. She would go to the shooting range with me sometimes and shoot the pistol I gave her."

"What kind was that?"

"The same as mine. Just a little smaller, easier for her to grip." Lange uncrossed his arms. "I need to get back to work."

It was apparent talking about his ex-wife softened the man, and her leaving had upset him.

"Can you think of any reason why Sigler would say you gave him your hunting tag?" Even though the man had been an unlawful hunter, he'd been adamant the D.A. gave him the tag. Yet, he'd tap danced around everything else that he was questioned about.

Lange shook his head. "I know he'd been in court a

couple times on hunting violations and a DUII, but other than that, we've never even talked."

Hawke had a feeling someone was out to get the district attorney. But why? And who?

He walked to his vehicle. The feeling someone watched him had Hawke looking up. In a window on the second floor of the courthouse, Assistant District Attorney Rachel Wallen looked out.

Pulling out of the parking lot, he spotted the court investigator walking toward a light blue sedan.

A thought struck him. He wondered what cases Lange was working right now. Could someone want to discredit Lange to get out of trouble with the law? But what about the envelope in Sigler's possession from the D.A.'s office?

Hawke knew he should leave the investigation of Sigler's homicide to Donner. But he'd found the crime scene, gathered evidence, and what made him a good tracker was not being able to ignore the oddities that usually uncovered the tracks or trail.

But he couldn't continue to follow the clues while on duty. He had to take the rest of today and tomorrow off. During the busy hunting seasons all officers worked the weekends. That was when the most hunters were out. And if he didn't take his days off, the Lieutenant chewed his ass.

He drove home, parked his work vehicle, and stepped out. Dog raced over, whining and showing his teeth.

"I'm home the rest of the day." Hawke scratched the dog's ears.

Jack nickered.

Hawke walked to the paddock. "I suppose you

three would like some exercise." He patted each one between their eyes and headed to his apartment.

A flick of the switch on the coffeemaker and it started brewing. He took off his uniform and slipped into his everyday clothes, pulling on his cowboy boots. After making and eating a sandwich, he wandered back down to the barn.

Darlene stood at the entrance to the arena, watching a young woman lope a buckskin mare. "I wondered when you were taking a day off this week."

Hawke stopped beside her. "This time of year, it's hard to get a day off." He nodded. "She and that horse are looking better each time I see them."

The woman next to him nodded. "She needed confidence and the horse needed consistency. They are both blooming."

"Are you using the arena all afternoon?"

Darlene faced him. "You want to let your three hooligans out here to run around?"

"If you don't need the space." Even though he'd be taking Jack and Horse up into the mountains on Saturday, they had been cooped up all week.

"Chelsea will be done in another thirty minutes. And the arena is all yours."

"Thanks." Hawke started to walk away and stopped. "I need to take dinner to someone tonight. Do you think I should grab something from the store that warms up in the oven, or order from a restaurant?"

Darlene closed the distance between them. "Are you talking about Justine or Dani?"

He moaned. How did he not think she'd have intuition it was a woman? "Justine."

"The one you just want to be friends with. Take

something already cooked." She pivoted, took a step, and tossed over her shoulder. "She's a good woman. Be sure you know what you're doing."

His gut tightened. Of course, Darlene would be rooting for Justine. She'd known her practically her whole life. Dani was new to the area and those who had deep roots here would be leery of her.

But he and Dani had even deeper roots than the so-called first families of the area. Their families were here before settlers arrived.

He walked up to his apartment, dug around in the basket on his small counter, and found the menu for Blue Elk Tavern in Winslow. They didn't have a huge selection of food items, but it was either that or the Rusty Nail. He didn't want to order food from the place where Justine worked.

He punched in the tavern's number and listened to the buzz.

"Hello! Blue Elk Tavern," Ben Preston, the owner, answered.

"Ben, it's Hawke. I'd like to place a to-go order for tonight at six-thirty."

"You must be off today to know exactly when you'll be here to pick it up."

"I am. I'd like two of your fried chicken baskets and two slices of apple pie." He knew ordering two would catch the man's attention.

"Two? Do you have company coming over?"

The insinuation in the man's voice was exactly what he was trying to avoid by going to Justine's rather than bringing her to the tavern for dinner.

"I'm having dinner with a friend. See you at six-thirty." He ended the call and checked his refrigerator.

He'd have to stop at the Winslow General Store and purchase a bottle of wine. A quick google on his phone for what wine to drink with chicken and he knew what kind to get.

Dog stood up and stretched.

"Yeah, it's time to take the boys out to play." He descended the stairs.

Darlene and Chelsea stood by the woman's truck and trailer, talking.

He haltered Boy, Horse, and Jack. Opening the stall gate, he gave Jack's lead rope to Dog, who led the gelding into the arena. He'd acquired both animals about the same time and the two had become friends. Having Dog lead Jack, gave Hawke two hands when he had to deal with Horse's mule attitude.

When all three were in the arena, Hawke unhooked the lead ropes. All three took off running to the other end. He and Dog stood by the gate watching the large animals run and cavort as if they were playing tag.

His phone buzzed.

Donner.

"Hawke," he answered.

"What did you find out when you asked Lange about his gun?"

"He couldn't produce it. Said it was stolen. I took his statement."

Donner cleared his throat. "What did you think? Was he telling the truth or hiding the fact he ditched his weapon?"

Hawke was surprised the detective asked his opinion. "He seemed genuinely upset when he reached in the glove box and the weapon wasn't there."

"Did he say the last time he saw it?"

"Yeah." Hawke relayed the whole conversation to the detective. "And while I initially believed Lange was hiding the fact that he gave the hunting tag to Sigler, I'm starting to think someone has set up our district attorney."

"What makes you think that?" Donner asked.

Hawke laid out all his thoughts on the set-up. "Sigler was adamant the D.A. gave him the tag. He really believed it. But I don't know why he didn't say anything about it during his arraignment. Unless he was saving the information for his hearing, but how would he know it would work more in his favor if he waited?"

"Like someone who knew the law coached him?" Donner offered.

"Yeah." Hawke watched as his horses and mule started to slow down and mosey around the big open area.

"Then there's the envelope. Anyone with access to the office could have sent the hunting tag to Sigler." Hawke hadn't worked out how they got the tag. It had been purchased with Lange's credit card.

"Are you thinking the Assistant D.A.?"

Hawke wasn't sure how the detective jumped to that conclusion, however, it was clear by Donner's tone, he found that highly unlikely.

"Or the previous assistant. The last one didn't leave the office on good terms with Lange." But he'd taken the District Attorney's wife. If anyone should be setting someone up it would be Lange setting up the assistant.

"Travis got away with Lange's wife. I don't think either one of them would want to upset what they have."

"Then we'll just have to keep digging. Might look

into the cases Lange has on the docket. Maybe one of those people is trying to upset the attorney to get their conviction overturned." Hawke didn't think there was a severe enough case coming up that would warrant this much work to overrule.

"I'll see what I can come up with and keep you informed. You do the same when you aren't chasing hunters." Donner ended the conversation.

All three geldings walked over to him. They'd had their fun and now wanted attention. He rubbed the wide space between their eyes, scratched the base of their ears, rubbed his hands up and down their necks and scratched their chests. When they started pressing closer and closer, he snapped the ropes on the halters. He and Dog led them back to their paddock.

Closing the gate on the three, he gave them grain and walked out into the late afternoon sunshine and cleaned out the water trough and refilled it.

All the time he did these mindless actions, his brain was trying to make sense of the evidence and clues they had. What nagged at him the most was the tale of the evidence at the crime scene. The shooter had to be someone Sigler knew. But why had he driven himself to the hospital? Calling 9-1-1 might have saved his life. Was he worried whoever shot him would have heard the dispatcher giving his address and the shooter would have realized they hadn't killed him?

Hawke climbed the stairs to his apartment and pulled out his laptop. Opening the case file on the homicide, he entered the notes from his visit to the D.A.'s office today. Sitting back and thinking about what Lange said about not having an alibi, he thought he might try to find a neighbor who saw him come home on Monday night.

A glance at the clock showed he had a couple hours until his dinner with Justine. Hawke grabbed his cowboy hat and coat and headed out of the apartment with Dog on his heels.

His dodge pickup sat beside the barn. It hadn't been started up in a week. Dog jumped in the cab when he opened the driver's side door. Hawke slid behind the steering wheel, held in the button that warmed the glow plugs, and turned the key.

The motor roared to life.

He smiled and ruffled Dog's ears. Animals and machines were reliable.

Thirty minutes later, he traveled along the road on the west side of Wallowa Lake. An area of large homes, mostly log. Some were all year residents and others were only summer homes. Several vehicles went around him as he slowly moved along, trying to get a glimpse of the house numbers. He knew Lange's house was on this road, but he wasn't sure which house was the district attorney's. Once he'd established the house, he could talk to the neighbors.

It turned out Lange's house was on the end of five houses in a row along the lake shore. The D.A.'s house was a little smaller and not as ostentatious as the others.

Hawke backed up and pulled into the driveway of the log house closest to Lange's. A golden retriever trotted around the corner of the house, woofing, its flag of a tail waving.

"Stay," Hawke said to Dog as he whimpered to get out and play.

Closing the door, he leaned down and patted the dog on the head. "How are you today? Anyone home?"

A man in his seventies walked around the corner of the house from where the dog had appeared.

"Can I help you?" he asked. He had on a thick coat, stocking cap, and warm boots.

Hawke pulled out his badge. "State Trooper Hawke. I wondered if you could answer a few questions for me?"

The man studied his badge and squinted at him. "How come you aren't in uniform? State Troopers are always in uniform." He glanced at the pickup and Dog sitting inside. "And that's not a state vehicle."

"It's really my day off but something has been bothering me and I wanted to get some answers."

The man nodded. "About what?"

"Did you happen to see Mr. Lange come home on Monday night?" Hawke knew this line of inquiry could open up a can of worms that he might not be able to shut.

Chapter Eight

The man studied him. "Why do you need to know?"

"It has to do with an investigation." Hawke wasn't going to throw the D.A. under the bus. He liked his job and didn't want to do anything that could get him tossed out of the State Troopers. "Did you happen to see him come home? And the time?"

The man rubbed a hand over his chin and patted the dog's head with his other hand as he thought. "Monday night. Let's see that would have been three nights ago." He thought some more. "They pick up garbage on Wednesday. I would have been putting the bin out on Tuesday night... The night before that..." He shook his head. "I don't think I remember seeing anything." He nodded to the house on the other side. "You might check with Rupert. He likes to take his dog for a walk in the evenings. You know, to wear the young pup out."

"Is he home right now?" Hawke asked.

"He's always home this time of day. From one o'clock on. He likes to do any shopping or appointments first thing in the morning. It's when his wife is at her best." The man did an about face, and started walking.

"Excuse me. I didn't catch your name," Hawke said, pulling out his phone to make note of the man's name for his records.

"Stewart Crossley."

"Thank you, Mr. Crossley."

Hawke walked out to the road and over to the cobblestone walkway up to the two-story log house. The door was four feet wide with carved wildlife images. He rang the bell.

Barking echoed inside the house.

"Quiet!" a male voice bellowed.

The whirring of rolling wheels grew louder. The door opened. A woman, most likely closer to seventy than sixty, looked up at him from a motorized wheelchair. Her body appeared shriveled up and boney.

"Hello," she said. "Rupert! Rupert! We have company!" she hollered over her shoulder.

"Marilyn, what have I told you about opening the door when I'm busy?" A tall, broad shouldered man with snow white hair walked into the entry. He caught sight of Hawke and hurried faster.

"We don't buy or donate to anyone who goes door to door." The man grabbed the door as if to shut it in Hawke's face.

He pulled out his badge. "I'm State Trooper Hawke. I'd like to ask you some questions about Monday night."

The man peered at the badge. "You aren't in

uniform."

"Mr...."

"Donaghey. Rupert Donaghey. This is my wife, Marilyn." He motioned for his wife to move her wheelchair.

She headed it out of the entry and called over her shoulder. "Take him into the dining room, Rupert. I'll bring coffee."

Mr. Donaghey shut the door as Hawke stepped into the house. "It looks like my wife feels up to a coffee klatch."

Hawke followed the man through a living room and into a large dining area with a thick timber table.

"Have a seat." Mr. Donaghey pointed to the chair to the right of the one he took at the end of the table.

Mrs. Donaghey entered from another door. She had a tray across the arms of her chair. Her husband took the three cups of coffee from the tray, setting them in front of Hawke, himself, and his wife as she moved up to the table.

"What do you want to know about Monday night?" the woman asked.

"Did you happen to notice when your neighbor, Mr. Lange, came home?" Hawke pulled out his phone and quickly added the couple's names.

"You want to know when Benjamin came home Monday night?" Rupert asked.

"Yes. And if he happened to leave any time later?"

The two glanced at one another.

"I was out walking Rasputin, our Airedale. I'm sure you heard him barking. I was kenneling him when my wife opened the door." He glanced at Mrs. Donaghey and gave her that look only people married

79

for a long time shared. "I'm pretty sure it was after six, probably closer to seven when he pulled into his driveway. He sat in his car for a while talking on the phone. It looked like whatever the call was about he didn't like it." Mr. Donaghey reached over and grasped his wife's hand.

"I shouldn't have stood in the shadows watching him, but he's been even more distant since his wife left."

Mrs. Donaghey jumped into the conversation. "When Lorraine was still here, the two of them would come to dinner a few times a year. But every time I invite Benjamin, he turns me down. And not in a polite way."

"That's why I thought maybe I should keep an eye on him when it was obvious he was having a bad conversation. We heard through someone else in this neighborhood that there are times Benjamin picks up his mail and has what our friend calls a temper tantrum after looking through it."

Hawke studied the two. They were both nodding slightly. What was so upsetting to the D.A. when he picked up his mail?

"What did he do after his phone call?" Hawke asked.

"He got out of the car and went in the house after kicking the garbage bin." Mr. Donaghey flinched at the memory.

"Do you know if he went back out that night?" Hawke had to make sure the man was in his house during the hours the forensic pathologists nailed down the time of death.

"I didn't hear any cars leave and when I walked

Rasputin the next morning before Benjamin left, his car was in the same place he'd parked it the night before. He didn't even go back out and put it in the garage."

Hawke's cynical mind wondered if the man left the car out so people would think he was home.

"Thank you. You've been helpful. Is there anyone else on this road who might have visited with Mr. Lange that night?" Hawke finished off his coffee.

"You could talk to Stewart next door. He sees more of Benjamin than we do, being right next door." Mr. Donaghey tipped his head the direction of the man who'd suggested he come here.

"I visited with him already. Thank you."

Mr. Donaghey walked him to the door. "Is Benjamin in some kind of trouble?"

"I don't know. Did he and his wife have a good marriage?"

The man glanced over his shoulder and whispered. "They weren't as compatible as my Marilyn thinks. I didn't tell her about all the arguments I witnessed on my walks. I think if Benjamin could get over the fact he couldn't keep her, he'd be happier alone or with someone new. Lorraine was a sweet girl, but she didn't like taking second place to his career."

"Do you think she could be the one he was speaking to on the phone Monday night?" Hawke wanted to make sure Donner got a warrant for Lange's phone records. While he was inching toward the feeling the man was set-up, he still wasn't sure the man couldn't have staged it to look like he was being set up.

"He could have been. But whoever it was, I've never seen him that angry."

Hawke walked out of the house. The door closed,

and he hurried down the road to his pickup. Dog whimpered in his ear as he slid behind the steering wheel.

"Yeah, I better hurry if we're going to pick up dinner and get to Justine's on time."

《》《》《》

Hawke pulled into Justine's driveway at 7:05. Dog stood up whimpering and wagging his tail. He knew he'd be able to play with other dogs while he was here. Hawke had adopted Dog from Justine five years ago. She not only bred bird dogs, she took in rescue dogs.

The minute he opened the door, the chorus of barking from the kennels filled the air.

Justine stepped out onto her porch. "Quiet!" She called out, not as an order but as a command. The barking calmed and slowly stopped.

"You're late," she said as he walked up to the porch with their dinner in bags.

"I couldn't make up my mind on what kind of wine you'd like."

Her eyes widened. "I prefer beer."

"Good. Because I gave up and bought a six pack."

Justine laughed.

He followed her into the kitchen. Hawke placed the bags on the kitchen table, set for two.

"Do you want it plated?" she asked, opening a cupboard.

"No. Just plates for us to eat. We can grab out of the boxes. Less dishes." He pulled the Styrofoam to-go boxes from the bag.

Once they were both seated, a beer each, and the food between them, Justine stared at him. "What is this about?"

His heart started pounding against his rib cage. His feet wanted to start running. He'd never been good at saying what he meant when it came to women.

"I want things back the way they were."

Her eyes widened before she lowered her lashes and picked up her fork, poking it into a chicken leg. "Seems we had a tough conversation over chicken before," she said.

They'd sat on the tailgate of her pickup having a picnic at Williamson Campground up the Lostine River as he'd told her that her sister might have killed someone.

He stabbed his fork into the chicken and scooped french fries out of the container. "I guess so. Then this shouldn't be so tough." He glanced up.

Justine watched him, her fork poised halfway between her plate and the Styrofoam container.

"Remember that dinner your sister made you invite me to?" He hated to bring up her sister when he was the person who'd arrested her.

Her expression turned hard. Her eyes narrowed. "Yes."

"We both said we only wanted to be friends."

"And?" She put her fork down and picked up her beer, avoiding eye contact.

She wasn't going to make this any easier for him. He saw that. Damn! Why did women always make the man feel like he was wrong when it went both ways?

"I've been avoiding you because the last time we spent some time together you were looking at me like you thought I would take our relationship beyond friends." He said it. His heart stopped hammering his ribs. He peered across the table at her. "And then there was your outburst in front of the Rusty Nail about Ms. Singer as if you were jealous."

Her cheeks reddened and her eyelids lowered, hiding her emotions. "You have been a good friend. Before and after my family turned out to be murderers." Her head came up. "I may have started fantasizing about what it would be like to have you in my life more."

He shook his head. "I'm not the marrying, or the boyfriend kind. I'm married to my job. I appreciate you for not kicking my butt when I brought you the news about your sister and father. I would like to remain friends. But if you're going to get angry when I don't come by or call, or you hear I've been seen with another woman, I don't think it would be a healthy friendship for either of us."

She nodded and forked fries onto her plate.

He waited, but she didn't say anything. Just started eating. Was she stalling, hoping he'd change his mind?

His stomach was in a knot. He didn't love Justine, didn't really feel anything more than he did for his sister. But she'd been a good friend since meeting her when he adopted Dog.

"I'm willing to go for just friends. I haven't seemed to be able to tolerate the people I grew up with since moving back to the valley." She picked up her beer bottle and held it out to him.

He picked up his beer and they clinked bottles. "To friendship."

His guts unknotted and he dug into the lukewarm food. He'd finished off a leg and a breast and a heap of fries when Justine cleared her throat.

"So… when do I get to meet the pilot that took

84

over Charlie's Hunting Lodge?"

Hawke choked on the chicken he'd just swallowed. He coughed and grabbed for his beer.

"I didn't mean for you to choke," Justine said, standing beside him, pounding on his back.

He waved her away. "I'm fine," he croaked and swallowed another gulp of beer. "Why do you want to know about Ms. Singer?"

Justine laughed as she sat back down. "Ms. Singer. So formal. From what I've heard, you two have had dinner at the Firelight several times, and you spent time at the lodge when you were recuperating from getting shot in the shoulder."

He studied her to see if it was jealousy that had her asking. All he saw was merriment at his discomfort. That was the friendship he'd missed the last few months. The one where they could laugh at one another.

"Okay. Dani. She's an ex-Air Force officer. She knows how to work on and fly air planes and helicopters. She's pretty handy with most everything." He realized how that came out and his ears burned.

Justine burst out laughing. "Oh, you have it bad for this woman. Does she know?"

Mortification struck as sure as a lightning bolt. "No. And if you are my friend, you won't spread rumors or say anything to her if you happen to meet."

Her merriment died. "You know how I feel about rumors. I don't spread them."

Rumors had ended her marriage. He nodded and opened the other bag. "How about dessert?" They finished the meal and cleaned up.

"Want a cup of coffee before you drive home?" Justine asked as they finished up the dishes.

"No. I need to get going. Still some things I want to check on the computer tonight."

"This have anything to do with Duane Sigler's death?"

He studied her. "Yes. You know something?"

"Not that I heard, but Ralph Bremmer has been saying a lot of things." She opened the front door.

"Like what?" Hawke stepped out, and Dog arrived by his side.

"You know I don't listen or repeat rumors. All I know is someone said Duane's name and Ralph set off on a whole long tirade."

"Thanks. I may just stop in at the restaurant tomorrow. Ralph gets there about eight, right?"

"Like clockwork."

"See you then."

Hawke and Dog climbed into his pickup and headed home. Ralph Bremmer. The man gave loans that ended up with people losing their vehicles and homes. Did Duane owe him money?

Chapter Nine

Horse brayed, waking Hawke from a deep sleep.
After leaving Justine's the night before, Hawke wrote
up a list of things for Donner to either get warrants for
or to check out. He'd sent the email off around eleven
and fell asleep. He'd slept the hardest he had in months.
It had to be from relieving the stress of his friendship
with Justine. He hadn't realized how much he'd feared
losing her as a friend but wasn't going to jump into any
other kind of relationship with her just to keep her
around.

He scrubbed his hands over his face, started the
coffeemaker, and took a shower. Clean, dressed, and a
cup of coffee in him, he walked down the steps with
Dog on his heels and greeted his horses.

"You're up early this morning for not going to
work," Darlene said, walking out of the room where the
grain was stored.

"Headed to the Rusty Nail for breakfast." He
loaded hay in a wheelbarrow to take out to throw in his

Paty Jager

horses' run.

"Then the dinner with Justine went well?" His landlord watched him intently.

"Yes. We've reaffirmed, we are just friends." He saw the bit of hope fade from her eyes. "All I feel for her is a brotherly fondness. That wouldn't be fair to her if I let her believe it was more."

Darlene nodded. "That's what we all admire most about you, Hawke. Your truth." She patted his arm and strode off to her house.

Hawke's chest swelled. If he were remembered after he left this earth for his truth, his spirit would be happy.

He rolled the hay out to the waiting horses and tossed it over the fence. A tug on the faucet handle started water flowing into the trough.

His phone buzzed. Kitree.

He smiled and answered. "What are you doing calling me so early in the morning?"

The ten-year-old giggled. "I wanted to catch you before you went to work."

"Well you're in luck. It's my day off." He'd met the child while tracking her and keeping her from the people who killed her parents. She'd bonded with him in the wake of her grief and since the Kimbals, Dani Singer's employees at the Hunting Lodge, had adopted her, he could visit with her whenever he wanted. She was the closest thing to a daughter or niece he would ever have.

"Sage said I could have a birthday party. I wanted to make sure you could come."

"I'm honored. When is your birthday?" His mind started flashing through what he should get her for a present.

"It was last week, but I knew you were too busy with hunting season to come to a party at the lodge."

"I can be at the lodge for a party this Saturday night. Can you and Sage put one together that soon?" Now he'd have to come up with a present today.

"You bet! See you then!"

The connection ended. Water splashed, overflowing the trough. He hurried to turn the faucet off. Darlene didn't like him wasting water.

He pushed the wheelbarrow back to the barn and whistled for Dog. They hopped in the pickup and headed to Winslow and the Rusty Nail.

《》《》《》

Hawke sat at the counter sipping his coffee, waiting for his meal and Ralph Bremmer to make an appearance. Justine acted like her usual self. He was pleased that after they fell into the patter of conversation as they had for the last five years, the other patrons stopped watching them.

Merrilee hobbled out of the kitchen and plopped his plate in front of him. "Now that you and Justine have things worked out, you going to be coming in here more regular?"

He stared at the old woman. Her eyes watered, her wrinkles had wrinkles from all her years of smoking, and her gray hair was ready for another dye job. Only the last two inches of the thin strands were orange.

"You know this is my busiest season. I can't stop in for breakfast every morning. But I come as often as I can to support you." He raised his coffee cup to her and the door jingled.

He didn't have to turn around and look. Bremmer's

booming voice greeted the people at the table where he always sat.

Hawke dug into his meal. He'd wait until he was ready to leave before he started up a conversation with the man. Hopefully, by then his friends that had already ordered would have eaten and left.

Justine refilled his coffee as he wiped up the last of the egg with his slice of toast. "You going to talk to him?"

"When I finish and more of his friends leave," he replied in a soft voice.

About then two of the man's cronies came up to the cash register and paid.

Hawke picked up his coffee cup and moved over to the table where Bremmer and a man by the name of Otis Powell sat.

"What are you sitting with us for?" Bremmer asked, in his booming voice.

"I have a few questions for you about Duane Sigler." Hawke raised his cup to his lips watching Bremmer over the rim.

"Why do you think I know anything about Duane?" The man's gaze flit around the room as if trying to assess who had given Hawke the idea.

Powell snorted and said, "You think the cops aren't going to find out how much money he owed you?"

Bremmer glared at his friend.

"That's the kind of thing I'm looking for," Hawke said, smiling at the other man. "Why did he owe you money?"

"He borrowed money to buy that camper he used to take people hunting." Bremmer leaned forward. "You think I can take that camper? It was my money that bought it."

Hawke shrugged. "I'm not a lawyer. Are you the only person he owed money?"

"As far as I know. The kind of money I loan, we don't ask for financial records." Bremmer started laughing. Powell joined him.

"How much did he charge to take people on hunting trips?" Hawke couldn't understand why the man hadn't made enough from his guided hunts to pay Bremmer back.

"I don't know. Didn't ask. But he called me Monday night and said he'd have all my money the next day. Then the dumbass goes and gets himself killed." Bremmer slapped his palm on the table, making all the dishes and the condiment basket jump.

"He said he'd be able to pay you back the next day? How much did he owe you?" Hawke had a feeling the poacher had called Lange to blackmail him. That had to be the call the neighbor saw. But did or didn't Lange go to pay the man? Or did he take his pistol, shoot the man, ditch the weapon, and then pretend he'd lost it?

"Three thousand. That included interest. He'd paid part of it back a month ago, I think when he booked the hunts." Bremmer raised his cup to signal he wanted more coffee.

Justine walked over with the coffee pot. She looked at Hawke. "You want more?"

"No. I'm good." He waited for her to fill the other cups and go back to the counter before standing. He tossed a twenty on the counter by the cash register and walked out to his vehicle. Dog had steamed up the windows in the cab.

He wasn't supposed to be at work today and he needed to find a birthday present for Kitree. But the pull of the office had him driving over and parking in the lot in front of the building. He let Dog out to pee on some bushes before they both entered the Fish and Wildlife offices in the front of the building.

"Hey, that dog is better looking than you are," one of the biologists called out.

Hawke just waved a hand, walked down the hall, and through the door that joined the Fish and Wildlife offices with the State Police.

"What are you doing here today? You said you were taking the day off." Sergeant Spruel walked out of his office.

"I just had an interesting conversation with Ralph Bremmer at the Rusty Nail. Wanted to add it to the report so Donner has it." Hawke walked over to his desk and sat down. Dog laid down beside him.

Hawke relayed to his superior about the possibility the man had blackmailed the D.A. After talking to Lange, he'd thought it was a set-up, but the only person Sigler would know to blackmail would have been the D.A. himself. And if Sigler had called him, why hadn't Lange mentioned it, if, like he said, he didn't kill the man.

"If Donner hasn't added the phone records into the file, you might want to call him and tell him it could lead to the victim's killer." The sergeant walked back into his office.

Hawke clicked the monitor button on his computer, entered his code, and opened the Sigler file. The phone records weren't in the file. Neither were the financial records. He pulled out his phone and scrolled through his contacts to find Donner. He hit dial and waited. It went to voicemail.

"This is Hawke. I learned today that Sigler may have been blackmailing whoever shot him. Need to see his phone records as soon as you can get them added to the file." He hung up, clicked out of the file, and turned off his monitor. There was nothing to do here until he had the records. He'd go pick up Darlene and have her help him find a birthday gift for Kitree.

"Come on," he said to Dog and headed back through the Fish and Wildlife offices.

Dog circled the pickup as Hawke held the door open, waiting for him to jump in. "What's the hold up?" he asked.

The dog finally hopped in. Hawke slid behind the steering wheel. He turned the key in the ignition and his phone buzzed.

Donner.

"Hawke," he answered, leaving the vehicle in park.

"Donner. I'm in Eagle if you want to come get the records and fill me in. I'm doing a follow-up on my other homicide."

"Can you meet at Al's Café?" Hawke asked.

"Yeah. That will work. I should be able to shake loose here in about ten."

"Copy." Hawke disconnected and put the pickup in reverse. The plus side to meeting Donner at Al's—it was across the street from Bremmer's gas station and towing business.

《》《》《》

At the café, Hawke parked so that Bremmer knew he was across the street. Even though it didn't make sense that the man would have killed someone who owed him money, he might have known more about the blackmail plan than he let on. While Duane Sigler could keep his mouth shut about bagging more wild game than was legal, he was known to be a bragger about everything else. It was hard to believe he didn't tell the man he was paying off, that he was getting the money from the district attorney.

Hawke walked into the small café run by Bart Ramsey and his wife, Lacie.

Lacie waved to the half a dozen tables. "Take your pick. It's the slow part of the morning."

He nodded and took a seat the farthest from the counter where two farmers sat. Facing the door, he flipped over the upside down coffee cup and the woman hurried over to fill his cup.

"Do you need a menu?" she asked.

"No, I've eaten. Just waiting for someone."

She nodded and went back to filling the salt and pepper shakers. Bart walked out of the kitchen, wiping his hands on the white apron he wore. He waved before pouring himself a cup of coffee.

Hawke had met the couple when they'd first moved to the county and purchased the café.

The door jingled and Donner walked in. He headed straight for the table with a folder in his hands.

"Sorry. I haven't had a chance to get these scanned and entered into evidence." Donner turned his cup over.

Lacie appeared at the table to fill his cup.

"Can I get two eggs over easy, bacon, and toast, please." Donner placed his hat in the chair next to him.

"Coming up," the woman said, cheerfully.

"Missed dinner last night. This was a good idea." Donner sipped his coffee and slid the folder across the table to Hawke.

He opened the file and started scanning the information as he filled Donner in on what he'd discovered since last talking with him. "Looks like Sigler did call someone and talk for five minutes at a quarter to seven. Then made another call that lasted five minutes and another one that lasted one minute. I'd bet the last call was to Bremmer, telling him he'd be paid the next day." He studied the numbers. He'd never contacted the D.A. by his direct phone. The only way Sigler could have the number would be if they had been in contact before, when Lange sold the tag. He didn't like the D.A. all that much, but he didn't like to think someone who had been putting people in prison, could himself, need to go there.

"Do you want me to find out who these numbers belong to?" Hawke asked.

Donner's gaze slid over him. "It appears this is your day off. I can get to them in the next day or two."

Hawke shook his head. "I don't work like that. Once I'm on the trail, I can't sit back and wait for someone else to follow it. It'll only take a few phone calls to find out who has these numbers."

"Suit yourself. If it was my day off in the middle of a busy season, I'd be at home with my family." Donner leaned back as Lacie placed his breakfast in front of him.

Hawke stood, taking the folders with him. "My need to find answers is why I do this job and why I don't have a family."

He put three dollars on the table for the coffee and walked out of the café. Sitting in his vehicle, he used the quickest method of finding out who the numbers belonged to—he started dialing.

The first number went to voicemail. It was a woman's voice. "I'm unavailable. Leave a message."

He shrugged. Why not. "This is Gabriel Hawke, could you give me a call back at…" he left his number.

The next call was a familiar male voice. "Price."

"Mr. Price, this is State Trooper Hawke. I was wondering why Duane Sigler called you the night of his murder?"

The man sputtered a few seconds. "He didn't call me."

"I have phone records that show he did at…" Hawke rustled the papers and looked. "At six-fifty a phone call from Sigler's phone was made to your phone. And you talked for five minutes."

"How do you know it was my phone?"

"Because I dialed the number on the record from his phone provider, and I got you."

A deep sigh whistled through the phone. "He called me saying not to press charges or go after him. He had a plan to make money and would pay me back every cent I gave him for my hunt, and he'd pay the hunting violations. I asked him how he planned to do that and he just said, I know people who would pay for certain information to not come out."

"Why didn't you tell me this when I talked to you?"

"Because it would make me look like I knew whatever got him killed. I don't, and I don't want whoever shot him to come after me." The fear in Price's voice wasn't fake. His tone rose an octave as he spoke.

"Thank you for telling me this." Hawke ended the

conversation. That first phone call had to be to whoever he was blackmailing. And it wasn't the district attorney.

Chapter Ten

"Kitree is going to love that book on making
pressed flowers. She'll be able to keep a dried flower
diary of where and when she finds the flowers,"
Darlene said as Hawke pulled up to the barn.

They'd gone to Prairie Creek, the town in the
county that had all the art galleries and tourist type
shops. While he'd enjoyed the bronze statues on the
streets and some of the artwork in a couple of the
galleries, he was ready to leave when they'd stumbled
into a store specializing in capturing your memories.

"I think she'll be happy with it. Thanks for going
with me." He carried the bag with the book toward the
barn.

"Do you want to come over for dinner tonight?"
Darlene asked.

"Thank you, but I have some things I need to check
on and get packed for heading into the mountains
tomorrow."

She waved and headed to her house.

Hawke was halfway up his stairs when his phone buzzed. It was the number Sigler had called. He slid his finger across the screen and answered.

"Hello?"

"You left a message for me to call you?" The woman sounded skeptical.

"Yes, I was wondering who you are?"

The line disconnected. Okay, this meant going about it the hard way.

He put the gift for Kitree in his apartment, went back out and fed his horses, and returned to the apartment and opened up his laptop. He accessed the forms to request the information about the phone number from the phone company. Once the form was sent off there wasn't anything else he could do.

He began packing clothing and digging through his small cupboard to see what he had for food to take on his three-day trek up the Minam back country to Charlie's Hunting Lodge.

《》《》《》

Hawke, Jack, Horse, and Dog wandered up to the barn at the hunting lodge about four in the afternoon Saturday. From the lights shining in the three cabins, it looked like he might have to sleep under the stars.

"Hawke!" Kitree ran out of the lodge and straight at him. She flung her arms around his waist and hugged.

He patted her head. "Hey, don't squeeze me in two."

She immediately released him and wrapped her arms around Dog's neck. "I've missed you," she said.

He wasn't sure if she meant the dog or both of them. The thought she meant them both warmed a spot in his chest, he hadn't thought had grown cold.

"How many hunters are here?" he asked.

"Too many, according to Tuck." Kitree giggled.

"Why's that?"

"There's a couple of them that call Sage sweetie and honey."

Hawke understood the man was being protective of his wife. "Is there a bed for me to spend the night?"

"Sage made one up in the bunkhouse with us." She led Horse into the barn.

He wasn't sure he liked the idea of sharing the bunkhouse with the family. He hadn't minded staying in there when Clive, Charlie's old wrangler lived there.

Hawke unsaddled Jack and took the pack off of Horse. He grabbed the canvas packsaddle containing his work items, Kitree's present, and his belongings. "Lead the way to my bunk."

The girl skipped ahead of him toward the bunkhouse.

On the way, Tuck joined them. "Sorry you have to stay with us tonight."

"Beats sleeping out in the cold," he replied.

"The last few days the hunters have been streaming in here. Dani turned away three people in the last hour." He opened the bunkhouse door. "I'll be ready to get out of here in two weeks."

"Why do you think there are so many more hunters using the lodge?" Hawke asked.

"Because Dani has made it more comfortable. And Sage's cooking." He said the later as if it were a bad thing.

"Be thankful you have a wife who can cook." His ex had barely been able to boil water. She'd been proud of that fact. How naïve and young he'd been when he'd married her. He'd looked beyond her selfishness because of her other attributes. But he couldn't overlook her wanting to ignore what he'd sworn to do—uphold the law. Carting her brother off to jail for selling drugs hadn't been a hard decision. Her leaving him had hurt, but she'd also done him a favor. He no longer had to stress over someone worrying about him.

"I know. Just ready to do woodworking and relax during the winter months." Tuck put an arm around Kitree's shoulders. "And get this girl signed up for school. She needs to be around other kids."

Hawke agreed with that.

"Clean up and come in. Dinner will be ready soon," Kitree said.

"Are all the hunters invited to the birthday party?" Hawke asked.

She wrinkled her nose. "No, silly. We'll have the party after dinner. When they all go to bed."

"I see you have this all figured out." He placed his pack on the box at the end of the bunk where Tuck pointed.

"I do." Kitree grabbed Tuck's coat sleeve. "Come on."

Tuck grinned and followed the child out the door.

Hawke was happy Kitree seemed to be fitting in with the Kimbals and life at the lodge. He stored his pack, pulled out Kitree's wrapped gift, and a clean shirt. Using the basin beside the woodstove, he poured water from a jug into the basin and put it on the stove to warm.

He took off his coat and shirt, washed his upper body with a bandanna dipped in the warm water, put on the clean shirt, and tossed the basin of water out the door. He ran his hand through his hair, shoving the two-inch long bangs off his forehead. It was rarely regulation length. He spent too much time in the wilderness and didn't want to look like a cop with the regulation crew cut.

Pulling on his coat, he left the bunkhouse and walked to the lodge. A tug on the door and he was met by warmth from the fireplace and scents of bread, roast, and something sweet.

Half a dozen men and two women sat and stood in the great room. He nodded to them and went in search of the owner. Expecting Dani to be in the kitchen helping out, he wandered that direction.

The dining room table was set and water glasses were filled.

He pushed through the kitchen door and found only Sage and Kitree in the kitchen, dishing up the food.

"What do you want me to do with this?" he asked, holding up the gift.

"You can set it up here," Sage pointed to the high shelf above the dishes. "Glad you could make it. Someone has been bugging me to see if you could come. She rode down to get some of our guests just so she could call you."

Hawke had wondered about the call. "I'm here. Where's Dani?"

"She and Tuck are discussing some hunt a couple want to go on tomorrow." Sage opened the cookstove and pulled out a large roast.

"Do you need help?" he asked, grabbing a towel and making to help carry the roaster.

"I'm fine." Sage placed the roast on the wood

counter in the middle of the kitchen.

He tossed the towel at Kitree and headed to the office at the back of the building.

Tuck and Dani were hunched over the desk. He walked in the room and saw they were looking at an Eagle Cap Wilderness map.

"Are you two conspiring to overthrow the world?" Hawke asked.

They both jumped.

Dani spun toward the door. "Anyone ever tell you it's not nice to sneak up on people?"

"I'll go help with dinner." Tuck waited for Hawke to step into the room and he stepped out.

"I heard you were invited to a birthday party," Dani said, folding up the map.

"Yeah. I had to come up here and keep an eye on hunters anyway." Hawke hated how he became as socially awkward as a teenager when he was around the woman.

"Well, I can tell you, you made that girl's day when you said you'd come to her party." Dani sat on the edge of her desk, facing him.

He didn't know what to say. Since their first meeting when he was angry with her for not telling him about her uncle's death, he'd been attracted to the confident woman.

"Anything exciting happening down in the valley?" she asked.

It was apparent she felt a need to talk rather than them just stare at one another.

Hawke leaned a shoulder against the door frame. "Yeah. A poacher was shot."

"Saves you the time and trouble of a trial."

He laughed. That was what he liked about the woman. She was direct and to the point. "True. But it is a homicide that has to be solved."

"How can you work that and be up here?"

"I'll head back down tomorrow. I'll have made enough of a presence here to hopefully keep the hunters wary and law abiding."

She laughed. "Are you planning to go out and shout you are here, in the woods?"

"No. I'll tell all the people sitting around the table who I am and ask them to show me their hunting license and tag." He grinned when she frowned.

"Isn't that the lazy way of doing it?"

"It's the best way to get the word spread hunter to hunter. Don't tell them I'm leaving tomorrow."

She laughed. "It's our secret."

"What is?" Kitree asked, popping into the room.

"That Hawke is a lazy game warden," Dani said.

"Hey!" Hawke protested.

Kitree laughed and grabbed their hands. "Dinner is ready."

《》《》《》

Hawke spent Sunday wandering back to the Minam Trailhead, checking hunters as he went. By the time he loaded up Horse and Jack, he'd checked close to twenty-five hunters. He'd never come across so many in one trip before.

His final parting to them all was to be safe and make sure it was an elk in their sights and that no one was behind the animal.

After starting his vehicle, he turned on his cell phone. The thing started dinging like crazy. The first voicemail was from Donner wanting to know what he'd gleaned from the file he'd given him. His email showed the phone company had sent him a reply.

He opened the email. The phone was listed as one that was registered to the Wallowa County, Oregon, Court System.

Hawke thought on that for several seconds. It was a woman who replied to his call. It wasn't Lange's phone. He wondered who he would have to go through to determine which county court employee had the phone. It appeared he'd be making a trip to the courthouse again tomorrow.

He pulled out of the parking area and waited until he was on Highway 82 headed back to the county before calling Donner.

"Donner."

"Hawke. Sorry I didn't give you a call back sooner. One call was from Sigler to the man he'd sold the elk tag to. Barney Price. He said Sigler called and told him he would be paying back all the money he paid for the hunt and would pay all his fines. The other call, was to a woman." He went on to tell him about the calls and receiving the information about who owned the phone.

"I'm headed home from being on the mountain. I'll go to the courthouse tomorrow and see what I can find." Hawke slowed down as he entered Eagle.

"There's a good chance he was blackmailing whoever gave him the tag," Donner said.

"Yeah. We'll need to see if she has any connection to Lange."

"We can rule him out. It sounds like a woman set him up," Donner said.

"It was his tag purchased by him. Maybe they are in it together." While Hawke had been leaning toward the district attorney not being guilty, he couldn't ignore the facts he'd dug up so far.

"What do you have against Lange?" Donner asked.

"Nothing. I just follow the trail and the facts. I'll bring you up to speed tomorrow after I go to the courthouse."

Chapter Eleven

Monday morning Hawke put on his uniform and called into dispatch that he was headed to the courthouse then out Zumwalt to check on hunters.

The courthouse was quiet. He walked to the Administrative Services Office and entered.

A woman of about forty with blonde hair and dark roots looked up from a computer. "May I help you?"

"I'd like to know who in this building has possession of this phone?" He handed her a piece of paper with the phone number on it.

"I'll call Dennis and see if he can help you." The clerk picked up the phone on her desk and punched a button. "Dennis. There is a State Trooper here requesting information." She nodded and replaced the phone. "He'll be right out."

Hawke remained standing even though there were two chairs over by the door.

Five minutes later, a man waddled out of the door behind the woman's desk. He appeared to be in his thirties, but the jowls and roundness of the face gave him a younger appearance. He had on a short-sleeved, collared, pull-over that hung straight down off his belly, placing the hem of the shirt a foot away from his thighs. He had on tan slacks and the non-tie shoes someone his size wouldn't have to bend over to tie.

"I'm Dennis Brooks. How may I help you?" He held out a puffy hand with thick fingers.

Hawke shook hands. "Trooper Hawke. I'd like to find out which county employee this number belongs to." He picked up the slip of paper he'd handed the clerk and presented it to the man.

"Why do you need to know this particular number?" The man pushed his eyeglasses higher up the bridge of his nose.

"I'd rather not say." Hawke hoped the man didn't give him the run around.

"This is a private number. Without a warrant or written consent from the person, my hands are tied." He handed the number back to Hawke.

"Judge Vickers is just upstairs. I'll be right back." Hawke pivoted and left the area. He'd witnessed the moment the man recognized the number. Was he covering for the person or was it really the protocol?

He climbed the stairs to the second floor and turned right, striding down the hall to the judge's office.

His secretary happened to be friends with Darlene.

"Hawke what brings you here?" she asked, glancing up from the computer.

"I need to request a warrant from Judge Vickers. Any chance I can get in and see him?" He stopped in front of the woman's desk.

"He's not in the office. His daughter is having a

baby. He and Sandra headed to Portland last night." She pointed down the hall. "You'll have to get the D.A. to issue the warrant."

"Thanks." Hawke walked out into the hallway and took a seat on the wooden bench along the wall. He was fairly certain the number wasn't the D.A.'s. But there was a good chance he might know who it belonged to without needing the warrant.

If the man knew the person and knew they helped Sigler get his hunting tag, he might withhold the information and not issue a warrant, trying to take care of things himself.

Terri, the D.A.'s receptionist, stepped out into the hall. Hawke stood up and hurried over, falling into step with her.

"Hi, Terri. You have a minute?"

She stopped and faced him. "Yeah. Mr. Lange wanted me to go to the bakery and get him a couple donuts. He hasn't been eating well lately." She frowned.

Thomas Ball, the district attorney's investigator, entered the hall.

"I'll meet you there." Hawke strode by the young woman, down the stairs, and out to his pickup.

He hopped in and drove the block and a half to park a street over from the bakery. With the slip of paper in his hand, he entered the bakery and ordered coffee. He took a seat at a table in the corner away from the window. The D.A.'s investigator always popping up, was starting to make him paranoid.

Terri stepped in the establishment. Her cheeks were rosy from the walk.

He nodded for her to go ahead and get what she

came for.

The young woman approached the counter.

"Hey, Terri. You here for the boss again?" a man in his twenties asked.

"Yes. Two cinnamon twists and a large coffee please." She held out a bill. The young man took the money, rang up the sale, and then retrieved the items.

Terri moseyed over to Hawke. "What did you want to ask me?"

He held out the slip of paper. "Do you know who this number belongs to?"

"I'm not good with numbers, but it's close to Ms. Wallen's." She studied it some more. "It's not hers, but close. Why?"

"It's a private number listed with the county. I need a warrant to get the information, but Judge Vickers left, and I didn't want to ask Mr. Lange for a warrant."

Her eyes widened. "Because you think he has something to do with the homicide in Eagle?"

That caught his attention. "Yes, why? Do you know something?"

"I'm not sure. When I was leaving last evening, Ms. Wallen was in Mr. Lange's office telling him she'd learned he was your top suspect in the case and that she wouldn't be surprised if you came to talk to her about moving forward with indictments."

Hawke's mind started whirling. That sounded like a threat from the assistant to her boss. "Is Ms. Wallen in the office right now?"

"No. She's taking a deposition in La Grande today."

"Terri, here you go," the young man at the counter called out.

"Thanks, Dane." Terri grabbed the bag and cup.

Hawke held out a card. "Could you call me when Ms. Wallen is in the office?"

She nodded and hurried out of the bakery.

He finished his coffee, tossed the cup, and walked out the door. The light blue sedan he knew belonged to the D.A.'s investigator, sat across the street from the bakery. Hawke walked to his vehicle, climbed in, and called to tell dispatch he was headed to Zumwalt.

《》《》《》

Dusk had turned to inky blackness as Hawke made his way from the dirt road onto the North Highway. His phone had buzzed several times as he went in and out of service. He pulled over at a wide spot in the road and looked at his messages.

Terri had called early afternoon to tell him Ms. Wallen was in the office.

Donner had called to give him an update on the forensics. There hadn't been any new evidence discovered.

Terri called again. This time she said Dennis down in Administration wanted to talk with him. She rattled off a number to call.

Had the man changed his mind about helping him discover who the phone number belonged to?

Hawke scribbled the number in his logbook and dialed. The phone on the other end rang until a recorded message announced the hours the Administrative Office was open. He checked the time. The courthouse had been closed for over an hour.

What had the man wanted to tell him? Hawke called dispatch. "Requesting a phone number and address for Dennis Brooks, Administrative Services

Director for Wallowa County." He continued on to Alder.

Ten minutes later dispatch replied. "Dennis Brooks lives at three-thirty-two Maple in Alder. His phone number is…"

Hawke wrote this down on the pad on top of his laptop. He pulled over again and dialed the number dispatch had given him. The phone rang and went to voicemail.

"Dennis. This is Trooper Hawke. I received your message and will be arriving at your house in ten minutes." He closed the connection and pulled back onto the road.

In Alder, he headed straight for Maple Street. A small, one-story house had all the lights on. He noticed a swing set in an enclosed yard to the side of the house.

Hawke parked and walked up to the door. The television and what sounded like children laughing could be heard on the other side.

He rang the doorbell.

Running footsteps and the door opened.

"Hello," a boy of about five said.

"Hello, is your daddy home?" he asked.

"Markie, how many times do I have to tell you not to open the door before I get there." The woman was tall, full bodied and wore a billowy blouse with a low neckline. Her brown hair looked as if someone had taken a weedwhacker to it. She had a tattoo on the side of her neck disappearing down into her cleavage.

"Oh! Officer. Why are you here?" Her voice lowered as she asked.

"I'd like to talk to Dennis. He didn't answer his phone." Hawke remained on the porch.

"He should have been home an hour ago. I'm not sure where he is." She pulled a phone out of her back pants pocket and pushed a button. Holding it to her ear, she herded the boy back to the television set. She returned, shoving the phone back in her pocket. "He's not answering." She stepped outside, drawing the door closed behind her. "He doesn't go to bars and is always home on time. What did you want to talk to him about?"

"A matter we'd talked about at his work." Hawke pulled his logbook out of his pocket. "What kind of vehicle does he drive?"

"A green Toyota pickup. You think he's in some kind of trouble?" Her voice started to rise.

"We won't know until we find him. Go back in the house. If you hear from him, give me a call." He handed her his card. "I'll give you a call when I find him." Hawke strode to his vehicle and typed in Dennis Brooks and his address in the DMV records. Up popped two vehicle registrations. He wrote down the license plate of the Toyota pickup and called dispatch, putting out an APB on the vehicle.

He decided to get something to eat in Alder. He could eat a burger and upload today's reports sitting in his vehicle.

On his way from the Brooks house to the Shake Shack, he drove by the high school. A lone vehicle sat in the parking lot. A pickup. A sick feeling squeezed his guts. Hawke drove into the parking lot.

It was a green Toyota license RTH 334.

He rolled up to the driver's side.

Dennis's head leaned against the head rest. His eyes were open behind his glasses. It was the gray and red blotch on his shirt that made Hawke curse.

Someone hadn't wanted him sharing the identity of the person who had the phone number. How had they known the administrator had contacted him?

Hawke put his hand on the mic at his shoulder. "Send the medical examiner, a deputy, and a city cop to Alder High School parking lot. We have a twelve-forty-nine A."

He didn't want to go back to Mrs. Brooks and tell her her husband wouldn't be coming home.

Chapter Twelve

"Why would anyone want to do this to Dennis?" Dr. Vance, the medical examiner asked, after pronouncing the man dead.

"Any idea of how long ago this happened?" Hawke asked. He'd sent the city cop, Profitt, to see if anyone nearby had heard a gunshot.

Deputy Alden wandered about the crime scene taking photographs.

"The body is still warm and rigor hasn't set in. I'd say the shooter was here within the last two hours." The doctor started to pull off her gloves. She stepped back to the open door and grasped the victim's left hand. "He's made a fist."

She opened his fingers. A piece of crinkled paper fluttered to the ground.

Hawke picked up the paper. It was the phone number he'd asked Brooks about. He turned the paper over. A name was scrawled across the back.

Travis Needham.

How could the man still have a phone from this county when he was the D.A. in another county? Hawke pulled an evidence bag out of the kit on the ground next to the vehicle and put the note in the bag.

"That must have meant something to you," Deputy Alden said, motioning to the bag.

"It's what got him killed." Hawke pulled out his phone and scrolled through his contacts for Donner.

"I heard you have another homicide," Donner answered.

"It ties in with Sigler."

"How?" The detective questioned.

"I asked the victim about the number that Sigler called the night he died. It was a private number." He went on to tell the detective about the number being registered to the county.

"When I called, it was a female voice, but the note in our victim's hand says the number belongs to Travis Needham, who was the assistant D.A. to Lange up until eighteen months ago."

Donner whistled. "You have quite a puzzle going on there."

"You want to hear the kicker. Travis Needham took Lange's wife with him when he left."

"You think this Needham and Lange's ex are trying to ruin him?" Donner asked.

"I don't know. But why? Needham is a D.A. now in Marion County, and I heard the ex-Mrs. Lange is pregnant, something she wanted. It doesn't make sense." This conversation was stalling what he really had to do. Notify Dennis Brooks' wife. "I have to go talk to the deceased's wife. You should send someone to talk with Needham and see if he still has the phone."

"I'll get a detective in that area on it in the morning." Donner ended the conversation.

Another thought struck Hawke. Had Dennis said anything to Terri when he went to her for the phone number?

Hawke scrolled through his phone and called Sheriff Lindsey.

"This better be good," Rafe Lindsey said.

"It's Hawke. We have a homicide. I know this person was in contact with Terri Wordell, the D.A.'s receptionist. She may be in danger. Can you put a car on her house tonight? I'm going over to find out if she knows anything as soon as I talk with the victim's spouse."

"I'll get a car over there immediately." Sheriff Lindsey disconnected.

Hawke entered his vehicle and looked up the address for Terri. She lived a mile out of town toward Prairie Creek. The opposite direction of the Brooks residence. The vehicle from the funeral home pulled into the parking lot as he exited.

Deputy Alden would do a good job getting all the evidence. Hawke had a feeling there would be little. It appeared whoever killed Dennis Brooks had walked up and shot him when he rolled the window down. He also had a suspicion the bullet would match that of the one that killed Sigler.

《》《》《》

Hawke drove out of town toward the Wordells. As he'd figured, telling Mrs. Brooks her husband was a homicide victim hadn't been easy. He'd waited until a neighbor came over to stay with her before he left. The children were small enough they didn't understand their mother's outburst or why Daddy hadn't come home.

He hated having to tell the survivors a member of their family had been taken from them. Whether it was by violence or a car accident.

It was after nine. He'd clocked in overtime once again. It was becoming a daily thing lately.

The porch light was on. Two vehicles sat in front of the house. The county car sat at the end of the driveway.

Hawke pulled up and a light went on at the barn he passed. That was a good way to indicate to the deputy on surveillance if there was someone sneaking around.

He stepped out of the pickup and walked up to the door. The muffled sound of a television could be heard from the other side. He knocked on the door.

A dog barked from inside.

"Shhh. Shhh, Curly," Terri said.

The door opened. A large man stood on the other side of the screen door. The light behind him was dim, hiding his features.

"Mr. Wordell, I'm Trooper Hawke. I'd like to come in and have a word with your wife."

The man opened the screen door and backed up.

Terri had her arms around the neck of a Chesapeake Bay Retriever. "Trooper Hawke, what are you doing here?" She released the dog and walked over to him.

"When Dennis Brooks came to you today and asked for my phone number, did he tell you why he needed it?" Hawke wanted to ease into the 'you may be in danger.'

"Only that you had said you'd be back with a

warrant and never returned." She studied him. "Why didn't you ask Mr. Lange for the warrant? I know Judge Vickers is out of town."

"I'd like to tell you, but you may already be in danger." Hawke stepped back as her husband, a man a good two inches taller than him, broader and younger, moved between them.

"What do you mean Terri is in danger?"

"We have a deputy sitting at the end of your driveway. Dennis was murdered tonight."

Terri gasped and ducked under her husband's arm and clung to his waist. "How?"

"That doesn't matter. What matters is that you don't go anywhere alone. He didn't tell you anything but whoever killed him may not know that." Hawke took a step toward both of them and looked them both in the eyes. "Were you working at the office when Travis Needham was the Assistant D.A.?"

"No. That was my grandmother, Anne Detmier. I took over when she retired. I'd helped out through high school and then went to business college and came back." She rubbed a hand up and down her husband's arm. "Is my grandmother in danger, too?"

"No. Can you tell me who might have seen Dennis in the office today?"

"He walked in right ahead of Thomas Ball, the investigator. He went into his office then came back out and went into Ms. Wallen's."

"All of this happened while Dennis was asking about my phone number?" Hawke wrote all of these movements into his logbook. "How did he know to come to you for my number?"

She shrugged. "I don't know. Maybe because

you're law enforcement and we're the D.A.'s Office?"

"Thank you. I'm sorry to bring you bad news. Stay inside the rest of the night. And don't go anywhere alone until we get this solved."

"Don't worry. I help with construction jobs this time of year. I'll take some time off and make sure I'm with her." Mr. Wordell dropped a kiss on her head.

"You can't sit in the D.A.'s Office," she said.

"We'll talk about it later." The man released his wife and walked him to the door. "Thank you for warning us. Dennis was a nice enough guy. He didn't deserve this. How is his wife taking it? I went to school with her."

"Not very well." Her tear-streaked, shattered face flashed in his mind.

"Good luck getting whoever did this." Mr. Wordell closed the door.

Hawke slid into his vehicle, drove out and had a few words with the deputy, and drove home.

《》《》《》

Tuesday morning Hawke drove to the State Police Office and walked into Sergeant Spruel's office.

"I'm going to be working on the two homicides. The first person I'm talking to this morning is D.A. Lange."

"Are you sure that's wise considering Judge Vickers isn't here to get any warrants? And what about the Price guy who was duped by Sigler?" Spruel stood, walked to the door, and closed it.

"He wasn't in the D.A.'s Office yesterday when Brooks asked for my phone number." Hawke paced from one side of the ten by ten room to the other. "Brooks knew who the number belonged to. He knew I had to go to Lange for the warrant. He must have figured Lange wouldn't give me the warrant and decided to help me. Donner said he'd send someone to talk to Needham about his phone. I'd rather go myself…" He glanced at his superior.

Spruel shook his head. "That's unwarranted hours. Someone in Marion County will conduct the interview."

Hawke knew the sergeant was right, but he preferred seeing suspects reactions when they were questioned. Many times that was more telling than the answers they gave.

"Talk to Lange, but don't accuse him. Be subtle. Use the self-control you show when interviewing suspects." Spruel leaned back in his chair. "Don't ruffle the D.A.'s feathers. We might need his help for other matters."

Hawke nodded and left the office.

"Which unit are you patrolling today?" Sullen, another Fish and Wildlife Trooper, asked.

"None. I've got two homicides I have to clear up." Hawke planted himself on the chair in front of his desk.

"Homicides? Since when are you a detective?" Sullen walked up beside him.

"Since a person I talked to yesterday ended up dead last night."

"Brooks."

"Yeah." Hawke hit the monitor button on his computer and glanced at his fellow trooper. "Did you know him?"

"He was related to my wife. In a distant way. Why?"

"Would he go to the authorities with information or

try and blackmail someone?" He'd thought about this all night. Why had Brooks gone to the parking lot to meet someone? Had he hoped to make something from the sale of the information?

"He was as law abiding as the pope is religious. He'd have only given information to someone he felt would do the right thing with it." Sullen studied him. "Why?"

"I don't understand what he was doing in the high school parking lot with the information I had asked him about gripped in his hand. Who lured him there?"

"Could he have thought you'd meet him there?" Sullen asked.

"How? Why would he think I'd be there? He left a message on my phone when I was out patrolling. When I tried to return his call is when I discovered something was wrong."

Sullen slapped him on the back. "Can't help you there. Good luck." He left through the back entrance.

Hawke wasn't sure what he would look up. He doubted any forensics had come back on Brooks. The link was the D.A.'s Office. Or the county court... Terri said Thomas Ball had seen Brooks in the office asking for his phone number.

He typed Thomas Ball into the government database. He'd been the Wallowa County District Attorney's investigator for as long as Lange had been in office. The man hadn't had any trouble with the law. Did he work for the county or for Lange? Could the man have killed Sigler and then Brooks protecting his boss?

A talk with the investigator might be in order, along with Lange.

Chapter Thirteen

At the top of the stairs to the second floor of the courthouse, Hawke spotted Mr. Wordell sitting on a wooden bench outside the D.A.'s Office.

"You're going to have a long day," Hawke said, stopping in front of the man.

He shrugged. "She's worth it."

Hawke nodded and entered the D.A.'s Office.

"Trooper Hawke, what brings you here this morning?" Terri asked, her smile not as welcoming as in the past.

"I'd like to speak with Mr. Lange and Thomas Ball."

Her eyes widened before she picked up the phone and punched a button. "Mr. Lange, Trooper Hawke would like to speak with you?" She listened and her cheeks reddened. "He didn't say what it was about." She listened a few more seconds and hung up the phone.

She cleared her throat. "He said, make an appointment and come back tomorrow."

Hawke glanced at the door. "Does he have someone in there?"

Terri shook her head.

Hawke glance down at the phone and didn't see any buttons lit up. "And he's not on the phone?"

"Correct."

Hawke walked by the desk and shoved the D.A.'s office door open.

"What are you doing barging in here?" Lange came up out of his chair. His face was red and contorted in anger.

"I'm investigating two homicides, and you are going to talk to me because you are in the middle of them." Hawke dropped his hat in the chair and stepped up to the desk, putting both hands palm down and leaning toward the smaller man. "I want straight answers. Two people are dead, and your receptionist could be in danger."

Lange's eyes widened. "Terri? Why?" He dropped into his chair behind the desk.

"Dennis Brooks, last night's victim, was in here yesterday asking her for my phone number."

"Why would Dennis want your number?" Lange's dark eyebrows rose, curling over his eyes like bushy caterpillars.

"I'd been to see him about a phone number Duane Sigler called. A private number listed with the county court." Hawke studied the man. He didn't flinch from the accusation. It appeared he was searching his mind. "He wouldn't give me the name of the person who had the number without a search warrant."

"Why didn't you ask me for one?" Lange leaned back and stared at him. "Because you didn't think I'd cooperate. Trooper, I've told you, I have nothing to do with the death of Duane Sigler. I'm willing to do whatever it takes to clear my name."

"Terri said she didn't tell anyone about Dennis' request. She also said that your investigator, Thomas Ball, walked through the outer office while Dennis was asking for my number."

Lange leaned forward. "Thomas and I have worked together for a lot of years. He'd never kill anyone or try to frame me."

"Are you sure?" Hawke had seen best friends and lovers turn on one another over jealousy and greed.

"Yes."

"Why would Travis Needham still have a phone issued to him from this county?" Hawke asked.

"He shouldn't. Is that the number you were looking for?" Lange spun in his chair and pulled out a drawer in a file cabinet behind him.

"Yes. That's the name that was with the number on the paper we found clutched in Brooks' hand."

Lange spun back around and plopped a file on his desk. "Right here, when Travis left, he turned in his phone, number..." he recited the number Hawke had been investigating.

"What happened to the phone?"

"It would have been assigned to the new Assistant D.A." He glanced up. "Why didn't the number have her name attached to it and not Travis's?"

"I'll have to ask her that question." Hawke picked up his hat and sat down in the chair. The next round of questions needed a bit more tact.

Lange peered at him, his eyes questioning behind his glasses.

"How do you, Travis, and your ex-wife get along?"

The man visibly flinched. He pulled himself together before answering. "As well as could be expected when a young colleague captures your wife's attention and she tells you you've grown into a curmudgeon at an early age."

"Would there be any reason for them to want you undermined?"

Lange sat up straight. "What do you mean?"

"Look at the facts. Sigler had a hunting tag with your name on it and purchased with your credit card."

"Is that why you insist I should have known about the tag?" Lange pulled his wallet out of an inside suit pocket. "Is this the number used?"

"I'm not sure." Hawke pulled out his logbook and wrote the number down. "I'll look it up on the fish and wildlife site."

"Why else do you suspect Lorraine?"

"Your gun went missing and your ex-wife and ex-assistant both knew where you kept it. And now the phone that was assigned to Needham is the one Sigler called before he was killed."

A thought struck Hawke. "Just a minute." He scrolled through his contacts and found Sergeant Spruel's number.

He hit dial and waited.

"Spruel."

"Sir, it's Hawke. Can you find out what happened with Dennis Brooks' phone and have someone look to see what number called him last?"

"I'll see what I can do."

Hawke put his phone back in the holster on his belt.

"Do you think it will be the same number?"

"No. He'd know that number and know it was a trap." Hawke knew his next words weren't going to make the man happy. "I have a suspicion the call came from your phone." He glanced at the one sitting on his desk. "What time did you leave here last night?"

"Around six-thirty as usual."

"Was there any time when you weren't at your desk after Terri had gone home for the day?" Whoever was framing the D.A. had to be in the courthouse.

"If this line of investigation is true then it wouldn't be Lorraine and Travis." He didn't answer Hawke's question.

"Were you away from your desk last evening?"

"I was up at Judge Vickers office coordinating court dates with his secretary after five." His fingers flipped the pages on the bottom corner of his desk calendar.

If Judge Vickers was gone, why would his secretary stay after hours to fill in his calendar? He studied the D.A. The man wasn't telling him everything. "She'll tell me the same thing?"

The tips of his ears turned red, but he nodded his head once.

Hawke stood. "Keep all of this to yourself. I don't want whoever is doing this to know I've been speaking with you."

Lange nodded.

At the door, Hawke did a quick glance over his shoulder. The D.A. was picking up his cell phone. He'd bet his horse, Jack, that Lange was calling Judge Vickers' secretary.

He walked out to Terri's desk. "Is Thomas Ball

in?"

She nodded.

Hawke didn't wait for her to call the investigator. He strode over to the man's door, knocked once, and walked in.

"Hey!" Ball slammed the phone down and stood at the same time. "What's the idea of barging in here unannounced?"

"Keeping you on your toes." Hawke sat down and opened his logbook. "Where were you Monday the twelfth from six to nine p.m.?"

"A week ago Monday?" Ball plopped back down in his chair. He wore his hair long, covering his collar. He had on a collared pull-over and a suit jacket with jeans and tennis shoes.

"Yes." Hawke waited patiently.

"I believe I had pizza at the Pizza Oven in Prairie Creek that night."

"Were you alone?"

The man grinned. "Not if I could help it."

"Could I have the person's name?" Hawke held his pen over his logbook.

"I wasn't with any one person." The man wasn't being helpful.

"I'll talk to the employees. What about last night between five and eight?" Hawke stared at the man.

His eyes twitched before he leaned forward. "Last night. I believe I was over at the Brewery. You know, the High Mountain Brewery, on the way toward Prairie Creek?"

"Anyone with you?" Hawke continued to wait for an answer to write down.

"It was a Monday night. There weren't that many

people sitting around shooting the bull."

"Can you remember one or two?" The man was doing all he could to be evasive. That only made Hawke more sure he was hiding his whereabouts during the murders.

"I think Bud Trager was there. And Delwin Saxon." He nodded. "Yeah, those are the ones I'm sure were there."

Hawke wrote the names down and asked, "What did you think of Travis Needham?"

"Why are you asking about Travis?" The man responded without missing a beat.

Nothing about the man no longer working here or that he'd left a long time ago. Ball was fishing to see what Hawke knew.

"I'm digging into some history here at the courthouse. I'm trying to figure out why someone would kill Dennis Brooks."

"I heard about that. I can't imagine who would want to off that poor slob."

"That's disrespectful of the dead." Hawke glared at the man. He didn't like Thomas Ball. Dennis had been doing what was right and shouldn't have lost his life over it. Shouldn't have left behind a wife and two children.

"Sorry, Chief."

Hawke stood and grabbed the investigator by the front of his shirt. It was rare a slur such as 'chief' raised his anger. This man had stretched his patience. "I'm not a chief. I'm a State Trooper. And I have the ability to put your ass in jail." He tossed the man back in his chair, picked up his hat, and walked out of the office.

And Spruel thought he'd sent a level-headed

officer to question people.

He walked over to Terri's desk. "Is Ms. Wallen in?"

"Yes."

Hawke strode to the assistant district attorney's door, rapped once, and walked in.

Her head snapped up from where she'd been looking at documents spread across her desk.

"Trooper Hawke. Why are you interrupting my work?" She herded the papers into a pile and tucked them under a folder.

"Do you still have the cell phone given to you by the administrative department?" he asked, taking a seat in the chair in front of her desk.

"Yes. Why? Do you want to call me some time?" She raised one eyebrow and smiled.

"I'd like to see it." He held out his hand.

She picked up the cell phone beside the landline phone on her desk. "I don't understand why you need to see my phone."

He took it from her, went to settings, and wrote the number down in his logbook. While there he also noted the numbers she'd called the night before. When he started to write them down, she came around the desk and took the phone from him.

"What is the meaning of this?"

"I'd like to know why you don't have the phone number that was assigned to you?" He read off the number.

"I lost that phone, and they gave me a new one with a new number."

She said it convincingly, but Hawke wasn't falling for it. "Then why didn't they have your new number on file in Administrative Services?"

"I don't know. Maybe they forgot to write it down." She sat back down, tucking her phone in a drawer. "What does my phone have to do with anything?"

"Where were you Monday, November twelfth between five and nine p.m.?" He poised his pen on his logbook.

"That was over a week ago. How should I know." She stared over his shoulder.

"You could look on your phone's calendar or the calendar on your desk and jog your memory." He waited as she debated which one to look at.

Ms. Wallen flipped back a week in her desk calendar. "I was down in the basement looking for a couple of old cases that pertain to a county regulation that Judge Vickers asked me to look into."

"That late at night?" It was his turn to raise an eyebrow.

"I didn't want to dig around down there during the day."

"Why not? What was so secretive?"

She gave him a half smile. "I didn't want anyone to hear me screech when I ran into a spider."

"You don't have to be frightened of spiders."

"Some bite and can make you sick." She wrinkled her nose in disgust.

"A rattlesnake can bite and harm you, but they would rather slither off and catch a meal. A spider is the same. Both creatures are useful for their own reasons." He didn't see where a creature that could keep down the population of a nuisance could be harmful.

"You love your nasty creatures, and I'll avoid

them." She stood. "Anything else? I need to be somewhere."

"Where were you last night between five and eight p.m.?" he asked.

"Why are you asking me all of these questions?" Her aggravation was evident in the anger in her eyes and the way a muscle in her jaw twitched. "Wait a minute. Do you think I had something to do with the two homicides? That's insane. I'm an Assistant D.A. I convict people who break the laws not commit crimes." She laughed. It felt put on and not as if she were truly laughing at the absurdness but more the audacity of him even thinking such a thing.

"Everyone has a point at which they are willing to go against their beliefs to get something they desire." He studied her.

"That may be so, but you won't get me to tell you my desires."

"I only want to know where you were last night from five to eight."

"I was here until five-thirty and then I went home." She stood. "Now, I need to go, or I'll be late."

Hawke stood, placed his logbook in his pocket, and left the office.

Terri stared at him. He winked at her and walked out into the hallway. The Assistant D.A. didn't know it, but she'd just become his number one suspect to have called Dennis.

Chapter Fourteen

As Hawke walked down the hall to Judge Vickers office, his phone buzzed. Spruel.

"What did you find out?" Hawke answered.

"Brooks was called from a number at the courthouse. District Attorney Lange's to be exact. At five-twenty."

"That's what I figured."

"How did you figure that?"

Hawke explained all he'd learned so far from the D.A., Assistant D.A., and the investigator. "I'm headed to check out all their alibis for the times of death now."

"Keep me posted," Spruel said before disconnecting.

Hawke continued to Judge Vickers office. He knew the D.A. had called the woman the moment he stepped into the office and her cheeks reddened.

"Trooper Hawke," she said, straightening papers, not looking at him.

She was several years older than Lange. But she

did have a pretty face and the soft body of a woman carrying a few extra pounds. Which Hawke himself liked over a bony woman.

"Mrs. White, D.A. Lange said he was up here with you last night after five. Is that correct?" He stood in front of her desk.

She tilted her head back and gazed up at him. "Yes. He arrived sometime after five and was here for nearly an hour." Her cheeks deepened in color. "We were having difficulties making the schedules work."

He could tell there had been more than merging schedules going on, but he refrained from making the woman any more uncomfortable. "Thank you."

At the door, he pivoted and asked, "Did you happen to call him a week ago Monday? Between six-thirty and seven?"

She ducked her head. "Yes."

He wasn't going to ask her anything else. He had a person who could fill him in on any details living only a hundred feet from his apartment.

His stomach growled as he opened his vehicle and slid in. Noon. A good time to try lunch at the Pizza Oven in Prairie Creek.

Pointing his pickup toward Prairie Creek, he called Donner to fill him in.

"The victim last night was shot with the same gun as Sigler. I think it's time we got a warrant to search Lange's home, office, and vehicle. It's the same caliber as the one he claims is missing." Donner's tone said he was beginning to believe the district attorney was guilty.

"Judge Vickers is on vacation, and Lange isn't going to give you permission to search his house."

They'd have to wait for Judge Vickers and it was possible he wouldn't sign off on it either.

"If we wait, he'll have time to get rid of the weapon." Donner was being hasty in his declaring Lange the killer.

"I believe this whole thing is a set-up. Did someone talk to Needham and his wife?" His gut was saying Lange wasn't a killer. He put them behind bars.

"The detective hasn't gotten back to me yet. You can't believe someone that far away did this," Donner said.

"The man stole his boss's wife, his old phone is the one that made a call to a person who ended up dead, and it was information about that phone number that caused another death. It's hard to not see a connection." Hawke pulled into Prairie Creek. "I'm going to check out Thomas Ball's alibi. Talk to you later."

He pulled into the small parking lot beside the Pizza Oven restaurant. It was a pizza, salad, and chicken joint that served beer along with soda. He'd only been in the place once when he'd met someone there to take their statement about a possible poacher.

The interior was dark, like a bar. Dimly lit lights hung from the ceiling above the booths. A pool table and old pinball games sat near the back, that was partitioned off to keep minors away from the lottery game machines.

He took a seat and waited for the waitress to come out of the kitchen. There wasn't anyone in the eating area. A couple of voices drifted out from behind the walled off lottery games.

A woman in her forties wandered out of the kitchen and picked up the two-sided sheet with the menu. She placed the menu on the table and asked, "What can I get you to drink?"

"Iced tea. Any chance you know Thomas Ball?" he asked.

The woman's indifference switched to interest. "I do. Why?"

"I wondered if you'd remember if he was in here the Monday before last? It would have been the twelfth." He picked up the menu.

"He comes in quite a bit. He just lives down the street." She tapped her mouth with her pen. "I really can't say yes or no. I'll see if my husband can remember."

"I'll take the personal sized Meat Locker." Hawke handed back the menu.

She smiled. "I'll bring the tea right out and get the pizza going."

Ten minutes after she'd returned with the tea and said her husband couldn't remember if Thomas had been in that night, a dozen teenagers flooded through the door. He guessed it was lunch time at the high school.

Several saw him and nodded. Others avoided him. His uniform had a way of making people uneasy. Mostly those that had a reason for being leery of the law.

His pizza arrived. He finished off every last piece and decided since he was this close to the lake and Lange's neighborhood, he'd have a chat with the neighbors about when Lange had returned home last night.

He paid for his meal and headed to his vehicle. A thought struck him. The waitress had said Ball lived close by. It wouldn't hurt to see if he had neighbors to vouch for him. He put the investigators name into the computer and found his address.

Ball lived three blocks away from the Pizza Oven on a short street of three duplexes. His residence was on the end of the block. They all could have used a coat of paint, and the grass in the yards appeared to have been trampled to death and no flowers anywhere. Either it was all bachelors living in these or working couples who didn't care what their place looked like.

There was a car in front of the middle building. He parked at Ball's place and walked along knocking on doors. It was the residence with the parked car that answered. A woman in her early thirties, shoved her dark brown hair out of her face. She had on pajamas and a large sweater. From her red-rimmed eyes and red nose, she was home sick.

"Sorry to bother you." He pointed to his badge. "I'm Trooper Hawke. I was wondering if you knew much about your neighbor, Thomas Ball?"

"Is he in trouble?" the woman asked, backing away from the cold air entering due to the open door.

"No." He stepped in and closed the door.

The woman collapsed back on the couch. A bottle of water, box of tissues, and a blanket proved that was where she'd been when he disturbed her.

"Do you know when he came home last night?" Hawke perched on the edge of a recliner and pulled out his logbook.

"Last night?" She blew her nose and wrapped the blanket around her. "His car makes a distinctive sound. I think it was close to nine when he came home. He's late most nights. He lives alone, and I think he goes to bars after work."

"Do you live here alone?"

"No. My boyfriend lives with me. He works for the city. I have a job in Alder, but as you can see, I'm not in any shape to be helping people. I'd just make them sick." She drank some water.

"What's your name?" he asked.

"Ina Tragg."

He wrote her name in his book. "And you think Thomas came home around nine last night? Was your boyfriend here at the time?"

"Yes. He was home right after work. I had him pick up some flu medicine for me." She blew her nose again. "I hope I'm well enough to work tomorrow. I don't get paid if I'm not there."

Hawke stood. "Thank you for your time and answering my questions. I can let myself out." He walked to the door and exited, hoping he didn't catch her cold.

Knowing Ball hadn't come home until nine the night before, he was going to skip checking out Lange's neighbors and go back to the Brewery in Alder and see if anyone there remembered what time Ball left. Or if he even was there.

《》《》《》

The High Mountain Brewery had half a dozen people eating a late lunch and trying the local brews. Hawke walked in and turned heads.

Desiree Halver, a young woman whose family he'd helped out once, motioned for him to sit at the bar.

He walked over.

She placed a cup of coffee on the counter. "What brings you here, Trooper Hawke?"

"Did you work last night?" He took a sip of the coffee.

"Until eight. When I come in at eleven to help serve lunch, I get off early." She nodded to the pool tables. "Be right back."

He watched as she poured three glasses of beer on tap and delivered it to the three men sitting at a table not far from the pool tables.

She returned with the empties and dunked them in the sink of sudsy water. "You were saying?"

"I wondered if you happened to see Thomas Ball in here last night?"

"The district attorney's investigator who thinks he's God's gift to women? No. I remember when he comes in. He's always hitting on me." She made a face.

"He said he was and that Delwin Saxon and Bud Trager could vouch for him." Hawke glanced around the establishment. He didn't know these men.

"It's a sure bet those two would have been here. They are here every night." She nodded to a man stooped over a table by the restrooms. "That's Delwin. I'm not sure he even went home last night. I've been serving him coffee and rolls."

"Thanks. I'll go have a talk with him." Hawke picked up his hat and his coffee and walked over to the table.

"Mr. Saxon? May I have a seat?" he asked.

The man glanced up. The bags under his bloodshot eyes were purple. His face was grayish. He didn't look well at all. He looked like Hawke's stepfather the last months before his death. If he hadn't been drunk and run off the road, alcohol poisoning would have gotten him.

"Mr. Saxon, do you remember if Thomas Ball was in here last night?"

The man raised a shaking hand to his cup of coffee. "He bought me and Bud a round."

"What time was that?" Hawke asked, pulling out his logbook.

"About eight thirty."

"Did you see him in here before he bought you a drink?" Hawke had a suspicion buying the man a drink was an alibi.

"I don't remember seeing him, but me and Bud were busy drowning our sorrows. Can't remember for sure." The man steadied his head and peered at Hawke's badge. "He in trouble?"

"No. Thank you." Hawke added the fact Desiree hadn't seen Ball in the brewery before eight to his logbook and stood.

He walked over, paid Desiree for the coffee, and left. The investigator didn't have a clear alibi for his evening last night.

Out in his pickup, his phone rang. Donner.

"Heard back from the detective who questioned Needham and his wife. Both have alibis. Needham said he turned in his phone to Administrative Services. He and his wife have no reason to want to harass Lange."

Hawke had thought they were a long shot, but they couldn't afford to let anyone involved not be investigated. "Thanks. I discovered that Ball has no real alibi for last night. He was at the brewery but not until after eight and he was home, according to a neighbor by nine."

"The death occurred between six and seven, plenty of time for him to show up at the brewery," Donner said.

"That's my thoughts. I know I can get a search warrant from Lange to search Ball's home and office. If he kept the gun from the first killing, chances are he'll still have it." Hawke would love to pin both murders on the cocky investigator.

"Get the paperwork rolling, I'll meet you at the courthouse to start the search in an hour." Donner disconnected.

Hawke smiled. He liked the idea of searching the smug investigator's office, home and vehicle. But what he didn't understand was what did the man get out of killing the two men and framing Lange?

Chapter Fifteen

Hawke parked in the lot behind the courthouse to see if Ball's vehicle was there. The man had access to a county vehicle and his own. Only the county vehicle was parked behind the building. He must have gone somewhere, unofficially.

Before exiting his vehicle, Hawke opened up his documents file on his computer and wrote up a warrant to search Thomas Ball's home, office, and vehicles. He sent the document to Lange's office.

Hawke entered the building from the back and saw the stairway down to the basement. He'd ask Terri to print out the warrant for Lange to sign and come back to the basement and take a look. See if Assistant D.A. Wallen had been down in the basement like she'd said.

He walked down the hallway and up the stairs to the second floor. Mr. Wordell wasn't sitting in the hallway. He hurried into the D.A's Office. Terri wasn't at her desk. Hawke strode by her desk and knocked on

Lange's door.

Nothing.

He opened the door and found the room empty. Where could they be? He walked over to Ms. Wallen's door, knocked once, and opened it. She was also missing.

Back at the receptionist's desk, he glanced at the calendar. They were all at a county meeting being held in the conference room on the first floor.

He texted Donner not to hurry. He wouldn't be able to get a warrant for two more hours. That was how long the meeting was marked out on the calendar.

Retracing his steps, Hawke headed for the basement. He moved his hand along the wall at the top of the stairs until his fingers connected with a light switch. Descending the stairs, dust, the acrid odor of fuel oil, and the scent of musty paper clogged his nostrils. The light cover at the bottom of the stairs was so dusty the light barely reached the edges of the first room and the two doors on either side. The main room housed old desks stacked upside down on each other, old heavy wooden chairs hung from the rafters or floor beams depending on whether you were above or below them.

The door to his right had the words "Boiler Room" stenciled in black. The fuel smell seeped through the cracks around the door.

He looked to the left and found a door with the words "Court Records" stenciled in black. He walked to the door and discovered it was locked. It was the type of lock that required a skeleton key. Before he pulled out his pocket knife, he reached up and felt along the door sill. And there it was, a skeleton key. If that was all the county did to keep people out of the records, he didn't see a reason why he couldn't poke around and see what Ms. Wallen had been searching through.

Since the computer became common place in businesses and courthouses, the records were now stored digitally. What she was looking for had to date back to the 1980s or earlier. He found the light switch. Once again, the dust had accumulated on the light fixture, making it hard to focus his eyes. Not that he was having eye problems. Only when he had to read for long periods. His computer monitor was still far enough out that he could focus, but it was getting closer to him needing glasses.

Hawke pulled the flashlight off his duty belt, raking the beam over the interior to help him see. He scanned the area for signs someone had been in the room recently. He stepped to the right inside the door and slowly placed one foot in front of the other until he stood three feet into the room. Twisting at his waist, he looked at the floor behind him to see if anyone else had disturbed the dust on the floor.

There was a faint set of footprints with a scarce amount of dust in them. They appeared to be high-heeled shoes, the type he'd noticed the Assistant D.A. wearing every time he'd seen her.

Twisting back around, he scanned the floor to see where the tracks stopped.

In front of a file cabinet.

He walked over and opened the drawer. The screech of the metal track pierced his eardrums. People all the way to the second floor should have heard it. He lifted the heavy drawer to try and minimize the screech.

When the drawer was halfway out, he skimmed

through the labels on the files. They appeared to be drunk driving violations. Why would she be looking into decades old drunk driving records? Did Judge Vickers really give her this assignment or was she looking through them for her own reasons? Time to do more digging on Ms. Wallen. To make sure there weren't any other type of records in the cabinet, he pulled out each screechy drawer and looked. That's when he noticed a paper sticking up a third of the way back in the third drawer down.

There was a good chance the file before or after this spot had been looked at or taken. He pulled the two files out and used his phone to take photos of the reports inside. He'd have a couple questions for Terri when he saw her.

Shoving all the drawers closed, he exited the room and relocked the door. At the top of the stairs, he turned to close the door and spotted Ball, walking up the steps to the back door.

Hawke quickly shut the door and strode down the hall. The meeting was breaking up. Employees of the county meandered out of the conference room.

Lange stepped out, and Hawke caught up to him.

"We need a search warrant," Hawke said in a low voice.

"Follow me to my office." Lange lengthened his stride.

Hawke glanced over his shoulder and spotted Ball and the Assistant D.A. visiting.

Terri's husband sat on the bench outside the office. He nodded slightly as they walked by.

Hawke had to give the young man credit, he was doing a good job of keeping an eye on his wife and not acting as if it were a drudge.

"What do you need the warrant for?" Lange asked as soon as they were closed in his office.

"Thomas Ball's office, home, and vehicles."

Lange's brow furrowed and his eyes widened. "My investigator?"

"His alibi for last night doesn't check out. We need to search his premises for the gun." Hawke could see the district attorney was torn between his job and his loyalty to an employee. It was commendable but if it wasn't Ball, it could come back on Lange.

The attorney glanced at Hawke's hands. "Where's the warrant?"

"I sent it to your office via email." Hawke nodded toward the computer on his desk.

Lange picked up the phone and punched a button. "Terri. Trooper Hawke sent a warrant to our office. It needs to be printed out and brought in for me to sign." He replaced the phone and sat down.

Hawke lowered himself into the chair in front of the desk.

"Do you think you will discover my gun in Thomas' possession?" Lange was shuffling papers on his desk.

"I'm hoping we find it. At the moment it is all we have that could reveal the murderer." Hawke studied the man. He looked older, more tired than their first encounter when Hawke had accused him of selling his elk tag. "The motive for Brooks seems to be linked to the death of Sigler. Finding who killed Sigler should close two murder cases."

A soft knock on the door, and Terri entered carrying papers. She placed them on Lange's desk and left the room.

Lange read through the papers and signed. "Are you starting with his office?"

"Yes. As soon as Detective Donner gets here." Hawke reached out, grasping the papers.

"I'll wait out in my vehicle for Donner." He stood and headed to the door. His phone buzzed. Outside the office he glanced at his phone. The detective was in the parking lot.

He texted back for the trooper to meet him at the D.A.'s office.

Hawke stepped out into the hallway and called the sheriff's office, requesting a deputy to come to the courthouse.

Ball appeared at the top of the stairs. His gaze latched onto Hawke. "You waiting for the D.A.?"

"No."

Donner appeared behind the investigator.

"Him." Hawke walked over and handed Ball the warrant. "This is a warrant to search your office, vehicles, and residence."

"What are you looking for?" he asked, skimming over the document. "A gun. Specifically, a Smith & Wesson 380. I don't own one." He tossed the paper at Hawke and started to walk out of the office.

"Where do you think you're going?" Donner asked, grabbing Ball by the arm.

"You don't need me to look around in my office." Ball tried to pull out of the detective's grasp.

"You're staying right here in this chair." Donner led the investigator over to a chair at the same time a deputy walked through the door. The office was getting full of people.

"Deputy Novak, keep an eye on Ball. If he takes his phone out of his pocket, confiscate that," Hawke said as he and Donner entered the investigator's office.

"He was being belligerent," Donner said.

"That's him all the time." Hawke started at one side of the room and Donner took the other. They met behind the desk. "You take the file cabinet, and I'll take the desk," Hawke said, pulling out the top middle drawer.

"Do you really think this guy is dumb enough to hide a murder weapon in his office in the D.A.'s office?" Donner asked.

"It's not a case of stupid. It's a case of he thinks he's smart. Where would be the last place you'd look for a murder weapon?" Hawke pulled out more drawers and looked for secret hiding places.

"The D.A.'s office." Donner slammed the last drawer shut. "Nothing."

"Here either. Let's go have a look at his vehicles." Hawke walked out of the investigator's office as the Assistant D.A. walked in the D.A.'s office.

"What's going on?" she asked when her gaze flicked from Ball to the deputy.

"We're conducting a search," Hawke said. "I suggest you stay in this office until we're finished."

"Why?" She crossed her arms and glared at him. "You haven't handed me a warrant."

"Because you and Thomas, here, are too chummy." Hawke motioned for Ball to stand. "Let's go take a look at your vehicles."

The three policemen walked down to the parking lot with Ball. Deputy Novak kept the investigator away from his vehicles while Hawke searched his private car and Donner searched the county car.

They both came up empty.

"Bring him in your car," Donner told Novak. "We'll head to his residence now."

《》《》《》

At Ball's house, they found a stash of marijuana, magazines with nude women, and cases of empty beer bottles, but they didn't find the gun.

"I told you I didn't kill anyone. It would be bad for my job." Ball said, when they walked out of his house.

Donner held up the bag of marijuana. "Keep it up and I'll book you for having over the legal limit of marijuana."

"What do you think Lange will say if we tell him what we found in your place?" Hawke added.

The man wasn't so belligerent now.

"Where were you last night? I know you didn't show up at the brewery until after eight and you were home by nine. What did you do from five to eight?" Hawke had the man backed up against the county car.

He narrowed his eyes. "I didn't kill Brooks. I was helping a friend."

"What friend?" Hawke could tell the man wasn't going to budge. They couldn't do anything about it. They didn't have a motive or the weapon. "Take him back to the courthouse," Hawke said to Novak.

He and Donner stood in front of Ball's house discussing what they had so far. It amounted to nothing.

"Sigler had to be killed because he tried to blackmail whoever gave him the elk tag. It wasn't Lange. Who had access to Lange's credit card?" Hawke's mind was tumbling around.

"Did they have access?" Donner asked.

149

"What do you mean?" Hawke studied the other trooper.

"As long as someone had all his information, they could have set up a credit card in his name. And had all the transactions go to an internet account they set up or their own."

"We need to take a look at the credit card in Lange's name that was used to pay for the tag. I have that information in my logbook. I'll go through it tonight and send it to you." Hawke shook hands with Donner. "Hopefully, by this time tomorrow we'll have a suspect."

"Send me the info and I'll get some specialists on it." Donner slid into his car.

Hawke climbed into his pickup. Just as he was about to call dispatch and tell them he was off duty, a call came in requesting backup at a drunk and disorderly in Winslow. Looked like he'd help with that and go to the office and add to his report on the murder cases.

Chapter Sixteen

Donner stopped in Winslow having heard dispatch's call. Hawke managed to calm down one of the regulars at the Blue Elk while Donner loaded the town drunk, Archie, into his car and hauled him to the county jail in Alder.

"Why would you want to beat up Archie?" Hawke asked.

"He said all hunters were murderers." The man slurred his words and his eyes were pinging around in his eye sockets.

"He has a point. Hunters do kill animals that are just minding their own business." Hawke pulled out his logbook. "What's your name?"

The drunk squinted, staring at him. "George Rawlins, why?"

"I need your name to take your statement. Who started the fight?"

"He did. By saying hunters are murderers." The

man wiped a hand under his nose and reached out to pick up the beer in front of him.

Hawke eased the bottle away from the man. "Did he throw the first punch?"

Rawlins drew his hand back, staring at the bottle. "Can't remember."

That was a pretty good indication he'd thrown the first punch. "What were you talking about that riled Archie?"

"This business with Duane."

"Sigler? What business?" Hawke was curious to see what the man had to say.

"Yeah. Him getting killed. Shot they say. You know, he was a nice enough fella. But he did cut them hunters short." The man licked his lips and made an effort to grasp the beer bottle.

Hawke placed the bottle on another table. "How did Duane manage to charge so little for his hunts?"

"By feeding them canned stew and telling them it was the full hunting experience. He was good at talkin' you into thinking his way." The man shook his head. "Looks like he couldn't talk his way out of the bullet he took."

"Do you think any of the hunters he shorted would be mad enough to shoot him?" Hawke didn't think it was a hunter because all the evidence was aimed at the district attorney, but one of them might have also had a grudge with the D.A.

"Naw. That's what don't make sense. Everyone can't believe he was shot. Not like he was. Maybe out in the woods, hunting, but in his own barn..." The man shook his head slowly. "Don't make sense."

Hawke managed to get the man out in his pickup

and haul him to the jail in Alder. It appeared he'd been the one to take the first punch. It wouldn't hurt for both he and Archie to sleep it off in the jail.

He drove home, fed the horses, and took a shower.

Dog sat on his bed as Hawke heated up a dinner in the microwave. He sent the photos he took of the records in the basement to his computer. It would be easier to read them in a larger format.

Pulling the steaming dinner out of the microwave, he placed it on the small table next to his computer. He opened up his email and then the photos one at a time. The files were for drunk driving violations that happened in the summer of 1988. He had a feeling neither one had anything to do with their murders. Someone, most likely the Assistant D.A. had taken the one that was important.

He pulled up the archives of the Wallowa County Chieftain, the county's weekly newspaper, and began skimming through the files for the summer of 1988.

A headline caught his attention. DRUNK DRIVER KILLS PASSENGER. He went on to read how two 16-year-olds were at a party drinking, and on the way back to where they were staying, there was an accident. One was thrown from the vehicle and killed instantly. The driver suffered injuries that required he be ambulanced to Grande Ronde Hospital in La Grande. The name of the driver was Benjamin Lange. Hawke scanned the story for the name of the passenger. At the end of the article it finally mentioned the other boy. Wally Reedy.

Why would someone try and take revenge on Lange almost forty years later? Did it even have anything to do with the other deaths?

Had Judge Vickers asked Ms. Wallen to find the

records or had she looked it up herself?

Too many questions and not nearly enough answers.

From what he'd learned of Lange, he grew up on the west side of the state. What was he doing here that summer?

Hawke scrolled through the next week's paper looking for more information about the accident and the two involved. There was no mention of the families or a funeral for the other boy.

He'd have to ask the district attorney about that summer. He made a list of the things he needed to check or have checked and sent an email off to Donner about what he'd discovered and what they needed to know.

The clock on his computer said it was midnight. He needed to get some sleep.

《》《》《》

Hawke was finishing up feeding his horses when his phone buzzed. Donner.

"Did you get—"

"I was reading your email. What is this about Lange killing someone forty years ago?"

Hawke sat down on the third step from the bottom and told the detective why he'd looked at the records in the basement of the courthouse and everything he'd discovered from that investigation.

A low whistle pierced his ear. "You are digging up all kinds of worms. Now you think Sigler and Brooks deaths are because of an old drunk driving accident?"

"I don't know, but it seems kind of a coincidence that the file that appears to be missing could have something to do with the D.A. and all the evidence in the murders is pointing to him." Hawke rubbed a hand across the back of his neck. "What I don't understand is Lange has alibis for all but the missing gun. People have vouched for seeing him at the times the murders were committed so whoever is trying to frame him isn't doing a thorough job of it."

"Maybe they don't want him convicted, just to squirm?" Donner asked.

"I don't know. I'm going to have a visit with Lange this morning. See if he knows who might have a grudge from that long ago." Hawke stood, wiping the dirt from the back of his pants.

"I'll see what I can find on the name of the boy in the accident." Donner ended the call.

Hawke glanced at his watch. It was too early to head to the courthouse. He glanced towards the Trembley's house. Maybe they knew about the accident, and he'd yet to ask Darlene about Mrs. White, Judge Vickers' secretary.

He walked over to the house and knocked on the back door.

Herb answered, worry wrinkled his brow. "Is something wrong?"

"No. Mind if I have a cup of coffee with you and Darlene?" Hawke waited on the step as the man studied him.

"Sure, come on in. You don't usually invite yourself over." Herb motioned to the table.

Darlene turned from where she was frying eggs on the stove. "Would you like breakfast?"

"Only if you have extra."

Herb placed a cup of coffee in front of him. "You must think we know something."

Hawke sipped the coffee and set the cup down. "Can you remember anything about a drunk driving accident that happened almost forty years ago? Two sixteen-year-old boys were involved. One died, the other was badly injured. I don't think they were from around here."

Herb sipped his coffee. Darlene stood by the stove, spatula in hand, staring at her husband.

"Forty years ago?" Herb asked.

"Our Jenny would have been about sixteen," Darlene said, lifting the pan from the stove and placing sausage and eggs on the two men's plates. She set the pan in the sink and turned toward the table. "I do remember something about two boys who were here camping with their families. They were invited to a party by a local girl who worked at the lake. The two boys were heading back to the lake when the accident happened."

"I remember now." Herb placed his cup on the table. "Wasn't there some talk afterwards about that's what out-of-towners got for trying to butt into a party?"

Darlene placed a plate of toast on the table and sat down. "I'm afraid there wasn't much sympathy for the families of the two boys." She shook her head.

Hawke had a feeling dragging the summer back up with Lange was going to be hard. He put jam on a piece of toast and asked, "What can you tell me about Mrs. White, Judge Vickers' secretary?"

Darlene studied him. "What do you want to know about Sarah?"

"Is she married?"

"Widow. Her husband had a heart attack about four years ago. She has the one boy still in high school."

Darlene skimmed a finger around the rim of her coffee mug. "Why are you interested in her?"

"I wondered why she and District Attorney Lange would use the Judge's office for a quickie."

Darlene spit coffee onto her plate.

Herb burst out laughing.

"Really?" Darlene asked, her eyes sparkling.

"Don't tell anyone. I only believe that because of their red faces when I asked why it took so long to coordinate calendars."

Darlene started laughing. "Oh, I'm happy for Sarah." Then she sobered and stared at Hawke. "I think it was Sarah who invited the two boys to the party."

"How much older than Lange is she?" Could she be toying with him to get him tangled in deceit?

"Maybe two, possibly three years? Do you think they know something about the accident all those years ago?" Darlene's usually jovial face had worry lines etched on her forehead.

"I'll find out today." Hawke finished off his coffee and stood. "Thank you for breakfast and the information." He walked to the door and stopped, facing the couple. "Remember, none of this goes out of this house." He peered at both of them, but Darlene the longest.

The couple nodded.

Hawke had today to work on this and then he had to take tomorrow off, to be able to check hunters on the weekend.

What was the coincidence that Lange and White found each other after forty years and that Lange was being set up for two murders?

Chapter Seventeen

The first thing Hawke saw when he stepped onto the second floor of the courthouse was Mr. Wordell sitting on the bench outside the district attorney's office.

The young man stood as he approached.

Hawke stopped.

"Do you have any idea how long I'll have to sit out here and protect Terri?"

"I wish I could say today is it, but until we catch who killed Dennis Brooks, we have to be watchful of Terri." Hawke patted the man on the shoulder and headed into the office.

Terri glanced up from the papers on her desk and gave him her full attention. "Any new developments?"

"Not that I can talk about."

Her expression sagged into melancholy. "Chad needs to get back to work and not sit out there."

"He could go as long as you make sure you are always with someone." Hawke had a feeling, Terri wasn't a target. But he also didn't want her to not be vigilant.

"I've tried to tell him that. He won't listen." She picked up the phone. "Do you want to see Mr. Lange?"

"Please."

She punched a button. "Trooper Hawke is here to see you." She replaced the phone. "You can go right in."

"Thank you." He walked into the D.A.'s office and was surprised to see Judge Vickers.

"Judge. Lange." Hawke took the vacant seat to the Judge's right.

"Have you learned anything new?" Judge Vickers asked.

"Yes. But I'm not sure what it might have to do with the two homicides." Hawke studied the attorney. The stress of the investigation was taking a toll on him. He wondered what the extent of the injuries had been from the crash all those years ago.

"If it has nothing to do with the homicides why even bring it up?" Lange asked.

"Because it could." He turned his attention to Judge Vickers. "Did you ask Ms. Wallen to find a file in the basement?"

The Judge stared at him. "What are you talking about?"

"Ms. Wallen told me that on Monday the twelfth, when Duane Sigler was shot, she was in the basement going through old records for you." He studied the judge.

His eyes narrowed and he shook his head. "I never requested she look up any old files for me. And I'm certain I didn't ask her to look up anything for me around that time."

"Well, she, or someone else who wears high heels, was in the basement. From what I could piece together from marks in dust, drawers' contents, and such, it could be the file about D.A. Lange's accident when he was sixteen."

Lange visibly blanched.

Judge Vickers continued to stare at Hawke. "What do you know about that?"

"What I found in the Chieftain and extracted from my landlords." Hawke shifted his attention to the D.A. "I know you and your friend were vacationing here. Do you know if there would be anyone from then that could want to disgrace you now?"

Vickers picked up Lange's phone. "Mrs. White, would you bring my bottle of scotch down to Lange's office. Thank you." He glanced at Lange. "You look like you could use a drink."

Lange raised a hand. "I don't touch the stuff. Haven't since then."

"Then I need it."

"Did you know about Lange's history when he applied for the Assistant D.A. position?" Hawke asked Vickers. It was rude asking the judge and not the man himself, but Lange looked as if he might need to be checked into the hospital.

"I was the Assistant D.A. when the accident happened. Back then they didn't push for as harsh a penalty for homicides from drunk drivers. And then Ben nearly lost his life in the accident and it didn't seem like something to drag him into court over. He'd lost a friend and nearly his own life. The decedent's family didn't press charges."

"Wally and I had been best friends from first grade." Lange started.

A knock on the door drew their attention.

"Come in," Lange said.

Mrs. White entered. Her gaze flit from the Judge to Lange and then landed on Hawke. She handed the bottle of scotch to the judge and turned to leave.

"You should stay," Judge Vickers said.

Hawke stood, offering his chair to the woman.

She glanced at Lange.

He nodded.

The woman sat, folding her hands together on her lap.

Judge Vickers stood, walked to the door, and stepped out.

Before Hawke could say anything, the man returned with several of the small plastic cups from the water cooler in the outer office.

"Sarah, want some?" Vickers asked.

Mrs. White shook her head.

"Lange? You look like you could use a swallow for color." Vickers poured the amber liquid to half fill the cup and set it on Lange's desk. Then he filled another cup and took a swallow.

Hawke settled his gaze on Lange. "You were saying, you and Wally were best friends."

Sarah gasped and leaned forward. "What is going on?"

Lange raised a hand. "It's okay, Sarah." He settled his gaze on Hawke. "Our families did everything together, making it easy for the two of us to spend lots of time together. That summer we were sixteen, and our families decided to camp at Wallowa Lake for our usual summer vacation together." He glanced at Sarah. "I met Sarah at the ice cream shop. She was older, but we had a lot in common. She told us about a party happening up at the old stone quarry. We went. And as stupid teenagers do, we drank, were made fun of, and left the party angry."

Lange rubbed a hand across his face and stared at Sarah. "I drove too fast, and we ended up leaving the road and rolling the vehicle half a dozen times. Wally was thrown out and crushed. I held onto the steering wheel or I'd have been thrown out too."

He sighed and leaned back in his chair. "As it was, I had severe internal injuries. I didn't know what had happened to Wally until three months after the accident. That's how long the doctors felt they needed to keep his death from me."

"As I said before, charges were never brought up against him. It was up to the boy's parents and they didn't." Vickers took another swallow of scotch.

Hawke didn't see how anyone in the county could have a grudge with Lange. "When you came back, did anyone comment on remembering you or the accident?"

"No." Lange shook his head. "As far as I know the only people who knew are right here in the room."

A knock and Ms. Wallen stuck her head in. "Ben, we have that deposition to get—" she stopped when her gaze took in all the people in the room. "Is this a meeting I should have been told about?"

"No. Go take the deposition," Lange said.

"But you said you wanted—"

"I've changed my mind. You're capable of getting the information." Lange waved his hand, a definite dismissal.

Ms. Wallen's gaze toured the room, landed on Hawke, and she disappeared.

"If you need to go take that," Hawke said. He wasn't sure that he'd learned anything more than he'd already discovered on his own.

"No. I'd rather have her out of the office." He frowned. "Especially after hearing she might be the one dragging up my history."

Sarah gasped. "That woman is the one causing you all this loss of sleep?"

"We don't know that. She told me Judge Vickers asked her to do research in the basement for him." Hawke waited, knowing the man would butt in.

"I didn't ask her to do anything for me," the judge stated.

"She was up in our office a couple weeks ago asking me strange questions," Sarah offered.

"What kind of questions?" Lange asked before Hawke could.

The woman blushed. "She was digging into our relationship. Or trying to."

Lange's gaze landed on the door. The anger in his eyes wasn't masked at all. "Why would she care? What did she ask?"

Sarah glanced at Judge Vickers and Hawke before staring at Lange. "How long had we been carrying on? Why were we keeping it a secret? They were all personal questions. I told her I didn't feel the need to tell her anything."

"Good for you. But why didn't you tell me this?" Lange reached across the desk, Sarah put her hand in his.

"Because I know you two already butt heads, and I

didn't want to give you another reason."

This was something Hawke had wondered about. "Why did you take on Ms. Wallen as your assistant? I've also noticed from the short trips I've made to your office that the two of you don't get along."

Lange sighed and glanced at the judge. "It was as a favor to a law school friend. His niece was having trouble getting a job because of her personality. He said she was good, knew her law, and would be an excellent courtroom lawyer. I thought, why not. She can't be that bad, since she would be the junior lawyer." He shook his head and pinched the bridge of his nose. "From the first day she moved in, she's been acting like the D.A. and bossing me around. It's one thing to be forceful in a courtroom and another to be forceful in the office. I've had to talk Terri out of quitting three times."

"Why not fire Ms. Wallen?" Hawke didn't see a problem.

"She has her talons into every case we have coming up. She's done all the research and leg work which makes her invaluable. I had planned to go to the deposition today with her to start getting more involved in the cases so she wouldn't know everything. But with these homicides linked to me, I've been staying close to the office where I have alibis if another death occurs that appears linked to me."

Hawke understood the man's paranoia. He glanced at Mrs. White. If she stayed with him at his home, he'd have an alibi. But Darlene had said she still had a son in high school.

"If any of you can figure out how the past may play into the two homicides, give me a call." Hawke let himself out of the office. *What a mess.*

He stopped at Terri's desk. "What did the Assistant D.A. do that had you wanting to quit three times?"

Terri took her time looking away from the computer monitor. Her lips were pursed in disapproval. "The first time, she tried to tell Mr. Lange I had lost important papers. I hadn't. She'd asked for them and when Mr. Lange wanted them, she couldn't find them and accused me of losing them. The second time, Mr. Lange had asked me to get him donuts and coffee. I grabbed a five out of petty cash, like I always do, and went to the bakery. When I came back and put the change in, there was money missing. When I told Mr. Lange, she said I stole it because I was the one in charge of it. She'd been in her office when I left for the bakery and wasn't there when I came back. The third time, she lied, but said I was the liar. I heard her tell Judge Vickers something that was false. I know, all of the correspondence and cases go through me. I know what is written down. When I told Mr. Lange, she said I was lying to try and get her fired. I gave Mr. Lange the case file, and he went up to see the judge. When he came back down, he told me I had done the right thing and he'd take care of Ms. Wallen." She shrugged. "Now I feel responsible for all of their arguments. I know it's because he doesn't believe her."

Hawke put a hand on the young woman's shoulder. "He's lucky to have his receptionist be knowledgeable enough to let him know when his help is not being truthful." He glanced at the Assistant D.A.'s office. "Is she in?"

"No. She went to take a deposition at the senior living center."

"Would you put together a file on her and email it

to me?"

The woman's eyes lit up. "I can do that."

Chapter Eighteen

His phone buzzed as Hawke drove toward Winslow and the office.

"Hawke."

"Donner. The tech boys checked into the credit card number used to purchase the elk tag. It was set up from a computer with an IP address at the La Grande library. The card has not been used for any other purchases."

"It was set up specifically to purchase the tag in Lange's name." Hawke had figured that was the case. This confirmed his thoughts.

"Looks that way. The only way we might be able to find out who did it is to see how the credit card bill was paid. I'm working on a warrant to get that information."

Hawke filled the detective in on what he'd discovered last night and this morning. "Any chance you can dig up background on Rachel Wallen?"

"I'll get someone on that and let you know what I come up with." Donner disconnected.

Hawke pulled into the Rusty Nail for lunch before going to the office and writing up his report on the morning.

Justine stood behind the counter, taking an order.

Hawke sat down at the far end and opened the menu even though he knew it by heart. Merrilee hadn't changed it in the fifteen years he'd been living and working in Wallowa County.

"Iced tea or coffee?" Justine asked, standing in front of him with a coffee pot.

He turned the coffee cup on the counter over.

She filled it. "What are you having?"

"Grilled cheese and fries." He put the menu back and spun to check out the other customers.

Ralph Bremmer was poking fries in his mouth as fast as he could. It wouldn't have caught Hawke's attention if the man hadn't glanced his way every ten seconds. The man was nervous. As if he didn't want Hawke to talk to him.

Hawke smiled, picked up his coffee, and walked over to the table where Bremmer sat. "Ralph, how's it going?"

"Fine. Why you sitting with me?" The man asked. His usual bellow was actually contained to a natural tone.

"You don't happen to know anything else about Sigler's death, do you? Like, did he happen to say where he was getting the money to pay you off?"

The man's eyes widened.

"You do know how he'd planned to pay you off. Was he blackmailing someone?" Hawke kept his face serious even as he laughed inside at the man trying to act like he didn't know anything while his leg under the table started bouncing. Hawke felt the vibration in the floor.

"No. Duane wouldn't try to blackmail anyone."

"Then why are you so nervous. Did he tell you who?"

The man's leg started bouncing faster.

"You aren't trying to blackmail that person for Sigler's death, are you? Because if you are, you could very well be the next body that needs a medical examiner." Hawke spotted the beads of sweat on the man's brow.

"Ralph, if you know who Sigler was blackmailing, you better let me know. It's the only way you'll be safe." Hawke hoped the man's fear was stronger than his greed.

"I don't know what you're talking about." Ralph threw money down on the table and scrambled out of the café.

"You want your meal here or there?" Justine asked.

"There." He walked back to the counter. "Did you see anyone unusual talking to Ralph in here this morning?"

Justine shook her head. "No, but he wasn't in here for breakfast. This is the first time I've seen him today."

Hawke nodded and dug into his food. The man knew something. Would he be greedy enough to risk his life? Was his hunch enough to have someone watch him? No.

But he had a day off tomorrow. He'd finish his reports and watch Bremmer tonight and tomorrow.

《》《》《》

Hawke changed out of his uniform, fed his animals, and walked over to where Herb was working on a tractor.

"Anything we told you this morning help your case?" his landlord asked.

"A little. Tomorrow's my day off, but I'm going to watch someone tonight. Any chance you could feed my horses in the morning? I'll take Dog with me." Hawke grabbed the part on the tractor Herb was loosening.

"I don't see a problem with that." He took the part from Hawke. "Thanks."

"You bet." He strode over to his pickup and whistled.

Dog raced out of the barn and straight into the cab. He was ready for a ride anywhere.

"You have to help me stay awake tonight." Hawke told the dog, who sat in the passenger seat staring out the window.

They headed to Eagle. He hoped to catch Bremmer before he left his gas station. If the man didn't go home, he could be going to meet the person responsible for killing Sigler.

Bremmer was still at the station when Hawke pulled up across the street and one block up. He watched the front of the building in his side mirror.

Dog sat in the passenger seat drooling. They'd picked up a burger, fries, and a soda at the small drive-thru on the edge of Eagle.

Hawke dug in the bag for a fry and fed Dog while keeping his gaze on the mirror. He was licking his fingers and Dog his lips when Bremmer exited his business.

"He's headed somewhere." Hawke started his

vehicle and eased out onto the street after Bremmer passed him in his Ford pickup.

The man wasn't headed home. Hawke knew where he lived.

They traveled out of Eagle, through Winslow, and at Alder, Bremmer pulled into the parking lot of the High Mountain Brewery.

He'd be spotted by Bremmer and whoever he was meeting if Hawke walked in the brewery. He looked up the phone number and dialed.

"High Mountain Brewery, this is Desiree."

The person he wanted. "Hi Desiree, this is Hawke. Do you know who Ralph Bremmer is?"

"No. I don't think so."

"He owns the gas station and towing business in Eagle." He began putting a description of the man together. "He is wearing a suit jacket and jeans. A dress shirt but no tie. He's tall, a round face, and about sixty."

"I see him. He's talking to Thomas Ball."

The investigator. "Is there any way you can hang out around them just long enough to hear a bit of what they are talking about then call me back?"

"Does this have anything to do with Dennis Brooks' death?" she asked.

"It could."

"I'll call you back if I hear anything."

The connection ended. Hopefully, Desiree would be discreet while listening in. He'd hang up his badge if something happened to her. He'd helped her family out when poachers were trespassing, cutting fences, and being vicious.

He and Dog sat in the far corner of the parking lot where he could see the door to the brewery and

Bremmer's vehicle.

His phone buzzed. The brewery number.

"Hawke."

"Desiree. It's a good thing the man you're interested in talks loud. I didn't have to get very close to hear him. But I'm not sure what Thomas's replies were."

"Did it look like they were arguing?"

"No. Just having a conversation. Your guy said he knew Duane's death was being hushed up because of who killed him." The question in her voice told him she was curious about that.

"Did he say who he thought did it?"

She hesitated. "He said 'your boss' to Thomas. And he didn't even flinch."

Bremmer accusing Lange was exactly what the killer wanted. Bremmer wouldn't be in danger as long as he kept believing Lange had killed Sigler. But why had he gone to Thomas? Why not the Assistant D.A. or Lange himself?

"Thanks. Call me back if Bremmer talks to anyone else or Thomas acts like he's meeting someone else." He didn't think Bremmer was in trouble, but he'd stay here and follow the man home to be sure. He might even ask the gas station owner why he'd met with the D.A.'s investigator.

《》《》《》

Hawke crawled out of bed about nine the following morning. Bremmer hadn't left the brewery until one and then showed up at a house, Hawke called in and discovered, belonged to a widow. Bremmer must have called her because she answered the door in a revealing night gown and pulled him in as she kissed him.

That's when he headed home and Desiree called.

"I don't know if this means anything. Thomas didn't really sit and visit with anyone else the rest of the night. But when I was leaving to go home, he got into a car with a woman. Her Mustang was parked beside his car in the parking lot."

He'd thanked her for the additional information, and when he'd returned home, checked vehicle data on the people he considered suspects. He'd discovered Assistant D.A. Wallen had a driver's license but there wasn't a car registered in her name. He knew there were county vehicles she could use when needing to drive somewhere, but given the address on her driver's license, she would need a car to get to work.

His day off may require a trip to the courthouse to determine what vehicle she drove.

Dog woofed to get in. Hawke had let the critter out around six-thirty when he'd figured Darlene was feeding.

He crossed to let Dog in. Opening the door, he noticed someone walking into the barn. It was a woman, and the build wasn't that of his landlady. This part of the barn was only for his horses, the tack room, and when Darlene gave lessons. There shouldn't be anyone else around.

Before he could call out to see who it was, Dog yipped and leaped down the steps, landing at the woman's feet.

Hawke walked into his apartment and pulled on his pants and a shirt. By the time he returned to the door, Dani Singer stood at the foot of his stairs.

"Good morning," she said, peering up at him.

"It's morning." He did a quick peek of his place

and decided it wasn't too bad. "Want to come up for a cup of coffee?"

"If it's not an inconvenience." She ascended, Dog pushing by her.

"What are you doing down here?" He hadn't planned to sound like an interrogation, but he was curious at her showing up at his place unannounced. The only woman he'd invited into his home was Darlene, his landlady, to show her any updates or work he'd done to the place.

"You ask like I'm not allowed to come off the mountain." She stood inside the door, her eyes scanning the one room. "Small, but comfortable."

He filled the coffeemaker with water and grounds and flicked the switch. "It works for me. How did you find me?"

"Is where you live a secret?" She had a smug smile on her lips as she sat on the one chair at his small table.

His blood whooshed in his ears. Damn! He had to stop acting like a teenager around this woman. But there was something about her that made his desires come to life and his mind and tongue jumble. "No. But I don't remember telling you where I lived."

"You aren't the only one who can ask questions and get answers."

The pot finished making noises. He filled two cups, placing one in front of her on the table.

He sat on the bed, holding his cup. "Why did you need to find me?"

"I flew in as soon as it was light this morning and decided while my supplies are being put together, I'd come ask you about something Tuck noticed."

"You could have called. We could have met for

breakfast somewhere."

She smiled. "My knowing where you live makes you uncomfortable, doesn't it?"

"No. But I am hungry. I just woke up. I was on a stakeout last night." He ran a hand through his hair and knew it was probably standing on end. Oh well, that's what she gets for showing up unannounced.

"I'm sorry. We can go some place and have breakfast. There's that Mom and Pop place in Winslow. The Rusty something."

"Rusty Nail. It's just a Mom place. Pop skipped out on her years ago."

"I see. So you frequent the place. That must mean it's good food." She stood and moved to the door. "Come on. You can eat while I tell you why I tracked you down."

He didn't want to go into The Rusty Nail with Dani. Justine was already curious about the woman and might ask a bunch of questions, not to mention the regulars would start making things up. "I'm fine. I'll just make some toast."

She frowned. "Are you scared to be seen with me?" She studied him.

His face heated.

"Or is it any woman?" She opened the door. "Grab your coat and get over it. You need to eat, and I could use a better cup of coffee. No offense."

Dani started down the stairs. That she sought him for help with a problem was the only reason he grabbed his coat and followed her down to her sedan.

"Get in. I have to come back this way to get to my helicopter anyway."

He grimaced at getting into the sedan. "I'll take my

pickup. I need to go to the office and file my report from my stakeout last night." He headed to his pickup, Dog on his heels. The two climbed in and followed Dani's car out to the highway and toward Winslow.

Hawke had less flutters in his gut when he faced an armed suspect than thinking about Justine and Dani meeting.

Chapter Nineteen

Dani parked in the lot behind the Rusty Nail. Hawke pulled up alongside her car even though all the way to Winslow, he'd told himself to park on the street and not make it look like they came there together. However, his chivalry had him walking her to the café and opening the door for her.

Justine's eyebrows rose when he and Dani sat at a table in the far corner where most of the locals didn't congregate.

"This is a throwback," Dani said, as Justine walked up to the table with a coffee pot.

"Coffee, Hawke?" Justine asked.

He turned over the coffee cup on the table.

Dani did the same. "This has to be better than what he makes."

Justine's brows rose again. Her gaze darted between he and Dani.

Hawke cleared his throat. "Justine, this is Dani

Singer. Dani, this is Justine Barrow."

"Pleased to meet you," Dani said, holding out a hand.

Justine shook hands and stared at Dani. "You the woman running Charlie's Hunting Lodge?"

"Yes, I am."

Justine's gaze landed on Hawke. He couldn't tell what she was thinking and wasn't sure he wanted to know. "I'm starving. I'll take my usual." He handed the menu back to Justine.

"I'll have toast, please." Dani handed the menu back as well.

"Coming up." Justine backed away from the table before spinning around and heading to the counter.

"Nice woman. Do you know her outside of the restaurant?" Dani asked.

"She's a friend. I got Dog from her. She raises bird dogs and rescues dogs." He figured that was all Dani needed to know. "What was it you wanted to tell me about?"

"Tuck found game cameras set up in an area where the elk like to bed down. But they weren't pointed toward the beds, they were pointed out. As if someone wanted to catch photos of people shooting the elk. Are they something the Fish and Wildlife put up?"

He shook his head. "Nothing that I've heard of. But you didn't have to come tell me about this. You could have waited until I was up there this weekend."

"Tuck said you might need to look things up." She pulled a small game camera out of her purse. "He took this one down. Thought you might be able to use numbers on it or fingerprints to find out who is putting them up if it's not Fish and Wildlife."

He took the camera, wrapped in a neckerchief. "I'll take it to Fish and Wildlife when I finish breakfast and check it for prints." He placed the bundle to the side of the table. "You still didn't have to come find me for this."

She smiled. "I guess I just wanted to see you."

His brain shot off fireworks that she had wanted to see him and at the same time his conscience, the one that told him daily he was happy with being single, had his heart back pedaling. "I see." The two words came out as strangled as they felt.

Her brow wrinkled, and her eyelids lowered, hiding her eyes from him. Her body which had appeared relaxed, now tensed and straightened.

Justine arrived with their food. Her gaze bounced between them before she tilted her head toward Dani.

Hawke shrugged.

Justine scowled.

Sheesh! When the waitress returned to the counter, he picked up his fork and said, "I'm sorry. I'm not used to women showing up at my apartment and telling me where I'm going to have breakfast." Damn! That had come out as sarcastic and chauvinistic as all hell.

Dani's gaze shot to his. Her eyes blazed, and her lips were pressed together.

"I'm sorry." He reached across, putting his hand on hers. "I didn't mean it to come out like it did." He shook his head. "I'm not good at this man/woman thing. That's why I'm single."

He drew his hand back and shoved his fork into the hash browns.

"You don't have to be good. You just have to be civil," Dani said, picking up her knife and spreading the butter around on her toast.

His day couldn't get any worse than it was right now. His friend who was female was watching him make a mess of his friendship with another woman.

Bremmer walked into the café. It was good to see the man alive, but then, he'd figured as much after hearing what he'd told Ball.

"Hey! Look at our resident trooper having breakfast with a lady friend." Bremmer's voice boomed throughout the café and Hawke flinched.

"Are you having your usual?" Justine asked Bremmer, directing his attention to her.

Hawke relaxed a bit, but felt all the eyes in the place on him and Dani.

"What is wrong with being seen with a woman? We had dinner at the Firelight several times," Dani said, peeling open a packet of jam.

"I don't frequent the Firelight. This has been my breakfast place since I was transferred here. I prefer to not let these people into my personal life." He sipped his coffee.

"And how's that going for you?" Dani raised one eyebrow and drew his attention to Justine watching them.

"Miserable. Can we just finish eating and get out of here?" He shoved egg on his toast and shoved all of it in his mouth. If he kept eating, he wouldn't be able to put his foot in his mouth.

Justine came over with the coffee pot and check. "Refills?"

"No." Hawke picked up the check. "Unless Dani wants to stay longer?" He said it only as a way to show they weren't together but when she smiled at Justine and said yes, he wished they were leaving together.

He put money on the table to cover both their meals and left the café. When he glanced through the window as he walked by, Justine was sitting across the table from Dani. His day had to get better from here.

At the office, he typed up everything he'd learned and done the day and night before.

"What are you doing in here on your day off?" Spruel asked, when he stepped out of his office and saw Hawke.

"Typing up information on the Sigler/Brooks case from yesterday and last night." He leaned back in his chair. "I think the D.A.'s investigator is mixed up in it. Either that or he's trying to keep tabs on the whole thing for someone."

"I would guess D.A. Lange." Spruel stood with his arms crossed. "Any idea when we'll get you back out checking hunting licenses?"

Hawke knew he was making them one man short by following the murder leads. "I'll head up Minam again tomorrow." He held the camera out to his sergeant. "This was found not far from Charlie's Hunting Lodge by their head wrangler. He said it was near an elk bedding ground but pointed away from the beds. I'm taking it over to Fish and Wildlife after I check it for fingerprints."

"This is your only day off this week. You shouldn't be in here dusting a camera for prints." Spruel picked up the bundle. "I'll dust it and get it to Fish and Wildlife with the notation they need to talk to you."

"Thanks." Hawke finished entering the information in his computer and decided to dig into Thomas Ball's information.

He appeared to have family who'd lived in the county for a lot of years. He had lived in the Pendleton area, studied Criminal Justice at Blue Mountain Community College, and became an Alder City Policeman. It appeared he'd spent eight years as a cop before becoming the D.A.'s investigator. Nothing popped as out of the ordinary. So, by talking to Bremmer did Ball think he was protecting Lange? Or was he working with someone else, a woman, perhaps Ms. Wallen, to shove Lange under the bus?

The best way he knew to find out would be to ask him outright. Hawke turned off his computer and climbed in his pickup. Dog started whining.

"You need a doggy pitstop?" Hawke asked as he slowly drove by the Rusty Nail. Dani had left. What had she and Justine talked about? He had a pretty good idea it was him. He groaned and drove out of town, pulling over at the first wide spot and letting Dog run into a field and take care of his business.

Hawke's phone buzzed. Donner.

"I just read your report. You think Bremmer knows who killed Sigler?"

Hawke let out a long sigh. "I think Sigler told Bremmer who he planned to get the money from to pay him off. I think he thought it was Lange, and now Bremmer thinks he can get something out of Lange to keep quiet. But he's going through Ball, the D.A.'s investigator. I don't understand that. I was just headed to have a conversation—"

A vehicle drove by and the driver laid on the horn. Dog ran through the field back to the pickup.

"I missed that. What did you say?" Donner asked.

"I'm going to have a visit with Ball."

"Let me know how that goes. Both homicides left us with little to go on. I'm still waiting for the DNA results from the gum. At this point it is the only thing we have that might conclusively tell us who shot Sigler."

"Or if we found the gun…" Hawke knew that was a long shot.

"Yeah. And I'm going to win a lottery." Donner ended the call.

Hawke opened the driver's door and Dog leaped in. The wind was picking up and getting colder. He wasn't looking forward to going up the Minam tomorrow. Each year when the cold set in, he was happy to remain patrolling in his warm vehicle rather than riding a horse up into the mountains.

He stopped at Trembley's long enough to drop off Dog. Then he headed to Alder and the courthouse in hopes of having a conversation with Ball.

《》《》《》

At the courthouse, he discovered everyone but Lange had gone to lunch. He sat in the reception area reading the three-year-old magazines and listening to Terri type and answer the phone. He was surprised by how many times the phone rang.

"Are there that many pending trials on the docket?" he asked Terri.

She stared at him blankly. "What do you mean?"

"All the phone calls you've been receiving." He stood and walked over to the desk.

"Oh, they are people returning Mr. Lange's calls."

"Calls about upcoming trials?" His interest was piqued.

"No. He's been having me find phone numbers for

people from his past. I guess he calls and leaves a message because they have all been saying they are returning his call."

"Can I see that list?"

She glanced at the district attorney's door. "I don't know if I'm supposed to give them to you."

"Are they people from around here?"

"Some are. Well, a good number of them are locals, from families that have been here for generations." She put her hands on her keyboard as if suggesting he leave her alone.

"What age range would you say these people are?"

"How would I know?"

He stared at her. "You just said they were from families around here. You have been here your whole life. You should know approximately how old they are?"

"Mostly around Mr. Lange's age."

Hawke wondered if they were people who had been at the party all those years ago when Lange's best friend had died?

Chapter Twenty

Thomas Ball and Assistant D.A. Wallen arrived back at the District Attorney's Office at the same time.

Hawke stood as the two walked through the door. He'd had plenty of time sitting in the waiting area to figure out how he planned to deal with Ball.

"Trooper Hawke, you've been spending a lot of time in this office lately," Ms. Wallen said, walking toward her door.

"This office is in the middle of a homicide investigation." He'd decided while sitting and waiting, to not pussyfoot around. They needed answers and he was tired of trying to not step on any toes.

Ms. Wallen glanced at Lange's office. "Does he know you're onto him?"

Hawke stared at her. "I'm on to all of you."

She didn't flinch but her gaze started to flit toward Ball before she caught herself. "That's choice." She laughed and disappeared into her office.

Hawke shifted his gaze to Ball. "I'd like to have a word with you, in private."

The man narrowed his eyes, but he opened the door to his office and walked in.

Hawke followed and closed the door behind him.

Ball sat behind his desk, leaning back in his chair, and propping his feet on the desktop. He looked about as relaxed as a cougar getting ready to pounce on its prey.

"Tell me what you know about Sigler's death." Hawke sat in the chair in front of the desk.

"Nothing."

Even though he wasn't on duty, Hawke pulled out a logbook. It was one he kept in his personal truck for when he came across accidents. He'd put it in his pocket before entering the courthouse. "I know you met last night with Ralph Bremmer at High Mountain Brewery. I also know he was telling you that D.A. Lange killed his friend Duane Sigler."

Ball's feet flipped off his desk. He leaned forward, putting his forearms on the desk top. "How do you know that?"

"I followed Bremmer. I had a suspicion he was trying to get the money Sigler owed him by doing his own blackmailing." Hawke shook his head. "But when he contacted you...I wasn't sure what was going on."

"He called me. Said he had information on my boss." Ball raised his hands. "I technically have two bosses. The D.A. and Ms. Wallen. So I went. Lange and I go back a long time. When Bremmer started saying he knew Sigler was blackmailing Lange and that he's the one who had to have killed his friend, I pretended I believed him and I'd see what I could do." He shook his head. "Frankly, I figured if you cops hadn't come after Lange by now, then you must not have hard evidence and Bremmer was blowing out his ass."

Hawke studied the man. He was lying through his teeth. So many little tells. His eyes didn't stay on Hawke as he talked. His voice tremored slightly as he tried to hide…anger. And his middle finger on his left hand, tapped ever so slightly. He was nervous. If what he said was the truth, he wouldn't be nervous.

"What woman picked you up at the brewery about two a.m.?"

It worked. The man slammed back into the chair. "What woman? What are you talking about?"

"I have a witness who saw you get into a mustang with a woman after the brewery closed." Hawke closed his logbook. "What woman picked you up?"

"It wasn't me. I went home alone as usual." His gaze was over Hawke's shoulder and his finger was twitching on the arm of the chair.

There was a reason he didn't want to name the woman. Hawke decided to take a walk around the courthouse parking lot. See if there was a mustang parked anywhere. After he asked Ms. Wallen if she'd picked up Ball.

Hawke stood and shoved the logbook back in his pocket. "If Bremmer contacts you again, I want to know about it."

He left the investigator's office, walked to the Assistant D.A.'s door, knocked, and walked in.

"You're making a habit of interrupting my work." Ms. Wallen stopped typing on her keyboard and glared at him.

"Where were you at two a.m. this morning?" he

asked.

"In bed asleep. Where every sane person would be." She shifted her attention to her computer.

"You didn't pick Ball up in the High Mountain Brewery parking lot?"

Her fingers stopped pecking at the keyboard. She peered at him. "Why would I pick him up? He's a big boy and knows how to call a cab if he drinks too much."

Hawke wondered why neither one would admit they had been together last night. "Thank you." He left her office, waved to Terri, and stepped out into the hallway.

A thought struck him and he walked back into the D.A.'s office.

Terri's eyes widened. "Back so soon?"

"Who's the biggest gossip in this building? Or would see the most that goes on?" he asked.

Terri grinned. "That would definitely be Earl Gehry. He's the custodian."

"Where would I find him this time of day?"

"Try the basement boiler room. Bottom of the stairs, first door to the right."

Hawke nodded and headed to the basement.

Standing outside the boiler room, the sound of 40s and 50s country music could be heard.

Hawke opened the door and found a man nearing his eighties, reclining in a beat-up old chair, smoking a cigar, reading a Zane Grey novel, and an old record player spinning a 78 on the table by his chair.

"Mr. Gehry?" Hawke said, approaching the man. He walked up to within four feet of the man before he was noticed.

"Oh! My!" Mr. Gehry grasped the front of his shirt. His mouth opened and closed like a fish seeking air. His book and cigar landed in his lap.

Hawke retrieved both and turned off the music. The volume on the player was all the way up.

"Mr. Gehry, are you okay?" Hawke asked.

"What are you doin' sneakin' up on me?" The man finally caught his breath.

"I wasn't sneaking. I knocked, then I called your name."

"Well, it's sneakin' when you about scare the life out of me." He shoved the footrest down on the chair and stood. "What are you looking for me for?"

"I wondered if you could give me some insights into the people who work in the courthouse?" Hawke pulled out his badge.

The man stared at it for some time. "Why do you want to know about people who work here?"

"It's for a homicide investigation."

The man nodded. "That would be Duane Sigler." Gehry shook his head. "That man was lucky he lived as long as he did, flirting with the law like that."

"Any ideas who killed him?" Hawke asked, leaning a hip against the wooden workbench.

Gehry walked over to a gurgling coffee maker. "Want a cup? I came down here for a coffee break. I always read while I wait for this old dinosaur coffeemaker to finish."

Hawke held back a snicker at the old man calling the coffeemaker, that was a newer vintage than him, a dinosaur. "If you have extra."

The man poured two cups and unfolded a chair hidden behind the boiler. "Have a seat."

When Hawke was settled on the chair, Gehry handed him the cup of coffee.

Gehry settled back in his recliner and sipped his coffee. Finally, he said, "If I had to pick someone, I'd say either the man he was thrown in jail with or the D.A."

Hawke leaned forward. "Why do you say the D.A.?"

"It's been a few months ago, I seen a letter sitting on the top of the mail I picked up to take to the post office. It was addressed to Duane. I thought it odd that it was coming from the D.A.'s office when I hadn't heard or seen that he was in any trouble with the law. Then one evening, I was cleaning the D.A.'s office. Mr. Lange was still in his office, but his door was open and he was the only one there when his phone rang. I was picking up trash and started to walk in until I heard him say, 'I didn't send you a tag. You blackmail me and I'll see you never blackmail anyone else.'" Gehry studied Hawke. "His voice was low and hard. At that moment, I could have seen him get rid of his blackmailer."

This was new. Lange never told him about the call. He'd have to go back over Sigler's phone records and see when the man had called him. And if he didn't, who had.

"Do you remember at all when this call was?" Hawke pulled out his logbook.

"I empty the trash Tuesday, Thursday, and Saturday on the second floor. Most Saturday's Lange is the only one in the office if there is anyone. But he doesn't stay until evening. So it was a Tuesday or Thursday."

He made a note to check and see who called Lange

on the Tuesday evening Sigler was shot. It could have been the person setting him up. Hoping he'd go see Sigler to be at the scene of the crime.

"What can you tell me about Thomas Ball and Ms. Wallen?"

The old man's gray eyebrows shot up and a conspiratorial smile turned the ends of his thin lips. "I caught those two goin' at it out in the parking lot a couple times. And they were both in the men's room on the second floor one day when I went in there to clean."

As he'd thought. "Do you know what Ms. Wallen drives?"

"Yeah, that dark blue mustang. They were in the back seat of that one day." The old man shook his head. "You'd think they could wait long enough to get to a bedroom. Dang young people these days think they have to move on a feeling the minute it strikes. There is so much more pleasure when you have to wait." His eyes glazed over, and he was off in another decade.

Sorry to break up his memory, Hawke cleared his throat. When the man focused on him, Hawke asked, "Is there anyone else in the courthouse that is hiding a relationship?"

"There's Lange and Mrs. White. Why they are hiding, I don't know. They're both single since Lange's wife dumped him for that assistant, Travis." He scratched his head. "And there's the young woman in the records office who has been meeting an older man behind the courthouse every day at noon. They drive off in a nice car, and he brings her back at five 'til one."

"What can you tell me about the Lange break up?" He was interested in the people around the D.A.'s office.

"I caught Mrs. Lange and Travis kissing several months before Mrs. Lange told her husband she wanted a divorce."

"And how did Travis and Mr. Lange get along before the marriage broke up?"

"Seemed to work well together. Travis was apologetic for taking Lange's wife."

"How did Lange take that?" Hawke asked.

"Not well. He was pretty grouchy for quite some time after the two left. It was Mrs. White who seemed to break through his anger and sadness." Mr. Gehry nodded his head. "And he hasn't really gotten along with Ms. Wallen. They butt heads nearly every day."

"That has to make Lange's job stressful." Hawke wondered once again at the relationship between the D.A. and his assistant. He'd learned the man took Ms. Wallen on as a favor to a friend, but making one's life miserable every day seemed like a lot to do for a friend.

Gehry nodded. "My break's over. Is that all?"

"Yes. Thank you for the coffee and the information." Hawke left the boiler room, ascended the stairs to the first floor, and exited through the back door.

There in the parking spot next to Lange's SUV, sat a blue mustang.

Chapter Twenty-one

The snow was coming down and Hawke had found fewer and fewer hunters as he'd ventured to the usual camp sites in the Minam Unit. The rest of the year, this unit would only be open to youth hunts. With only ten tags issued for the area, there was no sense in him coming back up on the mountain.

This being the last weekend of regular season hunting, he'd checked more of the animals hanging in camps. When it came down to the end of a hunt there was more likely to be illegal kills in a last effort to put meat in a freezer.

He'd gone to the elk beds where Tuck found the game cameras and took them all down. Fish and Wildlife said they hadn't put them up and no one had applied for permission to use game cameras for any wildlife study.

When he was headed back to the trailhead, and low enough to get cell service, his phone started buzzing.

Donner, Mr. Gehry, Ball, and Mr. Donaghey.

He dialed Donner first. "It's Hawke. I'm headed down the mountain, so the connection may be lost."

"I'll be fast. The info on Ms. Rachel Wallen came in. I sent the report to your email. She has a connection to Lange."

"Yeah, a college friend of his is her uncle." Hawke said.

"You'll want to look at the file." The call ended.

Hawke wondered why the detective was being so cryptic.

Next, he dialed Donaghey. "Mr. Donaghey, this is Trooper Hawke. You called me?"

"Yes. Something is going on at Benjamin's house. There has been music playing loudly since last night and his lights have been on all night. I knocked on his door. He's not answering." The man's worried tone troubled Hawke.

"Did you call the police?"

"I did. You."

Hawke sighed. "Did you see any other vehicles there?"

"No."

"I'll send someone to check it out and get there as soon as I can." He hung up and called Sheriff Lindsey.

"Lindsey."

"Sheriff, D.A. Lange's neighbor called. He said there has been music and lights on all night at Lange's house. He knocked and no one answered. You might send a deputy by to check on things." He didn't think the steadfast district attorney would take his own life, but if there was a death, Hawke figured it would be another murder.

He called Ball. "Hawke, why did you need to talk to me?"

"Bremmer is getting pushy about me not doing anything to help him blackmail Lange."

Hawke blew out a disgusted breath. "Tell him if he believes the district attorney killed his friend to take it to Sheriff Lindsey or the State Police, that you won't help him blackmail anyone."

"But that will hurt Lange," Ball insisted.

"Not as much as the person who has been framing Lange for the two homicides." Hawke hung up on the investigator. Ball needed to get his mind off his dick and into doing his job. Hawke was pretty sure Ball was stalling not for the sake of his boss, but to help Ms. Wallen.

Last he called back Mr. Gehry. "Mr. Gehry, this is Trooper Hawke. We talked the other day and you called me."

"Trooper, I think Mr. Lange is going to do something."

"What do you mean?" The hair on the back of Hawke's neck tingled.

"When I cleaned up his office Saturday afternoon, I found half started notes in his trash can that looked like suicide notes."

"Did you hang onto them?" Hawke's mind started spinning. The only reason Lange would kill himself was because he had gone against all he believed in and killed two people.

"Yes."

"Call Detective Donner." Hawke rattled off the detective's number. "Tell him you've talked with me and what you have."

Hawke was just about to the trailhead. As he'd talked with each person, he'd urged Jack to go a little faster to where they were now traveling at an extended jog which was dangerous on the slick trail.

He called back Sheriff Lindsey. "Has a deputy checked on D.A. Lange?"

"He arrived and found the house all locked up. A neighbor came over and offered a key. They were just entering the house the last I talked to them."

Hawke told him about the note and asked to be notified with whatever they found.

He'd reached the trailhead parking area. Hawke swung down off Jack, loaded the horse and mule into the trailer, then he and Dog jumped into the cab of his vehicle.

The drive from the trailhead to Eagle felt longer than the thirty minutes it took.

His phone buzzed. Hawke hit the speaker.

"Hawke."

"This is Deputy Novak. There is no sign of Lange at his house. His vehicle is here. Every light was on and a radio on high volume." The deputy's tone said he was wondering what was up.

"Did you talk to the neighbors, see if anyone knows when he came home and if there had been any other vehicles on the road?"

"Doing that now. The sheriff said to give you an update."

"Thanks. Let me know what the neighbors say. I'm taking my horses home. I've been up Minam all weekend."

"Copy."

He disconnected, and on a whim, took the road to

Sigler's house. On the street in front of the house sat Bremmer's pickup.

What was the man doing here? Looking for items to sell to get his money back? Hawke parked his vehicle and trailer behind Bremmer's pickup.

He checked out the Ford. It wasn't locked. A folder sat on the seat.

Hawke headed to the house. The front door was locked. He peered in the windows as he walked around to the back of the house. That door had been unlocked before.

A twist of the knob, shove of the door, and it swung open.

"Ralph? Ralph, are you in here? It's Trooper Hawke."

No reply or any other sound.

The sun was setting, throwing corners into darkness. He flicked the light switch. The interior lit up. No one. From the small film of dust, it didn't appear anyone had been in the house since the death.

He checked each room to make sure Bremmer wasn't hiding, thinking he'd be arrested for trespassing. The place was empty.

Hawke returned to the door, switched the lights off, and exited. He headed to the barn. The man had to be around here somewhere. He wouldn't have parked his vehicle here and driven off with someone else. That didn't make sense.

The interior of the barn was dark. Hawke grabbed the flashlight off his duty belt and clicked it on, moving the beam of light around the inside of the building. The elk that had been hanging up his first visit to the barn was gone. He figured Jed, the butcher, was instructed to pick it up. At least the meat would go to good use at the senior center.

Lowering the beam of light, he discovered a dark shape on the floor. He walked over and heaved a sigh.

It was Bremmer.

Hawke put his fingers to the man's neck.

No pulse.

A slow skimming of the light over the body revealed a hole in the man's jacket.

Hawke backed up and took photos from every angle before he rolled the body over. Blood covered the front of the man's shirt. The body had flopped over, unhindered by stiffness. Which meant it had lain here long enough for rigor mortis to have come and gone.

He straightened and pressed the button on his radio mic.

"Hawke. I have a twelve-forty-nine A…" He rattled off the address. "We'll need spotlights to check the crime scene."

He should have been off duty by now, but it looked like it was going to be another week of overtime.

While he waited for Donner, a deputy, and the medical examiner, he returned to his vehicle and grabbed a pair of gloves, evidence markers, and evidence bags. Back in the barn, Hawke took photos and videos the best he could with a flashlight. He searched the area around the body with his flashlight. It had to be the person who killed Sigler and Brooks. But if Bremmer had called Ball, trying to get him to roll on Lange, who else had the man called that would have met him here and killed him?

And where was Lange?

As if his thought conjured up an answer his phone

buzzed. Deputy Novak.

"We located D.A. Lange. He was with Sarah White. She apparently picked him up shortly after he got home on Saturday afternoon. He has no idea why his lights and music were on or how anyone got in and turned them all on."

This was interesting. "What about the note the janitor, Mr. Gehry, says he found in Lange's office?"

"I don't know anything about that," Novak said.

"Where is Lange now?"

"At his house."

"Tell him to stay there. Donner and I'll be by to see him when we can leave this crime scene."

"Copy." Novak ended the call.

Hawke glanced down where his beam was shining and spotted a glint off something metal. He reached down and picked up the shell casing. The same markings, right down to the dent from the firing pin. He dropped it into an evidence bag, placed a marker in the spot, and heard sirens coming.

Donner arrived in the door of the barn. "Who is it?"

"Bremmer. The man I believe Sigler told about his attempt at blackmail." Hawke looked at the detective's empty hands. "Didn't you bring some flood lights?"

"They're coming with a deputy." Donner walked in and noticed the marker. "What did you find here?"

Hawke handed him the bag with the bullet. "Smith and Wesson three-eighty. Same firing pin mark as the others."

"We know where Lange was. He has an alibi." Donner had a scowl on his face.

"You don't believe he was at Mrs. White's the

whole time?" Hawke found it hard to believe the woman would lie for Lange. But then people in love were the hardest to find fault with their loved ones.

"He's the logical person to have committed all three homicides. Yet, he always has an alibi. And his gun that fits the make and model of the weapon used, is missing. Kind of a convenient coincidence." Donner pocketed the evidence bag and pulled a flashlight out of his pocket. He began sweeping the light beam across the floor. "You haven't found anything else?"

"No." Hawke crouched at the body and checked the man's pockets. He came up with a receipt from the Rusty Nail and a paper with several phone numbers. The first two numbers he recognized. Ball and Lange. The other one, he didn't know.

"I think Bremmer called these three numbers trying to rattle the cage of the person responsible for the murders. I don't think he knew who would show up. My guess is the third number I don't know, is our killer."

"Why do you say that?" Donner walked over and took the paper.

"Because Lange has an alibi and Ball called me and told me Bremmer had called him and was trying to blackmail him or Lange, I couldn't tell which."

"I'll get someone checking out this third number and have Ball brought to the sheriff's office for questioning." He walked out of the barn, pulling his phone out of his belt holster.

Hawke returned to scanning the floor for more evidence.

Donner returned, a scowl on his face. "The DNA on the gum you found here at the first homicide came back without any hits anywhere. But it was male. We could connect it to the shooter if we have enough evidence to get a DNA sample."

Hawke wasn't surprised, while the killings had been premeditated and well executed, he had a feeling this wasn't someone who had a criminal record. But a person who did, could be orchestrating it.

"What did you find out about Ms. Wallen's family?" Hawke stood as the sound of vehicles arriving floated into the barn.

"The young man who died in the accident Lange was involved in was a cousin to Ms. Wallen's mother." Donner studied him.

"Does Lange know of this connection? If he and the lawyer are friends, you'd think the topic would have come up at one point or another, wouldn't you?" Hawke didn't know what to make of this. Had Lange known about his connection with Ms. Wallen? Was his past what always had them arguing?

"I would say Ms. Wallen should be brought in for questioning as well as Lange." Hawke stepped aside as Dr. Vance and the paramedics carrying a gurney entered the barn.

"Over there," Donner said, pointing the beam of his flashlight at the body.

Another vehicle pulled up and Deputy Corcoran carried in a flood light. Hawke hurried over and set it up as the younger man hauled in a generator.

Once the place was lit up with two floodlights, Dr. Vance knelt by the body, giving her short detail of what she could see.

"Gunshot, similar to the last two homicides. Will know better after the autopsy. He's been here a good twelve hours, possibly longer. His body temp is the same as the barn, no rigor, the discoloration on his face…" she looked up at Hawke. "He was face down when you found him?"

"Yes. I rolled him over."

Donner gave instructions to Corcoran to see what the neighbors saw and heard the last twenty-four hours.

Once the body was removed, Hawke and Donner did another sweep of the barn looking for clues before they headed to Alder to talk with the people they had pulled in.

Chapter Twenty-two

Hawke swung home to drop off Jack, Horse, and Dog. It was ten o'clock and he was running on the jerky he'd eaten mid-afternoon. He'd called Herb to see if the man could get the animals settled for him, since he wanted to go on to Alder for the questioning.

He pulled in and found the man and his wife standing at the barn doors.

Dog leaped over him and bounded up to the couple.

"Thank you for helping with Jack and Horse," Hawke said, stepping out of his vehicle.

"Not a problem. You have to be tired," Herb said, walking to the back and opening the trailer door.

"I'm more hungry. Thought I'd run up and throw a sandwich together." He headed into the barn.

Darlene stopped him. "I figured as much. Here." She held out a soft-sided lunch carrier.

He gave the woman a one-armed hug. "If you

weren't already married…"

She laughed. "You wouldn't marry me. You like being single."

"You have me there. Thanks again." Rather than waste time unhooking the trailer, he hopped in his pickup and headed out the driveway, unzipping the bag Darlene handed him.

He found two sandwiches, cookies, and a bottle of water. Herb was a lucky man.

By the time he parked in front of the sheriff's office, he was full and revived. He noted Donner's car was parked in front of the station. He hoped the detective hadn't started questioning anyone without him.

A county car pulled up alongside his pickup and Deputy Novak escorted D.A. Lange to the door of the building.

Hawke followed right behind.

"I don't understand why I couldn't drive myself," Lange said, as Sheriff Lindsey met him.

"It's just routine questioning," Lindsey said.

Lange caught sight of Hawke and walked over to him. "Is this your doing?"

Hawke shook his head. "Detective Donner requested you be brought in." He moved along to the sheriff. "Has he started?"

"Waiting for you in the interview room." Lindsey shifted his attention to the D.A. "Want a cup of coffee?"

"How long do you plan to keep me?" Lange asked, as Hawke headed down the hall to the interview room.

He stepped in and found Donner sitting across from Ball.

Ball's gaze landed on him. "Why did you drag me in here?"

Hawke glanced at Donner. "Did you tell him?"

Donner shook his head. It appeared he was letting Hawke ask the questions.

"When did Bremmer call you?" Hawke pulled out his phone to see when Ball had left the message to call him. Saturday around three in the afternoon.

"I don't know exactly. It was after noon on Saturday. Maybe one or two. Why?" Ball leaned back in his chair, trying to look relaxed, but Hawke could see his finger tapping on his thigh.

"Did you call anyone besides me?"

"You mean like the D.A.?" He was stalling.

"The D.A., Ms. Wallen, anyone else?" Hawke noticed Donner scribbled on a notebook, but the light on the recording device was green.

"I called Lange. Told him about Bremmer thinking he killed Sigler. We talked about it. He said to ignore the man, that he didn't do it. So, I did."

Hawke shook his head. "No, you didn't. You called and left a message on my phone at three. When I called you back this afternoon you told me Bremmer was trying to blackmail Lange. If Lange told you to forget it, why did you call me? Didn't you believe your boss when he said he didn't kill Sigler?"

The man squirmed.

"Why did you feel the need to tell me, unless you were helping to setup Lange for yet another murder?"

"What do you mean?" Ball leaned forward, placing his forearms on the table.

"Bremmer was shot some time Saturday afternoon or evening. You know anything about that?" Donner asked.

The investigator's gaze flit back and forth from Hawke's face to Donner's. "Nothing." He leaned back and crossed his arms.

Hawke had a feeling Ball knew a lot but was hoping to save his life by not talking. Sweat beaded his forehead, and his nostrils flared slightly. He was frightened.

Donner stood. Hawke followed him out of the room.

"He knows something and he's scared to tell," Donner said.

"I agree. We can't keep him. There isn't anything that puts him at any of the murders, though some of his alibis are shaky." Hawke didn't like that the man, an investigator sworn in by the state, would withhold information in a murder investigation.

"Let's put him in a cell for a bit until we can get someone to tail him." Donner walked down the hall to the jail.

Gregan, the older deputy in charge of the jail during the day, returned to the room with Donner and escorted Ball to the jail.

"Let's see what Lange has to say." Donner walked to the front.

Hawke snagged three cups of coffee out of the break room and walked into the interview room as Lange and Donner were getting seated.

"Thought this might help all of us," he said, hoping the D.A. understood this was a fact-finding conversation and not an accusatory one.

"Thanks." Lange took the offered cup and sipped.

"We brought you in because there has been another

homicide," Donner started.

"I heard. Novak's radio was on when he was escorting me here. You think it's connected with Sigler or you wouldn't have brought me in." Lange set his cup down and studied both of them.

Hawke nodded. "I believe Bremmer knew who Sigler was planning to blackmail about the elk tag with your name. Since you have been adamant you didn't purchase the tag and we discovered it was purchased with a card set up in your name, it seems, with the sole purpose of purchasing that tag, we—well, I believe someone wants to discredit you."

Lange shook his head. "That's what I don't understand. Who? And why get into my house and turn on all my lights and leave a radio blasting when I'm not there. I'm in the dark as much as you are."

"Who knew you'd be gone?" Donner asked.

"The only people I can think of would have been Sarah and her son, Jared. I don't have anyone to tell where I go and what I do." His knuckles whitened, he gripped the coffee mug so tight.

"When did you make the arrangements with Sarah to pick you up?" Hawke asked. Someone had to have overheard the conversation.

"I called her from the office Saturday to see if she wanted to go out to eat. I decided it was time we started dating in the open." His cheeks darkened in color.

"Why did she pick you up?" Donner asked.

"She said she wanted me to spend the night but didn't want my car sitting in her driveway." He shook his head. "Jared was going to be spending the night with a friend, and she wanted to be home, not come to my place." He glanced at Donner. "Somehow in her mind she felt me staying at her house made her look less desperate than her coming to my house."

Hawke found that interesting. The woman had morals but still broke them when it came to the D.A. "Who was in the courthouse when you called her?"

"As far as I know it was only Mr. Gehry. I'm about the only person who works on Saturdays. Everyone else has a life." He said it as if he found having a life overrated.

"That's interesting? Mr. Gehry found these in your wastebasket." Donner spread three pieces of wrinkled copy paper on the table.

This was Hawke's first glimpse at the letters the janitor had told him about.

Each one had a few more words written than the last.

"In my wastebasket?" Lange pulled the one with the most words toward him and read. "I don't understand. This sounds like a suicide note." He glanced up at Donner. "I'd never kill myself. That's the coward's way out."

"Take a good look. Is that your handwriting?" Donner asked.

"It's a pretty good replica. But I didn't write any of these." He thumped the paper down on the desk. "The lights all night, the radio loud, this note. Do you think someone was going to kill me and stage it as a suicide? And when I didn't come home it spoiled what they were up to?"

"That's a possibility." Donner leaned forward. "Did you know Ms. Wallen is related to Wally Reedy?"

Lange's eyes widened. "No. She's never said a word about it."

"She's been down in the basement of the courthouse. The file about your accident and legal actions is missing." Hawke watched the man.

"Rachel is behind all of this? I don't believe it. We may butt heads all the time, but I can't see her undermining me instead of coming right out and accusing me of killing someone in her family." He shook his head.

Hawke found it interesting Lange was standing up for the woman who had been caught in lies and may have pinned all the homicides on him. But he had the same thought. The woman he'd met so far, wouldn't have gone behind the D.A.'s back. She would have come right out and accused him of manslaughter, not set him up for murder.

"Have you asked her?" Lange asked.

"We're trying to locate her to bring her in for questioning," Donner said.

"You mean you can't find her?" Hawke asked. The hackles on the back of his neck tingled.

Chapter Twenty-three

After questioning Lange and swabbing him and Ball for a DNA sample, they put an all points out on Ms. Wallen. When the deputy went to her house to pick her up, she wasn't there. Neither was the blue mustang. Donner asked that the county put a deputy on Ball to see where he went and what he did when he was released.

Hawke wanted to follow him, but it was one in the morning and he was dead tired. He drove home and dropped onto his bed.

In the morning, Hawke was up early even though he was still a little groggy from lack of sleep. He hauled the hay out to his horses and was headed back to the barn to grab some toast before going in to work.

"Hawke!" Herb called to him from over by the equipment shed.

He changed his direction and walked toward his landlord. "What's up?"

"Was Ralph Bremmer's death the reason you went back out last night?" Herb held a can of starting fluid in his hand.

"You having trouble starting the tractor?" Hawke asked to change the subject.

Herb frowned. "You didn't answer my question."

"Might be a reason I didn't answer." Hawke raised his eyebrows and stared at the man in front of him.

"I see. Police business. Well, did you know Ralph was one of the "kids" at the party the night the district attorney had his accident?" Herb sprayed the fluid at the carburetor on the tractor. The oily, astringent odor tickled Hawke's nose.

He turned away and sneezed before saying, "How do you know this?"

His landlord shrugged. "Common knowledge. I could make you a list of all the kids that the officials knew were at the party."

"I'll grab some breakfast and come over and get that." Hawke started to walk away.

"Darlene has plenty of pancakes made if you want to just come to the house now." Herb climbed up into the tractor cab, started the vehicle.

Gray smoke spouted out the exhaust pipe as the tractor puffed to life and kept up a steady cadence.

Herb climbed back out of the tractor and started walking.

Hawke fell into step alongside Herb. Dog ran ahead of them as if he'd understood the conversation and wanted a pancake of his own.

Darlene greeted him with a plate of pancakes, eggs, and sausage links. This was another one of the times when he was glad he'd listened to Sergeant Spruel when he told Hawke about the Trembley's and the apartment they had for rent.

She placed a cup of coffee in front of him and leaned over Herb's shoulder as he wrote on a piece of paper. "What are you doing?"

"Making a list of the young folks who were at the party that caused the district attorney's accident." Herb tapped his lips with the pen. "Was it Molly or Martha Willey that was there?"

"The twins? If one was there, they would have both been there." Darlene refilled Herb's cup and sat down with one of her own. "Don't forget that Gehry boy. Dobey, Dooley..."

"Toby Gehry," Herb said.

Hawke had just been enjoying his food and half listening to the conversation. "Gehry, as in Earl Gehry who works at the courthouse as the janitor?"

"That's Toby's father." Herb glanced up from his paper. It looked as if he'd written down twenty names.

"That was a big party. Didn't the authorities break it up?" Hawke knew if that many youth assembled on the reservation, the party had to be held way off the roads or the cops broke it up.

"Around here if there's a party on private land it means the parents aren't concerned and the cops leave the kids alone." Darlene shook her head. "We always told our kids if we found out they'd been to a party, we'd discover who was there and tell all their parents. Which would have put our kids on the outs. They didn't want that. That's not to say, they didn't attend a party now and then. It's hard to know where they are all the time."

He knew that. His sister had lied so much to his

mom, he was pretty sure she quit asking where Miriam was going.

"These parties. Were there drugs?"

Darlene and Herb stared at one another for several moments.

Herb let out a long breath and said, "If Ralph Bremmer and Gehry were at the party, there was probably drugs."

Hawke wished he could get his hands on the file from the accident. Had Lange only been drunk or had there been drugs in his system. A thought struck. He could get a warrant for Lange's medical records at the hospital. "Is that everyone?"

"I think so." Herb held out the list.

"Thanks. This may help discover who is really behind all these killings." Hawke took the list. "Thank you for breakfast." He smiled at Darlene, plucked a pancake from the plate on the table, and headed to the barn. On the way, he broke off pieces of the pancake and tossed them for Dog to catch and eat.

"You have to stay here, boy. I'll be back tonight." He unhooked the horse trailer from his work vehicle and slid behind the steering wheel.

He called dispatch and told them he was on duty and in route to the Grand Ronde Hospital.

Then he called Donner.

"Any sign of Ms. Wallen?" he asked.

"No one has seen her or her vehicle. I've asked that they look for her at her mom's house. I don't understand why she is hiding."

"I have a list of the people who were at the party the night Lange had the accident forty years ago. Two of them were known to deal drugs. Our victim yesterday and Toby Gehry. I think it would be a good idea to put out an APB on Gehry."

"You think all of this has something to do with the accident forty years ago?" Donner sounded skeptical.

"The person being framed for two murders was a victim of that accident. One of the persons of interest that we can't find is a relative of the fatality that night. I think we need to look into the past to discover what has been happening now. I'm headed to La Grande. Lange was transported to Grand Ronde after the accident. Can you write up a warrant for Lange's medical records and have it signed by the time I get there? I want to see if they ran any drug tests on him back then." He ended the call as he drove through Eagle.

Where could Ms. Wallen have disappeared to? It was Monday. She should show up for work. Or had her digging into the past gotten her killed as well? That was something he didn't want to think about.

《》《》《》

At La Grande Hawke swung by the State Police Headquarters and picked up the signed warrant. Ten minutes later, he pulled into the parking lot in front of the Regional Medical Plaza off Sunset Drive and walked to the Information Services Center next door. Inside a receptionist greeted him.

"How may I help you?"

"I'm State Trooper Hawke. I have a warrant to look at hospital records from July twenty-third of nineteen eighty-eight."

Her eyebrows rose. "You'll have to talk to Mr. Parkwell. Have a seat while I call him."

Hawke took a seat and waited while the woman made the call.

"He'll be out as soon as he finishes a phone call."

Hawke nodded and pulled out his phone. He scrolled through his emails and opened the one on Ms. Wallen. She had indeed graduated with honors. With the good grades and accolades, he wondered at her uncle having to ask a friend to hire her. Or had that been a ruse to get her hired in Wallowa County so she could dig up the accident. Who wanted the accident dug up? Her? Her mother? The whole Reedy family? But why hadn't they just talked to Lange about it? Did they blame him? Was Ms. Wallen's goal all along to discredit her boss?

A man walked out of the door behind the receptionist. He walked up to Hawke and held out a hand.

Hawke stood and grasped his hand. "State Trooper Hawke."

"Stuart Parkwell. Follow me." The man was in his thirties, tall, slender with a bowling ball belly. The bald spot on the top of his head, reflected the hallway lights as he passed under them.

He stopped at a door with his name on it and motioned for Hawke to enter. Once inside, he indicated Hawke should sit in the chair in front of his desk.

Sitting, Hawke handed the warrant over the desk to the man. "I have a warrant for records from an accident in nineteen eighty-eight."

"That's a long time back. But it should be in the system." Parkwell took the papers, scanned the information, and began typing. "What exactly do you want?"

"This accident may have some bearing on a case I'm working on." He waited as the man tapped his keyboard, moved the mouse, and tapped more keys.

"Here it is. Would you like a paper copy?"

"Yes, please." Hawke held back from asking what the report said. The man hadn't said anything, but he acted as if the name had meaning to him. He didn't want rumors getting started that they were investigating the Wallowa County D.A. even though they were.

A machine whirred to life behind him. Parkwell stood and walked to the machine. "Anything in particular you're looking for in the report? I can decipher some of the medical codes for you."

"No, thank you. I have someone who can help me with that."

Parkwell handed him several pages. "Here you go. Anything else I can help you with?"

"Give me a minute. I'll let you know." He studied the pages. There appeared to have been drugs in Lange's system at the time of the accident. And not just marijuana. The district attorney seemed to be a person who liked to remain in charge of his faculties. The amount and type of drug found in his blood didn't make sense.

"Thank you. This is all I need." Hawke stood, shook hands with the man, and left.

Out in his vehicle he called the district attorney's office.

"Wallowa County District Attorney's Office," Terri answered.

"Hi Terri. This is Hawke. Is Ms. Wallen in?"

"No. She hasn't arrived. I've had to cancel several of her appointments. No one seems to know where she is. Thomas is in a foul mood, and Mr. Lange has been asking if I've seen Ms. Wallen every half hour. What's going on?"

"I can't say anything at the moment. Could you put me through to Mr. Lange, please?"

"Here you go."

There was a click and Lange asked, "Trooper Hawke, what have you learned?"

He explained what he'd found out from the hospital records. "Did you take drugs that night?"

"No. I had maybe two beers. That explains a lot of things. Why didn't they tell me this back then?" His question came out as a plea.

"Think about how you could have taken the drugs. I'm headed back to the county and will come straight to the courthouse to see you."

He hung up. This was a conversation he wanted to carry on in person. Where he could see the man's reactions. It might also be a good idea to have Mrs. White present. She had been at the party that night. Maybe she'd be able to shine some light on who might have drugged Lange and possibly his friend Wally.

Chapter Twenty-four

Hawke called Donner and filled him in on what he'd discovered in La Grande. The detective said Ms. Wallen was still missing, but Toby Gehry had been found. He'd sent a state trooper to bring him to the sheriff's office for questioning.

On his way through Eagle, Hawke drove by the Sigler residence. The neighbor who had confronted Hawke the first time he was at the place, happened to be out at his mailbox. Hawke hadn't had time to read any reports from the canvas of the area the night before.

He pulled up alongside the man and rolled his window down. "Mr. Douglas, did you happen to see any different vehicles on this road Saturday afternoon or evening?"

The old man leaned his arms on the window frame of the passenger side door. "There was a lot of traffic on Saturday. More Sunday night after you found another dead person." The man's bushy eyebrows rose up above his glasses.

"I want to know about Saturday. Did you recognize any of the vehicles?" From his first encounter with this man, Hawke realized Mr. Douglas knew what went on in this neighborhood.

"Well, Saturday Ralph's pickup came and went. He was here about noon. There was a blue mustang with a lady in it come by then left. Ralph left, and came back about two. Then one of them low-rider things that . rumbles came down the road. Not sure if it stopped or not. I know it wasn't ten-fifteen minutes and I heard it rumble back by."

The first car had been Ms. Wallen and the second Thomas Ball. The assistant D.A. couldn't have shot Bremmer because Mr. Douglas said Bremmer drove away and came back.

"Did Bremmer go anywhere after the loud car came and went?" Ms. Wallen could have instructed Ball to take care of the blackmailer.

"Ralph didn't leave after the loud car. But then another vehicle. An old Jeep rattled up the road and pulled alongside the camp trailer and disappeared back toward the barn."

Hawke studied the old man. "You didn't go check that out?"

"I knew Ralph was there. For all I knew, he'd found a buyer for some of Duane's stuff. It ain't a secret Duane owed Ralph money."

Hawke shook his head. "Did you tell all of this to the deputy on Sunday?"

"Yeah. Don't they keep you informed?"

"I was chasing down other leads. Thank you for the information."

Mr. Douglas backed away from the vehicle. Hawke drove down to Sigler's and turned around. Bremmer's pickup still sat at the side of the road. Hawke walked over and noticed the file that had been on the seat when he arrived on Sunday was gone. The vehicle contents should have been confiscated as evidence. He wondered what the file had been about.

Back in his vehicle, he called Donner.

"Donner."

"Hawke, mind if I sit in on this conversation with Gehry?"

"Works for me. I'll be there in about thirty."

"Do you happen to know where the evidence from the crime scene is? County? Or has it gone to La Grande?"

"It should be at the Sheriff's Office. Why?"

"I wanted to take a look at the file that was in Bremmer's vehicle."

Silence wasn't a good thing. Several minutes later Donner said, "There wasn't a file entered as evidence."

Hawke revisited the inside of the vehicle in his mind. There had been a file. "There was a file sitting on the console between the seats of Bremmer's vehicle. I saw it when I looked in before finding the body."

"I don't know what to tell you." Donner ended the call.

Hawke called dispatch. "This is Hawke. Could you have Deputy Corcoran call my phone?"

"Copy."

A few minutes later his phone rang as he pulled up to the Sheriff's Office. "Hawke."

"This is Deputy Corcoran. You wanted me to call you?"

"Did you find a file on the console of the victim's vehicle Sunday night?" He wanted to find that file. He had a feeling it would help the investigation.

"I didn't see a file in the vehicle."

"When did you look in the vehicle?"

"Shortly after I arrived. I was walking to one of the neighbor's and looked at the registration to see who it belonged to. Saw it belonged to the victim and put everything I found into an evidence bag." The deputy had a bit of a grudge in his tone as if he thought Hawke thought he hadn't done his job.

"From the time I arrived and saw a file in the vehicle and you took the contents from the vehicle, someone took the file. Thanks." That means whoever killed Bremmer had been hanging around. He was going to have another chat with Mr. Douglas. This time he'd ask who he saw up and down the street after Hawke arrived Sunday night.

Donner arrived as Hawke exited his vehicle.

"Learn anything new at the hospital?" Donner asked.

"It appears someone gave Lange drugs the night of the party. He said he didn't take them. He only had two beers. That's why he couldn't understand why he was so impaired when they were driving home."

Donner's eyebrows rose. "You mean someone intentionally drugged Lange and possibly his friend?"

"That's what it looks like. We may not be looking at Ms. Wallen out for revenge on Lange, but rather her digging into the incident is making someone nervous their part in the accident may come out." Hawke had a list of possible suspects thanks to his landlord's nosiness and good memories.

"Let's go have a chat with Toby," Donner said, entering the Sheriff's Office.

Hawke was surprised to find a taller, thinner version of Earl Gehry sitting at the table, his head resting on his crossed arms.

"Mr. Gehry, Toby," Donner said as he and Hawke took seats across from the man.

Toby raised his head and blinked as if the light in the room was too bright.

One look at Toby Gehry and Hawke didn't think the man had enough muscle or energy to hold a gun, let alone shoot it. And with the accuracy of the wounds.

"Where have you been the last couple of weeks, Toby?" Donner asked.

"Here, there. Not really sure?" He pushed back, leaning his body against the chair back. His head lolled a bit to the side and his hands in his lap, fidgeted.

"Have you been staying with your father?" Hawke asked.

The man's eyelids rose, showing jaundice in the whites of his eyes. This man was still taking drugs, forty years later.

"My father gave me a boot in the ass years ago. I have friends who help me out." He wrapped his arms around his body.

"Do you remember where you were on the twelfth of this month?" Donner asked.

"What month is it?" Toby asked, his brow furrowed.

Hawke decided to take a different tactic. "Do you remember a party back when you were in high school? One where a couple of vacationers showed up?"

Toby thought for several minutes and a smile

appeared, showing nasty black teeth. "Yeah. The two outies were sniffing around our local girls. Couldn't believe they showed up. We didn't give out information about parties." He scowled. "Found out later that Sarah gave them directions. Hell, she rarely even came to our parties. I think she was trying to impress them."

"You and the others didn't like these two out-of-towners crashing your party, did you?" Hawke watched. The man became more animated.

"No. We didn't. Locals only. Who knew what someone from somewhere else might tell the police?" He narrowed his eyes. "I had a hard time getting the one Sarah liked to drink a second beer."

"One you'd put drugs in?" Hawke offered.

Toby set his yellow, dilated gaze on Hawke. "It was Ralph's idea. He always has good ideas."

Hawke glanced over at Donner. It was evident the man hadn't heard about his friend's death. That ruled Toby out not only physically but he didn't seem to have a clue and no conscience of anything having gone wrong with his friend.

"Who besides you and Ralph knew you'd drugged the outie?" Hawke asked. There had to be someone else who wanted to discredit Lange for whatever reason and shut up Ralph once he began to put two and two together.

"No one. They didn't even say anything in the papers about the driver having had drugs when they crashed." He smiled. "Ralphie and me knew we didn't have to worry about it coming back to us."

Donner nodded to the door. Hawke followed him out.

"Do you think they were the only two who knew

about drugging Lange?" Donner asked.

"No. There is someone else. Someone who doesn't want that to come out. Someone who is willing to kill to keep it a secret. Either Ralph, or my money's on Toby, having said something to someone." Hawke walked down the hall to the dispatcher. "I'd like to get in the evidence room."

The woman nodded and took him to a room down by the jail. She unlocked the door and he signed his name.

Before she closed the door on him, Donner slipped in. "What are you looking for?"

"The stuff Corcoran took out of Bremmer's vehicle. He said there wasn't a file when he gathered the contents. I saw it when I arrived at the residence."

"Someone took it while you were investigating the body?" Donner sounded skeptical.

"I know it doesn't make sense. Not when the body had been shot the night before. Why hadn't the file been taken then?"

Donner handed him the envelope he was looking for. "We didn't send anyone around to Bremmer's house."

Hawke stared at the other trooper. "No one has touched his place?"

"Nope."

Hawke shoved the evidence bag back onto the shelf and headed out the door.

"You want me to come with you?" Donner asked, following him down the hallway.

"Only if you have nothing else to do." Hawke was in his vehicle and headed to Eagle before Donner backed out of his parking slot.

Rattlesnake Brother

《》《》《》

At Ralph Bremmer's house, Hawke knocked on the door. The man was a widower, his children had all moved away from the county. He hadn't expected anyone to be home but as a courtesy, he'd knocked.

Donner pulled up beside his vehicle as Hawke looked under rocks for a key.

Donner stepped up to the door and unlocked it. "I was slower because I went back to evidence and got his keys."

Hawke had been so single-minded about getting here and seeing what might help the investigation, he'd not considered how they would get into the residence. "Glad one of us thinks ahead."

Inside, the house was clean, well taken care of for there not being a woman in his life. But then, he had seen Bremmer rendezvousing with a woman the one night he'd followed him.

"What are we looking for?" Donner asked, flipping through a pile of magazines and envelopes on the kitchen table.

"Something that links the deaths with blackmail. Anything with Lange's name on it and possibly Toby's." Hawke found an old roll-topped desk. The rolling cover stuck halfway as he tried to open it. The desk was littered with papers and photos. As if someone else had gone through them, not caring what kind of a mess they'd left.

Donner opened a file cabinet drawer and whistled. "He has loaned money to a lot of people over the years. And all for a decent interest rate. Looks like he was actually helping others and not jacking them around."

Hawke was just as surprised that Ralph Bremmer

had a heart under that loud obnoxious demeanor he'd shown. He pulled a handful of the papers out and looked through them one by one. They appeared to be letters from his kids, photos of grandchildren. After he'd gone through all the loose papers, he started pulling out the stuff shoved into cubby holes.

"I don't see anything in this file cabinet that has anything to do with his death. They are all up and up loans." Donner shoved the bottom drawer shut. "I'm going to look in the bedrooms."

Hawke grunted and continued meticulously pulling out and reading each full and scrap paper he found. He was beginning to think whoever killed Bremmer had come here to find the papers that they later stole from his vehicle. But why, if they killed Bremmer, didn't they take the papers from his vehicle then?

He spotted something the size and shape of a business card in a cubby hole up higher. He tried to make his arm and hand contort to reach it, but couldn't. The partially open roller top was keeping him from getting to it. Hawke put the palms of both hands on the bottom of the roller top and shoved.

The crack of wood and tearing of paper brought Donner out of the other room.

"What are you doing? Tearing that desk apart?"

"No. It was stuck." The elusive paper he sought was a business card. Hawke plucked the card from the hole. Why was it laying there all by itself? He turned it over. *Rachel Wallen, Assistant District Attorney, Wallowa County Courts*.

"Why would Bremmer have Ms. Wallen's business card?" he asked, to no one in particular.

"You think she's behind all the murders?"

Donner's tone was skeptical.

"I think, she's been digging into her cousin's death and it upset someone." He pulled the rest of the items out of the cubby holes. Nothing else that seemed to have any significance. "Is she still missing?"

"Yes. Can't even find that blue mustang." Donner headed to the door they'd entered.

"She met Bremmer at Sigler's on Sunday," Hawke said, again more for his own thought process than to state something Donner should already know.

"I read Corcoran's report. So did Ball."

Hawke glanced at the detective. "I think we need to have another talk with the D.A.'s investigator."

Chapter Twenty-five

Hawke and Donner walked up the courthouse stairs and straight to the D.A.'s office. Terri's husband didn't sit on the bench outside the office. Hawke glanced at his watch. It was close to three. His stomach growled as if the time made it remember he'd forgone lunch to check out Bremmer's house.

Terri sat at her desk. "Trooper Hawke, Detective Donner," she said, glancing away from her monitor. "This office has had more police in it the last couple of weeks than we get all year."

Hawke nodded to the hallway. "Where's your husband?"

Her cheeks flushed. "I told him that no one has tried to do me any harm. He needed to get back to work."

"I think you're right. I also think that whoever hurt Dennis Brooks didn't follow him into this office." Hawke walked toward Ball's office. "Is he in?"

"I believe so. He's been going crazy because Ms. Wallen hasn't shown up for work today. No one seems to know where she is." Terri's gaze flit back and forth between them. "Do you know?"

"Sorry, we don't," Donner said.

"Has anyone been in her office this morning?" Hawke asked.

"Thomas was in there for about an hour around ten, when we all realized she wasn't coming in and hadn't called in." Terri's face paled. "Do you think something happened to her?"

"We're working on it," Donner said, knocking on Ball's door.

Hawke pushed by him, opening the door and walking in.

"What do you two want?" Ball asked, standing up behind his desk.

"Did you learn anything about Ms. Wallen's whereabouts by searching her office?" Hawke asked. There could be a woman's life in danger, there wasn't time to waste taking a long path when there was a shorter one that worked just as well.

"No. Whatever she's been doing, she must have all the files with her." Ball dropped back into his chair.

"She didn't tell you what she was up to? You two seemed to be close." Hawke noted the cynical twist on the investigator's lips.

"I've figured out she was using me to get the information she wanted."

"What information did she ask you to get?" Hawke leaned against a file cabinet and pulled out his logbook.

"First it was gathering names of the people present at the party that Lange and his friend had crashed before having a fatal car accident. I asked her why she cared about his past. She said, because she might need it for leverage someday." He grinned. "I like that she has high aspirations. The higher she goes, the higher I'd go, I figured."

"And you talked to everyone who was at the party? Bremmer, Toby Gehry…" Hawke pulled out the list Herb gave him and rattled off the names.

"Not the last two."

"What did you learn talking to these people?" Donner asked.

"That they were or are all locals. Back then they had a rule, no outsiders at parties. They were all unhappy that Lange and his friend showed up. I guess the only one who treated them nice was Sarah Price, who happens to be Judge Vickers's secretary, Sarah White. Fancy the two of them, Lange and Sarah taking up again after all this time."

"Did you learn anything else about that night?" Hawke asked. There had to be something that someone wanted hid. He wasn't sure if it was drugging outsiders or something else.

"Everyone seemed to say the same thing. They didn't think the two had had enough to drink to have an accident but when Sarah had wanted to go with them, her brother, Barney, threatened her to get her to stay at the party."

Hawke shoved away from the file cabinet. "Barney Price, the hunter from the Portland area who ended up in jail because of Sigler?" He glanced at Donner. "Why didn't he say he had family here or had lived here? He acted like he was a city slicker who didn't know anything about hunting and the laws."

"I'll go see if I can find out more about Mr. Price," Donner said, moving toward the door.

"And I'll go have a visit with Mrs. White." Hawke stopped at the door. "We still need to find Ms. Wallen. Have you called her family to see if she showed up there?"

Ball nodded. "No one has seen or heard from her for nearly a week."

"She must have discovered something and is on the trail or she was discovered by the killer and…" Hawke didn't need to finished the sentence.

"I'll go to her place and see if I can dig up anything." Ball rounded his desk.

"Keep us in the loop. This person has killed three times." Hawke stared into Ball's eyes.

"I will."

Hawke decided to make a stop before talking with Mrs. White. He motioned to D.A. Lange's door. "Is he in?"

Terri nodded and pointed to the phone. There was a light on.

Hawke nodded and strode to the door. He knocked quietly and entered.

Lange was scribbling on a pad on his desk. He glanced up, put up a hand to wait, and said, "Can you repeat that? Thank you." He put the phone down and motioned for Hawke to take a seat.

"I don't have time." Hawke let out a breath and started in with what he had to say. "It's starting to look like all these deaths stem from the night you and your friend went to the party and had the accident."

Lange's face pinched in anger. "Why do you say that?"

He laid out everything they knew to this point.

"You told me earlier I'd been drugged. You think Toby Gehry did it?" He tapped his pen on the tablet on his desk. "Is he related to Earl, our janitor?"

"Yes."

"That means he would have access to the courthouse." Lange tossed his pen down. "What about Rachel? Any word on her?"

"We're still looking. I want to talk to Sarah White."

Lange nodded. "She was there that night. She's the one who invited us."

"I've learned that. Did you also meet her brother?" Hawke watched the man.

"That night is a bit of a blur. I'm not sure. But I know she wanted to come with us when we left and someone grabbed her. I thought it was a boyfriend and she'd invited us to make him jealous." Lange's gaze snapped up to his. "You aren't telling me Sarah was involved in my drugging that night or involved in the deaths now?"

"All I can tell you is, it was her brother who kept you from taking her with you when you left that night and it was her brother who had your elk tag."

The minute it all sunk in, Lange's face went from pink, to red, to purple. "What in hell! Has she been setting me up to take the fall for all of this?"

Hawke raised his hands. "No. I think you and her getting together again set off her brother. We'll know when we get our hands on him. I'm headed up to talk to Sarah right now. I think it would be best if you stay here. But don't take this anger out on her. I think she's been a pawn for forty years."

Lange nodded his head, but his face was still as red as a Christmas ornament.

Hawke left the D.A.'s office.

Terri's face was white. She had to have heard her boss yelling.

"You're okay. He'll be calm in a few minutes." Hawke reassured the woman before he headed down the hall to Judge Vickers' office.

Mrs. White sat behind the desk, typing on the keyboard. She raised her gaze to the door as Hawke entered.

"Have they heard anything from Rachel?" she asked.

"No, we're still trying to find her." Hawke walked up to the desk and glanced at the judge's door. "Is there a chance you could go with me to the bakery around the corner?"

She studied him. "What for?"

"We have a lot to talk about." Hawke motioned to the phone. "Call the judge and tell him you have to run an errand and will be back in an hour."

"Are you really taking me to the sheriff's office to question me?" Her eyes were wide and fearful.

"No. We're going to the bakery to have a talk away from where you work. You're not a person of interest. I do, however, believe you have information that can help this investigation." Hawke touched the phone. "You can call him or I'll tell him I'm taking you for questioning."

She picked up the phone. "Judge, I need to run an errand." She paused. "Probably an hour. I know. I'll have that done tonight." Sarah replaced the phone. "I have some important papers to finish typing tonight. I hope this won't take too long."

"I hope so, too." Hawke helped her put her coat on. They walked down the hall, the stairs, and out the backside of the courthouse.

"This time of day the bakery isn't open," she said.

Hawke glanced over at her. "Is that why you thought I was taking you to the sheriff's office?"

"Yes."

He glanced up and down the street. "Where do you suggest we go?"

She pointed toward the park. "We could go to Olive's Café or…" She pointed to the front of the courthouse, "the Treetop Café."

"Let's go to Olive's. We're less likely to run into anyone from the courthouse or police station." Hawke walked beside her through the park and over to the overpriced, but quiet café.

They found a booth in the far corner away from the door or prying ears.

"I'll have coffee and peach pie," Hawke told the waitress.

"I'll have tea with honey and a piece of chocolate cake," Sarah said.

When the waitress hurried away, she asked, "What do you think I know? I've been spinning everything I think I know around in my head and can't figure out what you want me to say."

"I just want you to tell me the truth."

The waitress returned with their drinks and desserts.

"Thank you," Hawke said.

"About what?" Sarah squeezed honey into her tea.

"First, the night of the party where the locals were

unhappy with Lange and his friend showing up." Hawke saw the glint of awareness flicker in her eyes.

"Did they do something to Benjamin's drink?" She leaned forward, anger flushed her cheeks and darkened her eyes.

"You didn't know?"

She shook her head. "I wondered afterwards because he'd drank maybe one full beer. And then the crash." She poked at the cake with her fork. "I wanted to go to him at the hospital, tell him I was sorry to have invited him, but Barney kept telling me to forget him. He was an outsider, I didn't need to get mixed up with someone who would drink and drive and kill their best friend."

"Who was Barney? A boyfriend?" He knew the truth but didn't want to give all he knew away.

"My kid brother. But he always told me what to do." She laughed. "The irony is for all his talk about outsiders, he went to college, met a woman, and now lives in the city. I ended up stuck in the county, marrying a decent man, having children, and staying, with the people I despised while growing up." She shook her head. "Don't get me wrong, I've made some strong friendships. But while I was in school, I didn't like some of the 'politics' that happened in this county."

She sipped her tea and set the cup down. "Like the accident. If it had been local kids who'd wrecked a car and one was killed, it would have been in the papers for months, and I would have learned what had happened to Benjamin. But it was in the paper the week after it happened and that was it. As if because it wasn't someone who lived here, it was of no importance."

She stabbed the fork into her cake. "It was

235

important to me. I had fallen hard for Benjamin the week he and his family camped at the lake. He came into the ice cream shop every day, usually when it was time for my break, and we'd talk. It was my fault he had the accident. I encouraged him to come to the party. I knew it was the only way I'd get to spend more time with him. When I wasn't at work, everywhere I went I had to take Barney with me. It was my parents' way of making sure I had a chaperone all the time."

Hawke understood her frustration and thinking she'd get more time with the boy. "What about when Lange became Assistant D.A.? Did you two recognize one another right off?"

"We did. But we were both married. Then my husband died. We kept our relationship as friends until his wife ran off with Travis." She scowled. "I'm sorry his marriage didn't work, but I'm glad she left. I wouldn't have wanted to be the cause of their break up." Sarah peered at him. "I think if I'd been responsible for another tragedy in his life, he would have never forgiven me."

"Do your kids like Mr. Lange?" Hawke asked.

"So far, Jared is the only one who has actually met him. The other two have left the nest. But I've told them about him. They understand, it's been five years since their father died, and they don't want me to be all alone when Jared graduates and moves on." She smiled. "This weekend when Benjamin stayed with me, we talked about him selling his house and moving in with me. He said all he has are bad memories living in that house by the lake."

"Have you told anyone else about this arrangement?" He didn't want to come out and ask if her brother knew. Which brought up another thought.

"Didn't you realize the man arraigned on hunting with an illegal tag was your brother?"

She dropped the fork, clattering it on the plate. "He told me it was all Duane Sigler's fault for giving him a bad tag."

"When did you talk to him?" Hawke had a suspicion the man had still been in the county the night Sigler died.

"The night he was arraigned. He stayed with us." She stared at him. "Why?"

"That tag had Benjamin Lange's name and address. It had been purchased with a credit card set-up in Mr. Lange's name. But it wasn't purchased by the D.A. Someone tried to frame him for selling the tag to Sigler. Who is now dead. A phone that Ms. Wallen said was missing, was used to called Sigler the night he died. Dennis Brooks, the man, who was getting me the name of the person who had the phone, was killed." He watched the woman's eyes widen and her mouth form an expression of disbelief. "And Ralph Bremmer, one of the locals at the party that night long ago, was killed. According to Toby Gehry, it was Ralph's idea to drug Lange that night, but I discovered it was your brother that kept you from getting into the car with Lange and his friend."

"You think...You...." Sarah shoved the plate of cake away and stared at it.

"Of the ones who seemed to know what was going on that night, Toby and your brother are the only two still alive. Did you tell your brother you and Lange were back together?"

"He wouldn't. Why would he? He has a wonderful

life. He'd never want to mess that up," she said, rather than answer his question.

"Do you know where he is now?" Hawke pulled out his logbook.

"As far as I know he's gone back to Gresham. Isabelle, his wife hasn't called and asked where he is." She folded her hands on the table. "What should I do?"

"I don't know for sure he killed anyone, but he is a possible suspect. I don't understand how he could have had access to the courthouse." Hawke had a lot to think about and more trails to find to get to the truth.

"He helped clean the courthouse when he was in middle school. Mom never said so, but I think it was a punishment for something he'd done at school." Sarah slid to the side of the booth. "Can I go? I really have to finish that typing for Judge Vickers tonight. He needs the report for court in the morning."

"Just make me a promise. If your brother calls, don't tell him what I've told you and try to find out where he is and call me."

She nodded. "He took Benjamin away from me once. I won't let him do it again."

Chapter Twenty-six

The day was gone. Hawke headed home even though he feared for Rachel Wallen, wondered where Barney Price was hiding, and hoped he was finally on the right trail.

Dog greeted him as he pulled up to the barn.

His phone buzzed. Donner.

"Hawke."

"We've established Barney Price hasn't been home since leaving for his hunting trip. His wife doesn't know where he is and was getting ready to call the police when a State trooper contacted her."

"He has to be in the county. He spent a night with his sister, Sarah White, but she hasn't seen him since." Hawke was pretty sure given the anger she felt toward her brother butting into her life, she would let him know if the man showed up at her place.

"I'll have someone check the records to see if he has any property locally."

"Sounds good. I'll pick things back up in the morning." Hawke disconnected the call and stepped out of his vehicle.

Dog jumped up, making his happy sounds.

"I know. I've been spending long hours away." He rubbed the dog's ears and back before wandering over to the stall gate and the three heads hanging over waiting for a rub and grain.

"What would I do without all of you missing me?" He rubbed Jack's forehead, then Boy, and on the end Horse.

He turned to get their grain and headlights flashed on the shed across from the barn. Who would be visiting this time of night?

Hawke stepped out of the barn and watched Darlene exit the vehicle, wave, and head for the house. One of her friends must have picked her up for a meeting. He walked back in and finished giving his animals their grain.

Hawke had one foot on the bottom step when Dog started talking and headed to the barn opening.

Darlene walked in. "Hi. Herb said you were home."

"Only shortly before you returned." He motioned up the stairs. "I'm hungry, want to talk while I eat?"

"Sure."

Hawke led the way up to his apartment. While he took off his coat, vest and duty belt, Darlene started his coffeemaker.

He grabbed bread, peanut butter, and jam out of his cupboard. Seeing what he grabbed, Darlene placed a plate and knife at the table and took a seat on his bed. All he had in his small apartment was the chair for the small table/desk and bed to sit on.

Spreading peanut butter on the bread, he glanced up at Darlene. "You must have heard something at your meeting to come straight up here and talk to me."

She nodded. "It was a meeting of the cultural arts committee. It was held in Prairie Creek at the Alderman Gallery." She slipped out of her coat and walked across to the gurgling coffeemaker. "There was more talk about the deaths than what was on the agenda." She poured two cups, placed one in front of him, and sat back on the bed.

"I see." He studied her before opening the jam jar. "Did you say it might be connected to the accident forty years ago?"

She shook her head. "I didn't need to. A couple of the women there had been contacted by the assistant district attorney about their memories of that night. They went on to say that Ralph Bremmer, the third man killed, had been at that party that night. Which brought up talk about the party." Darlene sipped her coffee.

Hawke didn't miss how she had the mug cupped in her hands as if she needed the warmth. What had been said? He didn't ask. He took a bite of his sandwich and waited.

"They brought up the fact Sarah was the one who invited the two who had the accident. By the way, she wasn't at the meeting."

He swallowed the bite and asked, "Is she a member of that committee?"

"Yes. She's the secretary. That got more people speculating. Mr. Lange was brought up. They think he is trying to get back at the people who were at the party by having Ms. Wallen ask all the questions." She sipped the coffee.

Hawke set his sandwich down, gulped coffee to get the peanut butter off the roof of his mouth, and asked, "Why do they think he's trying to dig up dirt on that accident?"

She peered at him with wide worried eyes. "They say everyone but Sarah knew that drugs had been put in the two outsiders' drinks. And that it was Barney who bragged about it." She flipped a hand. "Barney is Sarah's brother."

"Did anyone say if they'd seen him lately?" Hawke held his breath. Maybe the gossip in this county would help him find the man and possibly Ms. Wallen.

"They all said for being so adamant about fitting in when he lived here, he went to college and only came back for Sarah's wedding and her kids' graduations." She sipped her coffee. "They all said even though he was younger than Sarah, he bossed her around and hated that she was a cheerleader and prom queen when he always had to impose himself into the parties. Sarah rarely went to the parties. And that's where he wanted to be. He tried hard to be a popular kid, but his temper." She took another sip. "They think she only went to the party that night because she'd invited the two strangers."

This was showing him more about Sarah White and more about her brother, who appeared to be like a rattlesnake, striking when it was for his own benefit.

"Do you happen to know where Barney and Sarah lived as kids?"

Darlene shook her head. "Herb might know."

Hawke finished off the sandwich and made another one. "Thanks for the information. I'll talk to Herb in the morning. Right now, we're focused on finding Ms. Wallen. She's missing."

"Oh no! You don't think…" The horror on his landlord's face said she worried the young woman had become a victim of Barney Price.

"We won't know until we find her or our murderer."

"I'll let you finish eating and get to bed. You have a lot of work to do tomorrow." Darlene stood, placed the mug on his sink, and left.

Dog, who'd been the poster dog for an obedience school while the woman was present, now begged. Hawke tossed him the last quarter of his second sandwich. "Price has to be the one doing the killing. He had a grudge with Sigler, Brooks was going to… What? What could the phone number have to do with Price? That doesn't make sense."

He made a note to ask Ball if Ms. Wallen told him about losing her first cell phone.

"There is a connection. All three were killed with the same gun—most likely Lange's."

This was getting him nowhere. Just more circles and uncertainty.

Hawke stripped, walked into his shower, and was thankful for the heat-on-demand water heater as he stood under the hot spray until his mind and muscles were mush.

《》《》《》

In the morning as Hawke took care of his animals, he kept a lookout for Herb. Finally, as he was getting ready to head to his vehicle and clock in, his landlord stepped out of the shop.

"Darlene said you were interested in where the

Prices lived forty years ago." Herb met him halfway between the shop and his vehicle.

"Yes."

"Their family moved to the county when Sarah was a first grader. They bought an old homestead up on the slope west of Alder. It was mostly timber, very little land to grow any crops on. The father was a sculptor and the mother a painter. They were throwbacks to the hippies of the sixties. Sarah was tolerant, but Barney was always trying to distance himself from his parents. Make Sarah act 'normal.'"

"Can you give me better directions than on the west slope?" Hawke wondered if the man who despised his childhood was using the old place to hide.

"Can't miss it. Go all the way to the end of Valiant Road. When you come to a gate, that's the place." Herb pivoted away, then back. "You think he's the one you're looking for?"

"We won't know until we find him." Hawke patted Dog on the head and told him to stay. He strode to his vehicle, called and told dispatch he was on duty, and drove out the driveway.

His first call was to Donner. "Any news on Ms. Wallen?"

"Nothing. I can't believe we can't even find her car."

"Yeah, that flashy car should be easy. I'm headed to the place where Barney Price grew up."

"Going to do some tracking?" Donner asked.

"Something like that."

"Good luck."

"Thanks." He disconnected the call and headed to Alder. If he saw any sign of traffic in or out of the place recently, he'd call for back up. Right now, finding the man there was just a hunch.

He wondered if Sarah asked her son if he'd seen or helped his uncle. He hoped the man hadn't implicated his nephew. The thought bothered him. He pulled out his phone and dialed Judge Vickers office.

"Judge Vickers Office, Mrs. White speaking."

"Sarah, this is Hawke."

"Did you find Barney?" Her tone was both hopeful and fearful.

"No. Did you happen to ask your son if he'd seen his uncle?"

The seconds stretched into a minute. "He has talked with his uncle, hasn't he?"

A sigh whistled through the phone. "Yes. I asked him if he'd seen Uncle Barney and he said he gave him money and a sleeping bag. I told him that Barney was wanted by the police and to let me know the next time he was contacted by him." Another sigh. "Jared wasn't happy with me siding with the police and not my brother. I didn't want to tell him he may have killed people. I'd prefer Jared stay away from him."

Hawke's thoughts started banging into one another. "Did Barney find him or did he call?"

"I don't know."

"Could you find out? And if he called, get the phone number, please." Hawke had an idea he knew what phone the man had used. It could possibly connect him with the Brooks killing.

"I'll see what I can do."

"While I have you, what were some of your brother's favorite places when he lived here?"

"That was a long time ago. Let me think… The

roller rink at the lake. The quarry. He liked to hike up the mountain behind our house. He hauled lumber up there one summer and built a small structure. It's probably not even standing anymore. He was only twelve when he built it."

"Thanks. Call me as soon as you get the information from Jared."

"I will."

Hawke ended the conversation and pulled over to add the information into his logbook. The quarry and Price place were in the same area. He'd check those and if nothing panned out, he'd head to the old building used for a roller rink and events at Wallowa Lake.

Chapter Twenty-seven

The quarry was vacant. There hadn't been any tracks made in the mud or patches of snow leading into the area. Not to mention there wasn't a place for Price to huddle up at night.

Hawke turned around and headed down to the main road on the slope, following it up to Valiant Road. He turned right, heading up hill, toward the mountain and thick forest.

The road had some activity. Mud puddles had been cracked by tires and patches of snow had muddy tire tracks. He continued until a three-string wire gate marked the end of the road. As he'd navigated up the gravel path, the snow became more constant and deeper. He stepped out into four inches.

The wind blew white crystals off the trees, making it appear as if it were snowing.

Hawke swept his gaze over the area in front of the gate. A vehicle had entered when there was snow on the ground, but the tracks were filled in with about two inches. He still had no real proof these tracks had been made by Price.

He pressed the button on his mic. "Hawke. Following tracks into the old Price place at the end of Valiant Road."

The radio crackled. "Are you requesting back up?"

"Not at this time."

"Copy."

He checked his duty belt and vest, pulled on his coat, and locked his vehicle before opening the gate and following the tracks onto the property.

The scenery, when he lifted his gaze from the tracks every ten feet was as breath-taking as being up on the mountain. Pine and fir trees stretched up to the sky. The underbrush was less invasive than at the higher elevation. The white ground with bursts of brown and green poking out was one of his favorite sights. The struggle of the living to not let the snow and cold of winter halt its existence.

A glance ahead and he spotted an old run-down shack. If this had been what the Prices lived in, he understood how Barney, the boy, could have felt a need to pretend he was something else. The shack reminded Hawke of some residences on the reservation where he grew up. Those homes were derelict because the occupants drank or did drugs and no longer cared about life.

This place still had some of the artist parents' flare. The front door had once been blue with what he was sure were large vibrant flowers. Macramé plant hangers looked more like giant spider webs from the years of weather. The door was open, hanging by the top hinge.

Hawke took the dilapidated state to mean he didn't need to knock. He stepped inside. Darkness, as if the lights had been turned out, met him along with the stench of animal inhabitants. He found his flashlight and flicked the switch. Furniture was tossed about as if someone had thrown a tantrum. Some pieces were broken, others upside down or on their sides. Wildlife feces on the floor and furniture were contradictory to the intricate paintings on the rough-hewn board walls.

This had been a place of inspiration. Sarah may have felt that, but it was apparent from her conversations and that with Darlene, her brother hadn't felt the same.

Hawke moved through the rooms. Someone had been in the kitchen recently. There was a spot where the dust on the counter had been disturbed. Shining the beam of light around the room, he couldn't find any other proof of a human inhabitant.

He retraced his steps and returned outside. The tire tracks moved on by the building. He followed the dual indentions in the snow one hundred yards past the building and found a blue mustang. The license plate matched that of the vehicle owned by Ms. Wallen.

Hawke cautiously approached the vehicle even though the two inches of snow hiding most of the blue meant the doors hadn't been opened since the last snow. Brushing the snow off the driver side window, he was pleased to not find a body in the front seat. A yank on the door and it opened. A purse sat on the passenger seat. An open wallet sat on top of the purse. Hawke pulled out his phone and took photos. He scanned the back seat. Nothing.

He pushed the trunk button. Just because there

wasn't a body in here didn't mean one couldn't be hidden in the trunk.

Walking to the back, he slipped his gloved hand into the opening and flipped the trunk lid up.

Nothing.

It was a relief, but it also meant there was a possibility Ms. Wallen was somewhere out in the woods, cold and injured, or worse, dead.

Hawke closed the trunk and pulled out his phone to contact Donner. Reception was limited. He grasped his mic and said, "Hawke. Requesting Search and Rescue and Detective Donner to my location."

"Copy."

His gut twisted thinking Ms. Wallen could be injured or dead somewhere in the vicinity of her vehicle. But his first action would be to walk back to the county road, open the gate, and drive his vehicle back here.

《》《》《》

Hawke was crouched at the driver's side door, staring at the top of the snow, when Donner walked toward him following Hawke's tire tracks.

"Any luck?" Donner asked, staying to the back of the vehicle.

He shook his head. "The snow has melted and new snow on top, making it hard to tell if that set of indentions heading to the back of the house are footprints or if the indentions heading into the trees are prints." He stood and shrugged. "Sometimes Mother Nature can't help but make things more difficult."

Donner laughed. "Mother Nature." His facial expression hardened. "How about the sick homicidal maniac we have running loose."

Hawke wasn't ready to judge the man a homicidal maniac. Yet.

The Search and Rescue arrived, following Donner's tracks.

"What do we have?" Deputy Novak asked.

"Possible female victim somewhere on this property. Not sure if we'll find her alive or not." Hawke scanned the faces of the men and women who had trained for this type of assignment. While their faces remained impassive, their eyes revealed their hope at finding her alive.

They split up into four quadrants. Hawke went with the one where he thought there could possibly be footprints going further into the woods. They spread out with twenty feet between them and began walking, searching under bushes, behind logs, and in indentions in the ground.

Hawke discovered a muddy print. He'd been right to follow the indentions. Fifty more yards and he came upon the shack Sarah had mentioned. He approached cautiously.

Cupping his hands to his mouth, he made the sound of a whippoorwill. The people on either side of him glanced over. He motioned for them to come toward him as he approached the building.

The door on this building had been repaired. The building was small, no more than five feet tall and five feet wide by six feet long. He grasped the leather pull on the door and swung it open. The dark interior captured very little sunlight through the opening.

He tugged on his flashlight and shone the beam into the small enclosure. A sleeping bag with a lump in it took up the middle of the room.

Paty Jager

"Anyone in here?" Hawke called out.

A muffled whimper came from the bag.

Relief rushed through Hawke. He had steeled himself to find another body. Knowing whoever was in the sleeping bag was alive, gave him hope.

He knelt beside it, drawing the zipper down. A disheveled Ms. Wallen, the side of her face bruised, blinked at him. She held bound hands up in front of her face.

Hawke turned to the person standing in the door. "Call and tell them I've found her and get an ambulance up here."

Within minutes, Donner and Novak arrived at the building.

Hawke had the Assistant D.A.'s bound hands and feet cut loose and she sat, leaning against the side of the building.

Novak handed her a thermos lid of steaming liquid.

"Thank you. I didn't think anyone would find me." She took a sip of the liquid and glanced at Hawke. "I'll have to say, I now believe all the stories I've heard about your tracking skills."

"Who did this to you?" Donner asked.

"I don't know. I received a phone call to come out here. Someone wanted to talk to me about the night Mr. Lange had the accident that killed my mother's cousin." She studied them. "You all know that's what I've been doing? Trying to figure out what happened?"

They all three nodded.

She sighed. "I should have brought Mr. Lange in on this from the start."

"You didn't see who called you out here?" Hawke asked. What she should have done was over. They had

252

to focus on finding the man responsible for so many deaths.

"No. I arrived at the house. Saw the door barely hanging and walked in. Something hit me in the side of the head." She barely touched the bruising on her face. "The next thing I know I woke up in this sleeping bag with my hands and feet tied. I stuck my head out but found it was easier to stay warm if I remained curled up."

"Did you take the file from Bremmer's pickup?" Hawke asked.

"What file?" She stared at him.

Without Ms. Wallen having seen her assailant, they couldn't be conclusive that Barney Price was the man they were looking for.

The siren of the ambulance split through the silence of the forest.

"I'll direct the EMTs back here," Novak said, backing away from the door of the building.

"We'll need all the files and information you've gathered," Donner said to Ms. Wallen.

She nodded slightly. "It's all in my car."

Hawke glanced at Donner. There weren't any files in her car. "No, they aren't."

She started to stand. Hawke grabbed her arm, helping her stay on her feet. "I had my folder, the recordings of my interviews, and my computer with all the information…" Her eyes blazed. "The son-of-a-bitch who hit me and tied me up, took it, didn't he?"

"Looks like it." Hawke wondered how he hadn't seen any other tracks from the car. But he had. The indentions leading from the car to the back of the house that he'd wondered about. The person had to have taken the incriminating evidence out of her car at the shack. That explained the marks on the counter. That's where he'd placed her files and computer. Then he drove back here, carried her to this building and went back to the shack in a different direction. Gathered the evidence against him and… where did he go. And when?

Bonnie and Roxie, the EMTs, arrived with a basket.

"I think she'll be able to walk back to the ambulance," Hawke said, getting out of the way so the two could check Ms. Wallen's vital signs.

He and Donner stood outside the building, staring deeper into the forest.

"What do you think?" Donner asked.

"About the world debt or global warming?" Hawke asked, knowing Donner wanted his opinion of where to look next.

"Very funny." Donner didn't sound like he thought it was funny.

"I have one other place to check. His sister mentioned he liked to hang around the Roller Rink at the Lake."

Donner laughed. "That place is falling down. They plan to knock it down and put in parking for the tram."

"It's not down, yet. I think I'll wander that direction and have a look." Hawke started back toward where his vehicle was parked.

"Keep me posted!" Donner called out as Roxie and Bonnie, with Ms. Wallen between them, emerged into the cold afternoon.

Chapter Twenty-eight

Hawke's stomach was twisting and gurgling from hunger. Before heading up to the lake, he pulled into a parking spot in front of the Pizza Oven and went inside. It was after school and the three pinball machines toward the back had a dozen middle school kids laughing and being loud.

He didn't have anything against kids having a good time, but he really wasn't in the mood for their boisterous attitudes. He started to turn around and leave when the owner's wife saw him.

"Trooper, here for an early dinner?" She placed a menu on the table next to him.

He slid into the seat with his back to the door, but his eyes on the mob of middle schoolers. "I'll have iced tea and a personal size Canadian bacon."

"That will be right out." She disappeared into the kitchen and before he could get his coat off, she was back with his iced tea.

"Did you ever catch up with Thomas?" she asked.

"Yes. I did." Her comment reminded him he had a phone call to make.

She walked away as he pulled his phone out. He called the D.A.'s office.

"Wallowa County District Attorney's Office, this is Terri."

"Terri, this is Hawke. Is Thomas in his office?"

"No, he isn't. Do you want his cell phone number?"

"Yes. And we found Ms. Wallen."

There was a hesitation and she asked, "Alive?"

"Yes."

"Thank goodness!" She rattled off the investigator's phone number. "I'll let Mr. Lange know the good news."

He disconnected and dialed the number Terri gave him.

The phone rang several times before Ball answered. "Ball, state your business."

It wasn't the first time, Hawke wondered at the man's competence to be an investigator for the D.A.'s Office. "It's Trooper Hawke. We found Ms. Wallen. She's frost bit and battered, but alive."

"That's good news." The man who had appeared to have a thing for the woman didn't say it with as much gusto as the receptionist had. "Where?"

"That's police business for the time being."

The waitress returned with his pizza. "Thank you," he mouthed to her.

"What do you mean police business? Didn't you get the jerk who had her?"

"No. She was all alone. You wouldn't happen to

have copies of the investigation she was doing into the district attorney's accident forty years ago?" It was a long shot to think he might have some of the information that was stolen.

"I might. I'll have to dig around in my emails. Why?"

"The person who abducted her stole all of her files, including her computer." He wasn't sure it was a good idea to tell Ball all of this, but he couldn't see any connection between him and Price.

"I'll see what I can do." He disconnected.

The abrupt end to the call had Hawke wondering what the man was up to.

《》《》《》

It was dark by the time Hawke finished his pizza and drove the length of the lake to the Roller Rink. The huge building boasted two wide stairways to a porch that ran the length of the building. Square logs formed the walls and many large windows allowed light to enter. The Edelweiss Inn looked every bit of its one hundred plus years. It was built as a dance hall and later became an event center and roller rink.

Hawke watched his step as he climbed the stairs to the porch. Each one creaked and groaned under his weight. Even crossing the porch to shine his flashlight through a window, he winced at each creak and crack of the wood.

Shining the beam of light around the open space inside, he didn't see anything that looked disturbed. He had a feeling Price was headed home. He had all the incriminating evidence against him, until the D.A. started his own inquiry. And if the man were headed home, his vehicle had an all points out on it, which meant he'd be picked up.

He eased off the porch of the old building and his phone buzzed.

Dani.

"Hello," he answered.

"Are you off duty yet?" she asked.

"I can be but I'm up at the Lake. Which means I can't get out of my uniform until I get home." He was ready for an early night, but if the woman suggested meeting somewhere, he wouldn't turn down a chance to get to know her better.

"Sage and Kitree flew out with me today. Tuck and Ty brought all the horses out yesterday. Thought we might get together and celebrate a successful season."

He laughed. "A successful season for you."

"Well, I feel like celebrating and wanted you there."

The wistfulness in her voice had him at war with himself. He wanted to be with her, but he didn't want her to think he was marriage material. Maybe this would be a good time to let her know where he stood in the commitment stage of a relationship.

"I can head home, shower and change, and meet you at the Blue Elk in Winslow at…" he glanced at his watch. "Seven-thirty."

"That works for me. See you there."

He shoved his phone in his holster and started up his vehicle. Visiting and eating with Dani was what he needed after the last few days. Maybe with his brain otherwise engaged, he'd have some enlightenment about the case.

《》《》《》

Dani was sitting at a tall table when Hawke walked

into the Blue Elk. She had her hands wrapped around what looked like a tall, clear, mug of tea. He liked that she didn't appear to be drinking since she'd have to drive back to Eagle after they ate and the roads were starting to ice up.

"You look tired," she said when he sat down across from her.

"It's been a busy few weeks."

The waitress came over.

"I'll have a cup of coffee," he said and picked up the menu. It had been a while since he'd had a meal in the place.

Dani pointed to the blue elk hanging above the bar with its own spotlight. "Was that there when they named the place or did they name the place and paint the elk?"

"I'm not sure. It's been here ever since I started working in the county." Hawke had never really thought about which came first the blue elk or the name.

The waitress returned and they ordered.

Leaning back in his seat, Hawke studied Dani. "You look good. When you said you wanted to celebrate a good season, I took that to mean you exceeded your expectations of guests?"

"It means that I not only was able to pay for all the food and supplies and pay my help, but I banked a small amount that I can use to purchase a couple new horses. Tuck says there are a couple that shouldn't go back up next spring."

"That is good news." He held up his coffee cup. She clinked her tea cup against it.

"What do you plan to do with all your spare time

this winter? I know last winter you were looking for employees." He sipped his coffee.

"I'm thinking about flying over to the tri-cities one week a month to give helicopter lessons."

"That's a good use of your expertise." He liked the idea of her keeping busy. Now that she had his number and it didn't seem to bother her to call him, he was glad she would be occupied.

She studied him. "You're glad I'm going to be busy."

He had to admit she was the most perceptive woman he'd come across. "You read me too well."

"I get you're a permanent bachelor. I'm not trying to tie you up in anything. I don't have many friends, and I'd like to think you are one." She sipped her tea and studied him over the rim.

Her words helped loosen him up. "Thank you. I was wondering how to start this conversation." He peered into her eyes. If there was ever a woman he'd contemplate giving up his bachelor life for, it would be her.

She raised her hand and the waitress arrived. "We'll have two of whatever beer you have on draft."

Hawke raised an eyebrow. "I thought we weren't drinking?"

"You can't toast to friendship with coffee and tea." She pushed her tea to the center of the table as the waitress returned with the two glasses of beer.

Hawke grasped one, and they toasted to friendship. He sipped the brew and knew he'd only drink half the glass.

Dani ran the tip of her finger around the edge of her glass, staring at the liquid inside. "I had a nice conversation with Justine the last time I was in town."

He took a swallow of beer and asked, "Are you two wondering why I only want to be friends?"

"That, and we decided to start a Hawke friendship club." She looked up, merriment shining in her green eyes.

"Very funny." He leaned back as the waitress delivered their food.

Once they'd added condiments to their burgers and started to eat, Hawke opened his mouth and told her about his failed attempt at marriage.

"Really? She ditched you for her drug selling brother?" The anger in Dani's eyes washed away some of the pain he'd felt every single day since his wife had made her brother the priority over her husband.

"I guess the saying 'blood is thicker than water' is true." He took a bite of his burger.

"No 'stupidity is hereditary' is more like it."

A deep belly laugh launched his bite onto his plate. He laughed and for the first time, realized he'd been holding onto the disappointment to help him justify being single and not letting another woman into his life.

"Hey, you almost spit that onto my plate," Dani said, smiling and pointing at the chewed-up food on his plate. "You might want to wipe your mouth." She pointed to his napkin by his plate.

Man, he liked this woman. She didn't get squeamish over anything. He had a feeling having her for a friend was going to lighten his life.

They finished eating and parted by nine. Dani driving off toward Eagle, and he headed to the Trembley's.

There was something about today's events that

kept nagging at his brain. But he wasn't sure what it was. He arrived home, tucked the horses in with their grain, and slipped into bed.

Dog curled up in his bed, and Hawke turned off the light. He lay there thinking about his dinner with Dani and her comment, stupidity is hereditary.

He sat straight up. There was only one person he could think of who would be helping Price. He knew for a fact it wasn't his sister. It had to be his nephew.

Hawke glanced at the clock. It was after ten. Did he dare call that late? Probably not a good idea. He wrote a note on his phone and tagged it to buzz him at seven in the morning. That would be early enough to call and ask Sarah a question.

Chapter Twenty-nine

The buzz of his phone woke Hawke. He glanced at his watch and shot out of bed. He'd overslept. He only did that when he came back from trips to the mountains.

The message he'd set the night before blinked at him. He dressed and headed down to feed the horses. Dog trotted ahead of him, before charging out of the barn. Once the animals were cared for, he returned to the apartment, made coffee, and dialed Sarah White's number.

"Hello?"

"Sarah, this is Trooper Hawke. Do you have a moment to answer a couple questions?"

The noises coming from her end of the call stopped. "Yes. I heard you found Ms. Wallen." There was a pause. "Did you find Barney?"

"We did find Ms. Wallen. She didn't see who assaulted her. No, we didn't find your brother. I was wondering, has Jared been taking off more than usual lately?"

She inhaled. "You think he's been helping Barney, more than providing money and a sleeping bag."

"Well, he's the only person I can think of, and he did give his uncle a sleeping bag. By the way, we found Ms. Wallen in a sleeping bag. We'll need you to go over to the Sheriff's Office and tell us if it's the one from your house."

"Of course! You know you'll get all of my help. I can't believe my brother is doing this, but at the same time, he's always had a bit of a mean streak. I remember in school, he was nasty to Toby. Made him do things and when Toby'd get caught, Barney wouldn't stick up for him."

"Do you know where Toby lives?" Hawke wondered if Barney still had a hold over the drug addict.

"No. I can ask Earl when I get to work."

"No, I'll come by and ask Earl myself. Thank you. Do remember to go by the Sheriff's Office."

"I will."

The connection ended. Toby Gehry and Barney Price. Two unlikely accomplices, but they both had a lot at stake if Lange decided to press charges of manslaughter against them for the death of his friend.

《》《》《》

The Rusty Nail Café was quiet when Hawke entered. Justine stood behind the counter, and Merrilee was flipping pancakes in the kitchen. He took his usual stool at the counter.

After he'd finished his conversation with Sarah White, he'd thought about going to the courthouse first, however, Donner had called and asked that he update the case file. Which led Hawke to breakfast in Winslow before he went to the office.

"You're looking pretty smug for having unsolved murders in the county," Justine said, pouring him a cup of coffee.

"My usual," he replied.

She scribbled on her notepad as she walked to the kitchen window. With a flourish, she snapped a ticket up on the wheel.

The bell over the door jingled. Hawke glanced over his shoulder as one of the usual morning patrons came through the door. Bob Gunther.

Seconds later the man sat down beside Hawke. He bumped Hawke with his shoulder. "Who was that woman you were laughing with at the Blue Elk last night?" the man asked loud enough for half the café to hear.

Hawke spun the night before in his mind. He didn't remember seeing Gunther there, but he hadn't scoped out the whole place or paid much attention to the people going in and out. Which was unlike him. Even when he wasn't looking for a murderer, he checked out everyone around him. But last night he'd been focused on Dani.

"A friend," Hawke said, not glancing at the man.

Justine walked over and filled Bob's coffee cup. "A friend. Anyone I know?"

Hawke grinned at her. "I was told you two are part of the Hawke's friendship club."

Her brow wrinkled and she stared at him for several seconds before she laughed. "Oh, you were with Dani."

"Yeah. She called and wanted to celebrate a good

season at the lodge." He shrugged. "We had burgers at the Blue Elk."

"That's quite the place to celebrate," Justine said sarcastically, picking up two plates at the kitchen window and delivering them to a table.

"Any chance I can get her name and number?" Gunther asked.

Hawke didn't have any claim on her and he was pretty sure she'd turn the man down, but he also didn't have the right to give her name and number to anyone. "I'd rather not. If you want her name and number, you'll have to ask Justine for it."

Justine delivered his breakfast at that moment. "Ask me for what?"

"I wanted Hawke to give me the lady's name and number." Gunther picked up his coffee cup. "Looks like he's keeping her to himself."

Before Hawke could spin his stool and reply, Justine slapped her hand on the counter.

"He's not keeping her to himself, he's protecting her privacy. I sure as hell hope you buffoons in here don't give my name and number out to every gorilla that comes through and asks for it." She smiled at Hawke. "Good for you."

He nodded and dug into his food. It seemed he'd picked a feisty pair of women to be his friends. And two that had a lot more in common than either knew.

After breakfast he headed to the office. He hung his coat over his desk chair, started up his computer, and strolled into the breakroom for a cup of coffee.

Sergeant Spruel walked into the break room. "Are we any closer to finding our suspect?"

"We're slowly getting there. At least Ms. Wallen

wasn't a fatality." The fact Price hadn't killed the woman still bothered Hawke. Why hadn't Price? He'd seemed to have no problem shooting the others. Why didn't he shoot the Assistant D.A. who will reconstruct her information and go back and interview everyone again?

It didn't make any sense to him. Unless she wasn't gathering information to blame anyone at the party, only the D.A.

"I think we have two things going on." Hawke went on to tell the sergeant what he thought about Price and the Assistant D.A.

"You're stretching things a bit to think Price is trying to save his face and Wallen is trying to get the D.A. position." Spruel pointed to the door. "Get your report typed up and find Price."

Hawke nodded and headed to his computer. He had all the new information from the day before typed in within the hour. He pulled up the files Donner had amassed on the deaths. He was particularly interested in Ms. Wallen's family. After reading the report and making a couple of phone calls, he'd determined that Ms. Wallen's mother was in need of medical care that was going to be expensive. He had a feeling the Assistant D.A. was hoping to get a cash settlement out of Lange with her information.

He added this thought into his report and signed off. Stopping at the sergeant's door, he said. "Check the file, I found the reason behind Ms. Wallen's interest in the old case. Headed out."

In his vehicle, he called dispatch and told them he was on duty.

A call came in of an accident along the Minam

River twelve miles out of Eagle as he was pulling out of the parking lot.

"One-zero-zero-two responding," he said into the mic and flicked on his lights and sirens, heading toward Eagle.

He arrived twenty minutes later. Trooper Shoburg was already on scene and Deputy Alden pulled up behind Hawke.

It was a suburban with a family that had slid on a corner and the front end hung precariously over the edge of the road, dipping toward the cold water below. The river wasn't deep but it was swift this time of year. It was also cold enough to cause problems, not to mention hinder a rescue.

"I have a chain hooked to the bumper," Shoburg said when Hawke drove up beside him with his window down.

Hawke waved Alden past him to flag down the traffic coming around the curve and then positioned his pickup to attach the chain. Once Shoburg had the chain hooked, Hawke put his vehicle in reverse and gradually pulled the suburban back onto the road.

"Check your vehicle for damage," Shoburg was telling the driver, a man of about forty. A pregnant woman and three small children stepped out of the passenger side of the vehicle.

Hawke spotted the woman grab her stomach and hurried over. "Ma'am? Ma'am, are you all right?"

She shook her head. "Contractions."

"Get this vehicle to the side of the road," he told the driver. "Your wife's going into labor. We'll need the back seat."

The man stood still, staring at his wife. "She…?"

Shoburg pushed by him to move the vehicle off the side of the road.

Hawke called for an ambulance and escorted the woman to the back seat. "Slide on in there and stay warm."

"Ooooo," she moaned and grabbed her belly.

"Ma'am, this looks like your fourth time at this, I imagine you know more about your stages than I do." Hawke glanced over his shoulder wondering where Shoburg had disappeared. He was a husband and father. He'd be a better person to help this woman than Hawke was. In all his years, he'd only had to deal with one birth. He'd been lucky and shown up at the tail end only moments before the ambulance.

"This is my first." She laid down on her side and moaned.

He glanced over at the three children gathered around the man. "Sir? Sir? Is there a chance you can come help your wife?"

"I don't know a thing about this."

"Uncle Joe, I'm hungry?" a small girl said to the man.

"Uncle Joe, wait until daddy hears about us hanging over the river," the little boy said.

"Ooooooo," the woman moaned.

Hawke returned his attention to the woman. He'd heard first time births took a while. He would keep the woman company until the ambulance came. He was pretty sure her rattled husband and the nieces and nephews wouldn't help the situation any.

"It hurts! It hurts!" The woman shouted and grabbed his arm, clenching like the claws of a large crawdad.

"The baby can't be coming yet, you just went into labor." He tried to settled the woman back down on the seat.

"The contractions started before we left Ontario. I didn't tell Joe because I wanted to get rid of the kids." She bit down on her bottom lip and moaned.

Hawke glanced around for Shoburg. He was no where to be seen. Taking a deep breath, he said, "Then you better take off your pants and underwear so the baby can come out."

She stared at him and nodded. "There should be several blankets in here from the kids."

Hawke closed the door and walked to the back of the vehicle. Opening the back doors, he found a blanket.

"What are you doing with my blanket?" the boy asked, running over.

"Your aunt needs to use it." He walked to the door.

The boy grabbed at the blanket. "It's mine."

"Your aunt is having the baby. She needs it to stay warm. Go back over with your uncle."

The boy stood beside him pouting.

"Now!" Hawke ordered.

The boy ran back to his uncle and grabbed his leg.

Hawke slowly opened the door. The woman had her lower clothing off. He placed the blanket over her legs and belly. He also noticed the seat was wet. Her water had broke. He wasn't sure if it had been before he went for the blanket or after.

The woman moaned again.

Hawke knew he should take a look and make sure everything was coming out okay, but he really didn't want to invade this woman's privacy.

A shrill whine grew in sound. His heart raced. The ambulance! He glanced down the road back toward Eagle and was happy to see the red and white ambulance barreling down the road toward them.

Roxie was the first to hurry up to the suburban. "What do you have Hawke?"

"A woman having a baby. She's all yours." He backed away.

"Did you check to see how far along she is?" Roxie had a smirk on her face.

"Her water broke, and she's moaning. That's about as medical as I can tell you." He stuck his head in the door. "Good luck, Ma'am. You're in good hands now."

He walked away from the vehicle and over to the man and children. "What caused you to run off the road?" Hawke pulled out his logbook.

The man nodded toward the vehicle where his wife was giving birth. "I was starting to slow for the curve and Madge cried out, scaring me and my foot pressed on the accelerator. We fishtailed and ended up hanging over the water." He stared at the cold rushing water. "I'm happy we didn't go any farther."

"Me, too. I don't feel like getting wet today." He asked for their names and added all the information in the logbook.

Deputy Alden had the traffic moving from his side. The traffic on the far lane had been flowing slowly by after they'd pulled the vehicle to safety.

Hawke returned to his vehicle, turned the heat up, and called in he was available. He needed to go see Earl, the janitor, and find out whether Jared White had been helping his uncle.

Chapter Thirty

At the courthouse, Hawke went down to the boiler room looking for Earl Gehry. The light was on in the room, but there wasn't a sign of the man. Hawke spent a few minutes nosing around. He spotted a photo of Earl and Toby that must have been taken when the boy was in high school.

There was also a photo of a high school track team. Toby and Barney Price were standing side-by-side. Toby had a big grin on his face, and Price looked pleased with himself.

"What are you doing down here?" a voice behind him asked.

Hawke faced Earl. "Looking for you." He held up the track photo. "What events did your son participate in?"

Earl took the photo from his hand. "He was good at the long races. Could have got a scholarship if his friends hadn't introduced him to drugs." Earl swiped a rag across the photo and replaced it on the shelf.

"Is he still taking drugs?" Hawke asked.

"You should know. You pulled him in the other day." Earl wasn't as friendly as Hawke's first visit to the boiler room.

"Where is he now? Where is he staying?"

"Why? You still trying to pin all those killings on him?" Earl studied him.

"I don't think your son killed anyone, but I think he's being bullied into helping Barney Price." Hawke figured letting the man know he didn't blame his son might get him more cooperation out of the janitor.

"That Barney has manipulated my Toby for years. I hated it, but I couldn't get Toby to see it for what it was—bullying." Earl sat down. His chin lowered to his chest.

"Has Barney been around asking Toby to help him with things?" Hawke pulled over a stool from the workbench and sat.

"I caught Toby in here a couple of times after hours the last few weeks. He wouldn't tell me what he was doing, but he'd be high the next day." Earl's head lifted, he peered at Hawke. "I think he's the one that made the phone calls, maybe wrote those notes I found... I'm not sure. I caught him here several times."

"What about Dennis Brooks? How would he have known what Dennis was going to tell me?" Hawke still had trouble putting a reason behind the administrator's death.

"I'm not sure. But I found this at home and was going to put it back in the Administrative Offices tonight." Earl pulled a cell phone out of the pocket on the side of his recliner.

Hawke picked up a rag from the workbench and lifted the phone out of the man's hand. He placed it on the wooden bench and found the number for the phone that had caused Brooks death. He dialed the number.

The phone on the bench rang.

Dennis must have called who had the phone and made a plan to get it back.

"Did Dennis Brooks know Toby?" Hawke wrapped the phone up in the rag and shoved it in his pocket.

"I'm not sure. Maybe." Earl's eyes watered. "What are you going to do with my boy?"

"I just want to talk to him. See if I can get him to tell me what all Price forced him to do."

"You believe me? It was Barney being a bully?" Earl sat up in his chair.

"There is a lot of hatred in Barney Price. So much, he would ruin his life to ruin his sister's life. I don't know what grudge he has against D.A. Lange, but it goes back to even before the party, I think." Hawke moved toward the door. "Please, if you see your son, bring him to the Sheriff's Department or call me. I just want to get to the truth before someone, possibly your son, gets hurt."

Earl nodded.

Hawke walked up the basement stairs and popped out beside the administrative offices. He really didn't have any questions for them. It appeared the phone had been in the office for some reason and Brooks realized it was missing and possibly who had taken it. They wouldn't know until he could get Toby to talk with him.

He walked to the stairs and up to the second floor. His mind was still on the fact there had to be a grudge between Lange and Price that happened before the party. Then something at the party had caused the young man to drug a stranger and keep his sister from leaving with him.

Hawke entered the D.A.'s office.

"Hi Hawke," Terri greeted him.

"Hi. Your boss in?"

"No. He's down the hall at Judge Vickers."

"Perfect, that's where I was headed next." Hawke swung out of the office and strode down the hall.

Sarah White sat at the desk. She glanced up and her expression saddened. "Trooper Hawke. I went to the Sheriff's Office and it was our sleeping bag. I've also discovered that Jared has been skipping first and second period classes the last week. When I get my hands on that brother of mine, I'll wring his neck."

"We need to get our hands on him first." Hawke nodded toward the door. "They talking important stuff?"

She glanced at the clock on the wall. "Benjamin has been in there long enough that business is finished. They're probably talking golf."

"I wondered if you and Mr. Lange could meet me in the conference room downstairs in fifteen minutes?"

She studied him. "I'm sure I can make that happen."

"Good. See you down there." Hawke left the second floor, went on out the back door and over to the bakery. He purchased half a dozen donuts and three coffees.

When he opened the conference room door, Sarah and the D.A. were sitting side by side talking quietly.

"You two must have come straight down." He held

up the coffee and donuts. "I made a side trip." Hawke handed out the coffee and set the box of donuts in front of the two. He took a seat across the table from them.

"Why did you want to see both of us?" Lange asked.

Hawke settled his gaze on Lange then Sarah, and back to Lange. "Because I think this grudge, hatred, obsession, whatever you want to call it that Barney Price has for you goes to more than you being a stranger who showed up at the party and now someone who could send him to jail for his drugging you and causing the death of your friend."

Sarah inhaled. "What do you mean?"

"Tell me about the summer you two met? Where did you meet, how, and most importantly, did your brother see the two of you before that party?"

Lange stared at Sarah. "We met Tuesday after my family arrived at the lake for our week vacation. Wally and I went to the ice cream shop and Sarah waited on us."

"I remember thinking you were cute, but shy. Wally did most of the talking, but you were the one who I remembered that night when I went to sleep." She smiled.

"I went back there every day, with or without Wally," Lange said.

"I liked the days you didn't bring him. Then you talked to me." She stopped. "I remember Thursday, Millie, the girl Barney liked was there with her cousin." Sarah's eyes narrowed. "Remember, she tried to talk to you and keep you from visiting with me?"

"That's right. We finally walked outside on your break and barely got you back to work before your break was over, we'd walked so far talking." Lange scratched his head. "Was she at the party?"

Sarah's eyes widened. "She was! She ran over to you when you drove up. But you brushed her aside and walked over to me."

"That's right. She came over and told you your brother wanted to talk to you." Lange squinted his eyes as if thinking. "I remember her wrapping her arm around mine and trying to make me walk off with her. I pulled my arm out and went looking for you." His eyes widened. "Barney had a hold of your arm and you looked like it hurt."

"That's right, you hit him in the eye, and we went for a walk. When we came back, that's when Toby offered you the beer. You drank a few sips and then several of the boys started taunting you and Wally. When you wanted me to leave with you, Barney held my arm tight and told me if I went with you, he'd tell our parents I…" her cheeks darkened. "that you and I…"

"I get the picture," Hawke said. "I believe his resentment of you was rekindled when Sarah told him she was dating you. I think he had hoped to get you in trouble with the law and when that didn't work, he resorted to framing you for murder."

Sarah grasped Lange's hand. "I'm so sorry."

Lange kissed her hand. "It's not your fault." He shifted his gaze to Hawke. "What steps are you taking to catch him?"

"We have to find him. I believe Toby Gehry has been helping him." Hawke was going to help stakeout the Gehry residence.

"Poor Toby. I hope he didn't have anything to do

with the deaths," Sarah said.

《》《》《》

Hawke talked Sergeant Spruel into letting him head up surveillance on the Gehry residence. Deputy Novak and Alder Policeman Don Profitt were parked in their own vehicles two blocks down in each direction from the small house. Hawke sat in his personal pickup a block up the street from the house that sat on the corner of Ponderosa and Third Street.

An older Jeep, that matched the description from several neighbors on Sigler's street, drove up the street and parked in front of the house. Toby stepped out of the passenger side, carrying a pizza box. Barney Price stepped out from the driver's side.

That was why they couldn't find him. He was driving a different vehicle.

Hawke texted the two officers on surveillance. *Suspect entered the house. You two take the back, I'll knock on the door in five.*

He quickly typed the vehicle license in his computer. The Jeep belonged to Toby.

Hawke exited his pickup and walked across the street toward the house. He wondered if Earl was inside. If so, he hoped the old man didn't try to be a hero to save his son.

He glanced at his watch. Thirty more seconds.

Muffled sounds of canned laughter came from the television. The second hand blipped to twelve on his watch.

Hawke knocked on the door.

"Toby, get that!" Price shouted.

The door opened.

Toby Gehry stood in front of him his mouth

278

hanging open. "I didn't—" he started to say.

Hawke pulled him outside. "Sit right here on the porch. We don't want you. Is your father inside?"

"He's at work."

Hawke stood up as Price walked toward the door, "Toby who was—"

Price changed direction and ran to the back of the house. Hawke pursued, wanting the man to run into the two waiting for him.

"Police! Hands on your head!" Profitt shouted.

Hawke hit the kitchen in time for Price to spin around, grab something, and hurl it.

Hawke ducked, but didn't move out of the door. He raised his Glock. "Hands in the air."

Alden stepped in the door behind Price and grabbed one arm, snapping the cuffs on and pulling Price's other arm behind him.

The easiest part was done. Now to make the man confess to killing three people.

Chapter Thirty-one

After Price was put in the back of Deputy Alden's car. Hawke asked Toby, "You want to ride to the sheriff's department with me?"

Toby stared at Price. "I don't have to be with him, do I?"

"No, you're only being questioned. He's under arrest." Hawke turned to Officer Profitt. "Don't let anyone in or out of the house or near the Jeep. I'm going to get a warrant. We need to find the gun and the evidence that proves he kidnapped Ms. Wallen."

Hawke led Toby to his pickup. "Did you see Barney with a gun?"

The man nodded.

"When?"

"He gave it to Dad before he went to work. He told him to put it in D.A. Lange's office. Where it would be found." Toby stared at his feet. "Dad didn't want to, but Barney laughed at him and said, 'Toby is all you have old man.' I don't know what he meant, but Dad's face went white, and he took the gun."

"Come on." Hawke closed the door on his passenger and rounded the hood of the cab while talking on his phone.

"Donner. Write up a warrant to search Earl Gehry's house and Toby Gehry's Jeep. We arrested Price but need to find all the proof against him." Hawke slid behind the wheel of his pickup and followed Deputy Alden to the Sheriff's Office.

At the jail entrance to the building, Hawke told Alden to hold Price in booking and have Toby wait in the interview room. He'd be back.

Hawke walked over to the courthouse and tried the back door. It swung open. Did Earl always leave the door unlocked?

The rumble of a cart rolling on the second floor drew Hawke to the stairs. Halfway up, he heard voices. A man and a woman's. He slowed his ascent and listened.

"What are you doing?" the man's voice, Earl asked.

"Looking for that gun."

Hawke tensed. What was she doing at the courthouse so late?

"I don't know what you're talking about," Earl said.

"The gun Barney Price gave you. I know you have it. Toby told me." The authority in Ms. Wallen's voice proved she'd known more about the whole thing than she'd ever let on.

"Toby takes drugs. He doesn't know what he's saying most of the time." Earl said the words almost convincingly. But not quite. He couldn't talk bad about his son.

Ms. Wallen laughed. "Who do you think gives him the drugs?" A pause. "Don't look so surprised. He's the one who's been helping me build a case against my boss. He's the one helping me get the District Attorney position."

"I don't understand?" Earl said, the rumble of his cart excelled. He appeared at the top of the stairs and continued on down to the first floor.

Hawke burst by him and found Ms. Wallen digging through Earl's cart.

"What are you looking for Ms. Wallen?" he asked.

Her body stiffened, and she swung around. "That man, Earl, I believe he is the one who has been killing everyone." Her hand continued to dig through the trash bag hanging on the cart.

If she got her hand on the gun, he knew she'd use it on him and blame it on Earl.

He pulled his Glock for the second time in one night. "Get your hands in front of you where I can see them."

She slowly pulled the one in the bag out. It was empty.

"Next to the wall, both hands on the wall above your head," he said, walking closer.

She walked over to the wall and placed her hands as he'd requested. "I'm not the criminal here. It's Lange. He had the janitor take his gun. I bet if you look in his office, you'll find the files and my computer. He's the one behind all of these killings."

Hawke grabbed one hand and slapped his cuff on it, then the other one. He walked her over to the top of the stairs. He started to holler for Earl when the janitor and Deputy Alden appeared at the foot of the stairs.

"Earl, come show me where the gun is." Hawke handed Ms. Wallen over to Alden. "Take her to a holding cell, but far enough from Price they can't talk."

Alden nodded and escorted the Assistant D.A. down the stairs.

"The gun's in that tool box." Earl pointed to an old rusty tool box on the bottom of the cart.

"Toby told me Price threatened killing him if you didn't put the gun in the D.A.'s office." Hawke pulled out his phone and took a photo of the box. Then he picked up the tool box and opened it. The gun sat on top. He snapped another photo and closed the lid, tucking the box under his arm. "I'll need you to give a statement, just like Toby."

Earl nodded.

"Can you unlock D.A. Lange's office? I think Ms. Wallen left incriminating evidence in there."

The janitor walked over and unlocked the door.

Hawke walked in, flicked the light on, and scanned the area. The man had everything in its place. Which meant the files sitting on the file cabinet had to be what the woman had planted. He took photos of that and then picked up the files, flipping through the papers. Bingo.

"Come on Earl, let's go put all the pieces together."

《》《》《》

Hawke sat in the room with Price. It was noon the next day. They'd let him sit in a cell while they processed the house, Jeep, and the weapon.

Donner was talking with Ms. Wallen, whom they'd let stew overnight in a cell as well.

Price had his lips clamped shut.

"We have the gun. The one you told Earl Gehry to plant in District Attorney Lange's office. The one you stole from Lange's vehicle."

Price shook his head.

"No? We have both Toby and Earl's statements that say you threatened Toby's life if Earl didn't put the gun in Lange's office. And since you had possession of a weapon that has been proven to be the gun that shot the bullets that killed, Duane Sigler, Dennis Brooks, and Ralph Bremmer, we have you on three counts of homicide."

"I didn't take the gun." Price stared at him. "Toby did."

"I know. You bullied him, just like back when you told him to take that beer to Benjamin Lange at the party. A beer you'd put a large dose of cocaine in." Hawke studied the man. He didn't show any remorse.

"Why did you do that? He was causing no harm."

Price leaned forward, slamming his handcuffed, fisted hands on the table. "He was an outsider. My sister and Millie acted like they'd never seen a boy before. They both hung all over him. He was nothing. He'd be leaving in a few days. They needed to pay attention to those of us who would be there for them."

"Are you sure you weren't jealous? Jealous that he had a car and could summer at the lake and live somewhere else? You were stuck in the county, with parents who lived like hippies, and a sister who was happy with the way things were. But you weren't, were you?" Hawke knew a bit of the jealousy the boy felt. He'd had it whenever the sport teams would travel to other towns and he'd see nice houses, a nice school, and bleachers filled with parents cheering for their kids.

Few of the reservation parents attended the sporting events. They were the minority and didn't like to deal with non-reservation people.

"I hated it here!" Price spit the words out. "I hated my parents, was jealous of Sarah who fit in." He slammed his hands down again. "I made it out. I used a track scholarship to get the hell out of here and make a new life."

"What do you think your wife and children are going to say when they discover your jealousy and hatred killed three people?" Hawke never did understand the craziness that made a person with so much, do something that ripped not only their world apart but their family's world as well.

He dropped his face into his hands and sobbed.

"The best thing to do for you and for them is to tell me everything." Hawke had already started the recording device. He pulled over a pad of paper and poised a pen over it.

Price finally pulled himself together. "It started when Ms. Wallen contacted me. She wanted to know about the party her boss attended the night he'd killed his best friend. It brought back all that anger I'd felt. Then a couple days later, Sarah called and was telling my wife about how she'd reconnected with a boy from her past. When I heard who it was… I had to make sure he suffered."

"That's what I don't understand. Did you or Ms. Wallen get the credit card in Lange's name? I'm assuming it was she who used a computer at the La Grande library to purchase the elk tag and the person who sent it to Sigler, trying to implicate her boss in impropriety."

285

"Yes, the tag was all her idea. I went along because I wanted him to feel what it was like to have something you wanted ripped away from you." His red-rimmed eyes stared at his hands.

"Why did you kill Sigler? Did he figure out something was wrong when he called Lange and the D.A. denied knowing about the tag?" Hawke had puzzled out a lot of what happened. But they needed Price to say it.

"He did call Lange. But the secretary wouldn't let Duane talk to him. She put him through to Rachel. She told Sigler she'd get to the bottom of it, then called me and told me something had to be done about Duane. And she knew where Lange kept a gun."

"That's when you bullied Toby into taking the gun from Lange's car."

"He'd always been a wuss. It helped Rachel was supplying him, so he did anything we asked him to do."

"Except kill." Toby had said the two had tried to talk him into killing the first man.

"Yeah. I knew he was too much of a coward for that." The whole time Price was talking, he kept his head bent, his gaze on his hands. It was apparent now that he'd been caught, he wanted to unburden but not see condemnation in anyone's eyes.

"Dennis is the one I don't understand," Hawke said, opening the door for that murder.

"He figured out that Rachel had lied about losing her first phone. She'd started using it to call me and Sigler and realized it could be traced to her. So she said she'd lost it and was given a new phone. Brooks called her and asked her about the first phone. Said he wanted to know the truth before he saw you. She set up a meeting with him in the high school parking lot. But I rolled up and acted like I was just going to ask him a question and…"

Hawke hated it was his curiosity over the phone that caused Dennis Brooks' death. "And the killing continued."

"Yeah. That damn Duane had told Bremmer about the elk tag. He called Rachel trying to blackmail her. She set up the meeting at the barn. Figured we got away with one murder there, might get just as lucky with the second."

"What I don't understand is why did you turn on Ms. Wallen?" Hawke had been trying to make sense of his attack on the one person who's help he could count on.

"She said she had enough to get what she wanted. That I needed to go home and forget what had happened. But I'd done all the killing. She wasn't near as dirty as I was. When I told her I wanted her written word she'd not turn me over to the police, she laughed. 'It's your butt in a sling not mine.' Those were her words. She would have turned me in as soon as anyone thought to look at her."

"But you didn't kill her?"

"I didn't have the gun. It was at Toby's. I figured no one would find her before she froze to death." He glanced up. "I figured sure as shit when I heard she'd been found the cops would have been all over me."

"She said she didn't know who attacked her." Hawke studied him. The man was astonished.

"Why do you think she didn't turn on me?"

"Because she is just as much a part of the murders as you pulling the trigger. She knew that, but you didn't." Hawke leaned back in his chair. "Are you happy knowing you will be locked up for life and your sister will go on living her life? One you tried to ruin because of your unhappiness?"

Price stared at him as Hawke walked to the door. He called in the deputy standing outside the door. "Watch him until I get back with his statement to sign."

He walked over to the room where Donner was questioning Ms. Wallen. A door at the end of the hall opened and Donner walked toward him.

"What did she tell you?" Hawke asked.

"That Price coerced her into helping him." Donner's eyebrows rose.

"Do you believe her?" Hawke believed Price's version. He had nothing to gain by lying.

"Not all of it. She was not only after Lange's job but she also felt she was getting revenge for her cousin's loss of life at the hands of Lange. Her words."

"Before you take her statement in to be signed, you might want to read Price's." Hawke said.

"Better yet, you print out Price's and go have a talk with her." Donner ripped up the pages he had in his hands.

Hawke liked the idea of seeing how the woman wiggled her way out of the truth. "I'll just use my notes. I want to conduct my interview before she has time to think about what Price might have said."

He stepped into the room.

Ms. Wallen stopped picking her cuticles and smiled. "I really don't understand what is taking so long for Trooper Donner to get my statement to sign."

"While we're waiting, I have a couple more questions that came up during my interview with

Price."

Her eyes widened before she hid her feelings. "What questions are those? You know he is the one who hit me and left me to die?"

"How do you know that? You didn't know who hit you when we found you." He smoothed the notepad as he placed it on the table in front of him.

She trained her gaze on the paper. He'd been sure to leave a blank piece on top, allowing him to flip through the pages underneath for his notes.

"I was so cold and he'd knocked me in the head. They do say the head is a computer. I think the hit short circuited my memory. But I remember it now. Price was the one who hit me and left me to die. Will that go on his arrest sheet? Attempted murder?"

"That along with you being an accomplice in the other three murders."

"I what? You are mistaken. I had nothing to do with him killing those people." She tried to look innocent but to Hawke it only made her look more guilty.

"How did Price know where to find D.A. Lange's handgun?" Hawke watched her.

Her hands were clenched tight enough to give her white knuckles. "I'm sure his sister told him."

Hawke shook his head. "She didn't know about the gun." He flipped a page on the notepad. "And you were the one who contacted Price about getting information on Lange to put him out of office and hoist you into his place."

"I started my investigation to help my mom find closure."

"Started it for that. But when you realized it was a

way for you to move up the ladder quicker, and get money to help with your mother's doctor bills, you began the campaign to discredit the district attorney." Hawke picked out each word she misused and used it against her.

"He is a killer. He should have been charged with manslaughter for my cousin Wally's death." Her indignation didn't fool Hawke.

"He was a boy. A boy who by your own records was drugged and didn't know. Several people told me he only had one drink. Not enough to impair him as much as the accident details show. And the records from his hospitalization back then showed he had drugs in his system."

"I'd like a lawyer." Ms. Wallen stared at him her mouth crimped shut.

He could tell there would be no more coming from her, but she knew they had all they needed to get her charged with the murders as well as Barney Price.

Hawke turned off the recording device and picked up his notebook. "It's people like you that give lawyers a bad reputation."

He walked out of the room.

Donner met him, waving some papers. "Price signed his statement."

"She did break. Lawyered up." Hawke tapped the notebook. "She didn't like what I was asking her."

"I read through Price's statement. All of this stemmed from his unhappy childhood." Donner shook his head. "I'm surprised we aren't putting more people behind bars if that is all that sets them off."

"Everyone has their own way of dealing with their past. Just like a rattlesnake they can choose to change their path or they can strike. Price chose to strike."

Hawke drove to the office in Winslow and typed up his report.

"You have three days coming to you," Spruel said, stopping by Hawke's desk.

"I was hoping to get a full two." He'd had to cut his days off short since the murder of Sigler.

"Take three. The large game season is winding down. The others can handle things. You just solved a triple homicide." Spruel walked away and stopped. "By the way. Good job."

"Thanks." Hawke turned off his monitor and his phone buzzed.

Dani.

"Hello," he answered.

"Hi. I decided to have a dinner party tomorrow night. You interested?" she asked without preamble.

"Who all is invited?" He wasn't sure he wanted to spend one night of his time off with people he didn't know.

"Kitree, Sage, Tuck, and Justine."

At Kitree's name he was interested. He missed the girl. Sage and Tuck made sense since they were now Kitree's family. Justine….

"That's an interesting group."

"I just wanted my closest friends."

He heard something in her voice. "Since when is Justine a close friend?"

"Since we bonded over our friendship with you."

Hawke groaned.

"Is that a yes?"

《》《》《》

Leaving a review is the best way to show your appreciation to an author for entertaining you. All you have to do is leave a brief sentence or two about why you liked the book or what about the book interested you and a star rating. That's it!

The number of reviews a book has enables an author to do promotion and get seen by readers who read other books in the same genre.

Coming Fall 2019

Chattering Blue Jay
Book 4

Killer on the loose.

Tracking Rivalry.

Conceit could get them killed.

Fish and Wildlife Oregon State Trooper Gabriel Hawke is teaching a Master Tracking class at a law enforcement conference in Idaho when a dangerous inmate breaks out of prison. The man was last seen floating down the Snake River headed to Hells Canyon.

Hawke is enlisted to find the escapee, but a rival at the conference takes off on his own to try and find the man before Hawke. The man's over confidence has the trackers becoming the tracked.

About the Book

Thank you for reading book three in the Gabriel Hawke Novels.

Continue investigating and tracking with Hawke in book 4, ***Chattering Blue Jay*** releasing Fall 2019.

As I stated in the beginning. I grew up in Wallowa County and have always been amazed by its beauty, history, and ruralness. Many say Alaska is the last frontier, but there are so many communities in the western states that are nearly as rural as Alaska. After doing a ride-along with a Fish and Wildlife State Trooper in Wallowa County, I knew this was where I had to set this new series.

While you're waiting for the next Hawke book, check out my Shandra Higheagle Mystery series.

Paty

About the Author

Paty Jager is an award-winning author of 37 novels, 10 novellas, and numerous anthologies of murder mystery and western romance. All her work has Western or Native American elements in them along with hints of humor and engaging characters. Paty and her husband raise alfalfa hay in rural eastern Oregon. Riding horses and battling rattlesnakes, she not only writes the western lifestyle, she lives it.

You can follow her at any of these places:

Website: https://www.patyjager.net
Blog: https://writingintothesunset.net
FB Page: https://www.facebook.com/PatyJagerAuthor/
Pinterest: https://www.pinterest.com/patyjag/
Twitter: https://twitter.com/patyjag
Goodreads:
http://www.goodreads.com/author/show/1005334.Paty_
Jager
Newsletter- Mystery: https://bit.ly/2IhmWcm
Bookbub - https://www.bookbub.com/authors/paty-
jager